SHE
CAME
BY THE
BOOK

SHE CAME BY THE BOOK

MARY WINGS

BERKLEY PRIME CRIME, NEW YORK

SHE CAME BY THE BOOK

A Berkley Prime Crime Book
Published by The Berkley Publishing Group
200 Madison Avenue, New York, NY 10016

The Putnam Berkley World Wide Web site address is
http://www.berkley.com

Book design by Rhea Braunstein

First edition: March 1996

Library of Congress Cataloging-in-Publication Data

Wings, Mary.
    She came by the book / Mary Wings. — 1st ed.
      p. cm.
   ISBN 0-425-15147-6 (hardcover)
   ISBN 0-425-15144-1 (trade paperback)
    1. Women detectives—United States—Fiction. 2. Lesbians—
United States—Fiction.   I. Title.
PS3573.I53213S47   1996
813'.54—dc20
                                              95-21205
                                            CIP

PRINTED IN THE UNITED STATES OF AMERICA

10 9 8 7 6 5 4 3 2 1

For Eric Garber
who carries moonbeams home in a jar

ACKNOWLEDGMENTS

Special thanks to my mentors on Bernal Hill: Joan Holden, Kris Kovick and B. Ruby Rich. Their example of just how well life and writing can be combined continues to be an inspiration. And a tip of the hat to Cindy Cooper, who offered the title, and to book antiquarian Celia Sack, who knows just what vellum feels like.

TRACY PORT—executive director of the Archive

RENQUIST FALKENBERG—city supervisor

DEBORAH DUNTON—president of the board, couples counselor

ALLEN BOONE—assistant curator

HELEN THOMAS—mystery author, keynote speaker

BERNIECE ABLE—board member, Pulitzer poet

CARLA RIBERA—board member, fashion photographer

LARRY BOZNIAN—painter of Archive mural

FRANCESCA ALCAZON—Gertrude Stein expert

ROSE BAYNETTA—donor, in the security business

LEE TURGO—donor, chiropractor

~~**FRANCES COHEN**—physician and researcher~~ *canceled*

EMMA VICTOR—donor

History there = is no disaster = Those who make history =
Cannot be overtaken = as they will make = History which they
do = because it is necessary = That every one will = Begin to
know that = They must know that = History is what it is =
Which it is as they do . . .
—GERTRUDE STEIN, from WE CAME, A HISTORY, 1930

CONTENTS

PROLOGUE

As a lesbian, I never thought that I would mind another woman wearing the same dress to a big event. But the woman was Tracy Port, and the dress looked great on her even while she writhed, poisoned, at my feet.

My eyes unwillingly watched Tracy's body convulse. I felt guilty. Not because I'd felt bad about Tracy Port wearing the same dress to the Howard Blooming Lesbian and Gay Memorial Archive Dinner. And not because, even dying, she looked better in it than I did. But because, somehow, I thought the disaster that had ruined the dinner, that had taken Tracy's life, just might have been my fault.

I tried not to focus on the death mask taking over Tracy's features. But we were all transfixed, staring at Tracy clutching her throat, the black sequins of our dress blinking like a few thousand blinded raccoons. On the marble floor, the hem of the dress was rising to reveal the muscularly developed legs of the executive director of the Archive. Spectacular legs which had taken her over many a finish line. And on publicity jogs with politicians like the potential senator, Renquist Falkenberg. But Tracy had been dancing with an invisible demon of death and now the dance was done. Tracy lay at my feet. Dead.

Get a grip, Emma Victor. Figure out just exactly what you're doing here. And why someone is tugging on a box at the end of your arm. A box of history that you're supposed to be guarding with your life. It started with an errand. It has ended in death. Hold on tight.

HISTORY, PART I

The fog was spilling over the edge of the hills like a cloud from a bad Aladdin's lamp. It poured through the split in Twin Peaks and filled the Castro, so thick it blanked out the "C" and the "A" on the sign of that landmark plaster movie palace, the Castro Theater. Only a bright pink "STRO" shone through the mist, gilding with neon the happy queer people who roamed the streets buying chocolate chip cookies, renting videos and browsing in Cliff's Hardware Store. Couples clutched each other in the fog and laughed. San Francisco, where it never rains but the streets are always wet.

I was going to visit another les/bi/gay landmark, Rainbow House. An old Victorian homestead bought in the mid-seventies like so many other dwellings. With a lot of disposable income at hand, gay men had bought up the properties which surrounded the Castro Theater. Slowly they displaced the working-class Irish who were escaping queers and crime by moving to the suburbs. The new residents turned the formerly beige and white Victorian

1

houses into multi-colored gay homesteads with perfectly pruned rosebushes and flower boxes up front. Not a dead leaf dangling. The property values shot up sky high. Gaylandia was a realtor's dream. Rainbow House, the residence of former gay State Representative Howard Blooming, was a dream come true.

I banked the car's wheels against the curb of the steep hillside and struggled against gravity to open the door. Stepping into that cool shroud of fog, I shivered and pulled up the collar of my leather jacket. I looked up at the familiar house, its numerals shining in solid brass.

I wondered how long David would stay this time. Then I didn't wonder anymore. A big FOR SALE sign swung on a pointy-topped post in the middle of a recently tidied garden. David was selling the place. That was all right with me. History could move on, as far as I was concerned. Other people could live in the past, I thought. At least, that's what I thought then. I had forgotten that we are sometimes a sum of the things that have happened in the past. And that the past could dictate your future as if it were written in stone. Or etched in polished brass.

Howard Blooming had lived in this house with his lover, David Stimpson. Originally a mild-mannered chemist, Howard had had the honor of being our country's first elected gay official. And its first martyr.

A horseshoe arch led into a portico where a bas-relief had been lovingly revealed and restored. Howard Blooming had spent a weekend with dental tools and a hand-held acetylene torch removing the paint off the wooden carving. A moon, sun and star had been gilded onto a background of blue. Its original meaning was lost when City Hall burned in 1906 and most of the city's records were destroyed. A lamp shed a sad, refracted glow through beveled glass across the kind of porch where men and women would share a pristine kiss in times gone by. Or women and women.

Howard Blooming's kisses had never been pristine. As his press secretary, I hid Howard's proclivity for young men in uniform. It wasn't easy keeping secrets from David, but it was absolutely necessary. He had always suspected an affair between Howard and his protégé, Renquist Falkenberg, although that was one pairing I couldn't imagine. David was a bit paranoid, and we handled him with kid gloves. Of course, this was twenty years ago. I pushed the spring button of a brass doorbell. Somewhere inside, the Windsor works chimed as they had always chimed in Howard's house.

Bing, bing. Tanya, luggage, third floor. Tanya, Tanya.
I'd been shopping at Macy's when my pager went off. I drifted through cosmetics and found a bank of phone booths by the elevators. I called the number indicated on the digital display; it was Willie's office. Willie Rosini was a lawyer who had handled some of Howard Blooming and David Stimpson's legal affairs. I handled some of Willie's affairs, most of which could never go on the public record. Evidence that would never be used. Tracks that might never have been followed. But tonight would be different.

"Emma, it's Willie. David Stimpson just got in from Paris. He needs some help. I said I'd give you a call and see if you were available to go over to Rainbow House—"
Bing, bing. Elissa, hosiery. Elissa, hosiery.
"Aren't you going to that gala thing tonight? It will be on your way," Willie rasped. I could just hear the rhythm *pro bono, pro bono* starting up. David Stimpson was notoriously cheap. And dramatic.

Bing, Marguerite, Marguerite, handbags, bing, bing, bing.

I watched people moving in and out of the elevators. After Howard had been assassinated and a suitable period of mourning had passed, David Stimpson had made himself available for public appearances in Howard's name. He had slipped on the mantle of professional widow like a simple black sheath. The Widow of Howard Blooming was no mean position in Fairyland, but it wasn't an act I admired. However, I knew that David had loved Howard. Being a professional widow had been fulfilling, but it hadn't made up for the loss.

And then Renquist Falkenberg's political career had picked up, Renquist running on endless energy, a policy wonk who could stay up all night and all day. The high wattage of Renquist's ascent cast a big shadow over little David Stimpson. David Stimpson was without an agenda, just a few widow's weeds, a nice piece of real estate and too many memories. David rented out Rainbow House and moved to Paris.

"It'll be hardly out of your way. Just a little errand," Willie said.

"I'm not convinced."

"Do it for Howard's sake."

"How about for money?"

"Sorry, Emma, this comes under the heading of civic duty. But I think I've got a better gig coming up for you soon."

"Such as—"

"Surveillance."

Surveillance. Sneak and creep. Could mean sitting in my car for a long, long time for the bigger bucks. And civic duty and curiosity still had a draw. "Okay, I'll go."

"I have to warn you." I could hear Willie drawing in on

her cigarette. "He's a little upset. He *thinks* someone has been following him."

After I hung up the phone, I dodged a saleslady who brandished a bottle of perfume in my direction with a wink. There sure were a lot of dykes working at Macy's, I thought as I weaved my way out of the store.

Standing at David's door, I watched that familiar, thin shadow flickering behind the etched glass. Closer and closer, loping down a long hallway of time until the dead-bolt slid open and the brass knob turned.

"Emma!" The small eyes were wary and he hung back; we would not be engaging in the California hug routine. David and I had never engaged in niceties, especially not after Howard died. A wilted version of his old topiaried mustache curled over his lips; a small cellular phone perched in his pocket, antenna collapsed.

"Thanks for coming, Emma."

"That's okay, but I don't have much time." The hallway was long and hollow; Howard used to balance little windup toys on the plate rail above the wainscotting. But they were all long gone.

"It's nice to see you again." My voice echoed, tinny, dishonest. David's upper lip trembled. "What can I do for you?" I asked.

"I hate it here, Emma." I braced myself for the "white whine," the long overture of details David would tell me about his life that I didn't want to hear before getting to the climax, the errand he wanted me to run for him. I just wanted to get the errand done. I wanted to put on my tux and watch Frances slink into the black sheath I was carrying in a Macy's box.

"I'm finally packing up, Emma." Palm waving at the

5

empty hallway, David's skin was flecked with age, his arms still nicely biceped. "I thought I would be able to return after twenty years, but I still haven't got the heart for it. There have been strange noises in the house. I could be being followed—"

"Switch to a hard line phone, David." I gestured at his shirt pocket, but David, ever the retail queen, was eyeing the box from Macy's. The low-cut back was going to frame Frances's downy-skinned shoulder blades to perfection.

"You got something at *Macy's*?"

I nodded.

"I *never* shop at Macy's anymore."

"I'm trampled, David." But I was also curious. "Have you gotten an offer on the house yet?"

"Two million."

Two million. "Two million? What is this, Pacific Heights?"

"It's the only extant example of Queen Anne architecture of the period, not to mention the—" The little lips tightened defensively and he began over again. "I've got a two million offer. Firm."

"Two million. *Mazal tov.* Who's buying?"

"It was an anonymous offer. Willie Rossini is handling it." He sighed dramatically. "It will be good to get away. Away from all the memories. Howard never should have made that speech, never, never."

I watched David wind himself up like one of Howard's little toys.

"Could we linger in the present for just a moment David? Or do you want to turn back the clock and camp out at the one second that changed history?"

"The death threats *had* been coming on a regular basis, Emma. Ever since Howard appeared at the baptism—it was that gay schoolteacher thing. I still don't see why he had to be in the public eye so much of the time."

"Oh, David—" But there wasn't anything left to say. We all knew the facts of twenty or so years ago. They weren't going to change. The Universal Community Church baptism had been the incendiary event that had set off the right-wing fundamentalists. It was the moment when Jeb Flynne first identified Howard Blooming as the enemy to destroy.

The church had sponsored a multidenominational baptism of infants from parents of all sexual persuasions. The truly rainbow event was joyous for the San Francisco community. It had been even better for the press.

The right-wing fundamentalists had gotten wind of it and had staged a massive protest. Flynne became obsessed with the politician. He began penning a flurry of letters, which escalated in their gory prose. Flynne murdered Howard a year later in his office while Howard was quietly answering his mail. David persisted in seeing the baptism as the moment that set his lover up to be killed. That's how it all worked in David Stimpson's mind. And it was still all my fault. My grievous fault.

"Emma, I begged you not to let Howard do that speech after the baptism. He would have listened to you but you said *nothing*. It was more than bad judgment. It was *negligence*. You robbed me of the only man I loved."

Here we went again, that well-traveled path.

"David, take the nails out of your hands and climb down off the cross. It wasn't *my* job to protect Howard. I was his *publicist*." The ashes of my anger were cold now. David was still trying to pass on his guilt. The fact was, *he'd* flounced off in a huff when Howard had refused to be frightened

7

from delivering his speech. Howard had been killed before they made up.

I was the one who'd held Howard in my arms as he was dying, I was the one who'd heard his final words. David had missed his opportunity to become the Jackie Kennedy of queers.

"I just want to get rid of Howard's journals—"

"Howard's journals?" The words hung in the air, making their way through the packed-up boxes. Forgotten memories, like mice scurrying across the pages of a few bound books.

"You have Howard's journals?"

"Yes. Now *you* can have them. To take to the gala."

He ushered me into the Victorian-style parlor, where David's taste had reigned supreme. In its former days, it would have made Mary Todd Lincoln proud. But now, shorn of red brocade curtains, hand-knotted lace sheers and rococo mirrors, without its gold cupids poised on tip-toe, the room looked forlorn. An abandoned bordello, a room that had always amused Howard.

Now the panoramic view was worth two million dollars. The fog had wrapped around the Twin Peaks television tower like a furry white scarf. Lights pinpricked the gentle folds of hills. The merry-go-round colors of the houses faded in the dusk. All kinds of friends and families would be coming home from work to put dinner in the microwave.

I looked around. This home had long gone. Rows of boxes were carefully labeled and organized.

"Emma, I want Howard's final journals housed at the Lesbian and Gay Archive," he said with ceremony.

"The *Howard Blooming* Lesbian and Gay *Memorial*

Archive." I said gently, "You know they named it after Howard."

"*What?*" David's body shuddered and a sad look crept over his face. "I guess I *am* out of touch. In any event I want Howard's journals at the Archive. I mentioned it to Willie. She said you were going to the gala dinner tonight."

The journals. The diaries of Howard's last two years; the journals, which I knew he'd kept, but which David had insisted had disappeared. I'd never trusted the story of their alleged disappearance.

David left the room and returned with a faded, flowered, old-fashioned box. From Macy's. Where David never shopped anymore. I looked at the box and wondered at the history it now held. Had it originally held a set of champagne glasses? A present, perhaps from David Stimpson to Howard Blooming, marking a happy moment at the beginning of their relationship?

A twisted string handle was threaded through opposite sides of the box and rested on the lid. David looked at me a long time. Once I had the journals, he would be rid of the final secrets of Howard Blooming, the secrets that might still haunt David Stimpson, the secrets he could probably sell to a publisher, naming his price in the booming lesbian and gay book market. Before he had a chance to wrestle with his conscience and lose, I spoke up.

"It's the right thing to do," I said.

"Yes." David seemed relieved. "I made an appointment for you with Allen Boone, Assistant Curator. He's delighted, of course." David looked down at the box. "The last diaries. And letters." His voice was soft. "And, uh, some personal clutter, memorabilia. It's all in there."

My hands reached out and took hold of the package. It

was evenly covered with two decades of dust. Something, like a marble, rolled across the floor of the box.

"There's something loose in there." David grinned wanly. "Howard tucked a few extra mementos in, I guess. He was always so, so . . . disorganized."

Howard's image as the faintly absentminded chemist had served him well. But he'd had a mind like a trap when it came to the zoo of San Francisco politics. I stared at the box in my hands. It was heavy. I tried not to smile.

"Oh, and there's one more thing, Emma. The most important thing. The journals may not be read until everyone who might have been mentioned in them has died. The box must be sealed, Emma. Sealed for sixty years. It was Howard's wish. I know I can trust you to see to it, *can't I?*"

I walked down the stairs with the two boxes from Macy's. The sun had set into the foggy horizon. The dappled light of dusk came through the trees and fell upon the boxes. An old box housing the record of a les/bi/gay past that no longer existed. A new box for a glitzy les/bi/gay event that no one could have imagined back then.

I descended toward the street. Empty, although I could hear traffic just below the crest. The Howard Blooming box bumped on my hip. I shook it. Some kind of bead or button was rolling around, a troubling, disturbing sound. Something loose inside a box to be sealed for sixty years. My imagination ran wild with history and supposition. I stood for a moment, temptation and loyalty to Howard warring in my mind. I could open the box now and no one would know. Take a seat in my car, travel back to Howard Blooming's death and beyond. The street was quiet as a coffin. No one would know. My car beckoned silently. I would not look into the box.

I stepped from under the canopy of eucalyptus trees, glad to be out of the shadows. The street was quiet, a few leaves scraping along the pavement in a swirl of wind. Queen Annes, Edwardians and Italianates stood majestically on the hillsides, tumbling with blue sprays of African violets. I heard the historic cheers of Howard's people, our people, the whispered rumors about Jeb Flynne, as I held the box full of Howard's family skeletons. I looked up at the bay windows off the master bedroom. They'd been a hassle for the security guards. Howard had liked to take his coffee there in the morning in his houndstooth plaid flannel pajamas. I would brief him there. Ah, Howard.

Before he became political, Howard used to spend all his time puttering around the house, in his workshop down in the basement with his Bunsen burners and test tubes. He had been a dedicated chemist, but he gave it up for the chance to make history, and, some said, LSD. One of the skeletons in his closet was Laurie Leiss, a suspected terrorist and a cousin. But everybody has bad apples in the family, I thought, feeling the presence of windows around me. Windows behind which people were making new secrets. Bits of history, important to someone, doomed to disappear.

The mist was extending its clammy fingers. The first evening star made it through the fog, and I realized I was leaving Rainbow House for the last time. A convertible, top down, tried to make it up the hill. The occupants were laughing, their faces a blur behind the windshield. The black man's arm was slung around what looked like a white drag queen, in a futile effort to keep him/her warm. I squinted.

Then their car had clutch trouble; I'd seen it often enough on a hillside in San Francisco. Coming to a stall at

11

forty-five degrees, a loss of nerve as you reached the steepest point of the incline. Better to get up speed at the bottom and use momentum to get it up the worst, but this pair was stuck mid-hill and the only choice was to back up or burn out their clutch.

The driver chose the latter. The clutch whined in protest, smoking as they laughed. I could see the headlights, the low-digit license plate as it made the crest of the hill. Fog and the smell of burning clutch. It was a moment I would never forget, because it ended in a choke, a vicious clamped arm around my throat which threatened to snap my neck.

I bared my teeth, and bit into the sleeve of a heavy leather jacket, but the arms tightened. I threw my head forward and back, hoping to hear the satisfying sound of skullbone making contact with cartilage, nose flattened out of shape, a pleasing celery sound that never came. My fingers tightened around my burdens.

The arms closed tighter and the world began to grow black at the edges. I aimed my boot behind me, seeking any kind of way out of the hold, something that would keep the lights from going out in front of me. I found a groin, a foot, in that order, but my attacker was immune to pain. The choke hold tightened. The Macy's boxes were pulling away from my wrists as my heel finally found a crotch. It could have been a direct hit, but I was outnumbered.

A second assailant flew out of the blackness like a dark arrow aimed at my head.

"Waaaa!" An obscene peal of laughter from the open convertible as it made the top of the hill. My wrist twisted and someone yelled and all was dark. The rough feel of concrete on my cheek was my last conscious memory. Someone had picked up the sidewalk and thrown it at me.

IAMBIC
PENTAMETER

Footsteps running in the darkness and Frances's dress was twisting above me from a tree limb. Strange fruit doing the shimmy, an invisible form squirming inside. The dress danced above the sidewalk to the tempo which was crashing through my head. Where were Howard's journals?

My eyes scanned the sidewalk searching for the old Macy's box. Then I saw it. Lid cockeyed, but still in place, the octagonal package jauntily claimed a spot on the concrete, its twisted string handle reaching for my fingers. I just caught the tail lights of the convertible with the smoking clutch, a convertible which must have interrupted my mugging. It had all been over in a couple of seconds.

My fingers crawled along the pavement, found the string of the handle, grasped and pulled. Howard's journals. I cradled it in my arms and reached for the back of my head. A large swollen lump of pain lived there. But Howard's journals were safe.

I remembered the arms of my attacker, remembered my moves, moves that didn't work. If I could have turned,

13

gone for the eyes, I could have taken him. But I couldn't have taken two. If it hadn't been for the convertible—someone had yelled, driven away—mugging interruptus? I checked for my wallet and found it. They hadn't gone to that much trouble to steal a dress.

Or not. I knew that there was a gang working the Castro and this was their M.O. They mugged women on the street and lately the robbers had been getting more violent.

I found my car, started the engine and focused on the street, trying to get my vision in order. I still had Howard's journals. I folded Frances's dress. Miraculously, no sequins had been pulled loose. I returned it to the bed of tissue paper, pulled down the window, and took a deep breath of the comfortable, homey perfume of Northern California. Eucalyptus and exhaust.

Ten minutes later I pulled up to our home, a flat-faced Italianate in the Mission. The Victorian duplex was the working-class cousin to Howard and David's Queen Anne. I heaved the car door open with the two boxes on my lap. I crawled off the vinyl seat like I was a hundred years old. My hand was finding the back of my head and doing things that were making my headache much worse, but my hand couldn't stop. A face emerged out of the darkness.

There were times when I didn't want to see our house partner and upstairs neighbor, Laura Deleuse. This was one of them. She sucked on a cigarette and eyed me. "You don't look so good, Emma."

"No, really?"

Laura was a cop and I was a legal investigator; it didn't leave us with much to say. But we'd knocked back a few beers together when we were in the mood to tell the world to go to hell. Tonight it wasn't the world that Laura wanted to go to hell. It was me. Laura squinted through the smoke of her cigarette and said nothing.

"What's with you, Laura?"

No answer.

Then, "You don't know?"

"I'm too tired to guess. I just want to get dressed for my fucking date, Laura." I tried to move past her with the boxes in my hands.

"Then you'd better wash your hair. Your neck is bleeding." Laura waved the orange coal of her cigarette at me, then turned her back and trudged up the front stairs, one step after the other; each leg had to make a separate decision. Each leg deciding to carry that tired torso of Sergeant Laura Deleuse, of the San Francisco Police Department, to her lair. Civil servants busy as bees serving and protecting. It was almost enough to make me cry. "I don't care what you do, Emma," she said at the top of the stairs. I could tell I was going to hear what the problem was. Soon. "I just wish you wouldn't do it in *my* backyard. You know the laws have changed. And the Feds are in town." She closed the door firmly and chained, bolted and deadlocked it.

Okay, okay. So *that's* what it was about. *The garden.* Laura was pissed about the garden. I ran my hand over my hair and down the nape of my neck. There was a small spot which was sticky with blood. Thanks for the warning, Laura. The Feds. They said the Feds would take your car away if they found a joint in your glove compartment. They said the Feds would take your house away if you grew pot in your garden. And San Francisco had always been special territory so the Feds might be serving notice. Maybe I should cut the plants down.

I looked up at the Victorian front of our house, the

color of blue hydrangeas, its features iced with white scrolling. I saw the cobalt glass light, a propane flicker coming from Frances's office as I opened the front door.

I heard the distant hum of the refrigerator and Frances scribbling hastily. The big living room was dark. We'd knocked out interior walls and now the room stretched out before me, filled with books and laid with red jeweled kilim carpets. I flicked the switch. A string of halogen lights spotlit the spines of the books and splashy silkscreens on the walls. There were two matching leather couches with chrome frames. Frances used to wear black leather. Now she sat on it.

Mink the cat groomed herself on the cowhide. She stopped licking and stared at me intensely, two yellow accusing eyes that dipped suddenly toward the boxes.

Mink followed me lazily to the kitchen where I set both boxes on the floor. She sniffed the edges of the older box, her triangle nose recoiling once or twice as if shocked. Upon further investigation, she decided that the older box was her friend and rubbed up against it, removing dust with the swipe of her fur and revealing brighter colors of pansies.

"Where have you been, honey?" came a voice from the office.

"Just a sec—" I went into the bathroom and wiped the spot of blood off my neck. I shook my head, trying to get the taste of the sleeve of that leather jacket out of my mouth, the horrible taste of old leather, salty with sweat and reeking of aggression. I looked myself over carefully in the mirror. I didn't think there was any way Frances would notice I'd been mugged, and I wouldn't tell her, I decided. There was no reason to spoil the evening. Frances was busy writing.

I went to the tool cupboard and found a roll of silver duct tape. I surveyed the box. The lid rested uneasily on it, the corners splayed out, the paper crackling along the edges. That bead or button was still rolling around in there. I picked up the duct tape.

My fingernails pried the edge loose, gummy surface sticking to my fingers. With a tug and a squeal the tape parted from the roll. I held it over the box. Very sticky. Once it landed on the faded flowers, it would never come loose. Big secrets. Big deal. I laid the tape across the top of the box where it clung to the old paper. I ran my fingers over the material, paying particular attention to the juncture between box and lid. Around and around until the duct tape was completely used up. Howard's journals were mummified. Mission accomplished. I had won out over my own curiosity.

I leafed through the mail. Pacific Gas and Electric, a postcard from St. Croix. I flipped it over. For Frances. I flipped it back and looked at the warm sand, the ocean waves frozen in photographic moment. Frances and I needed a vacation. There was a thicker envelope at the bottom, addressed to us both. I tore it open.

"Just a minute, honey—" Frances called from her office, her voice distracted over the noise of a scribbling pen.

Civil Rights Campaign Fund . . . Circle of Friends World Cruise . . . your tickets are enclosed . . . The words circled a gold-embossed globe. *Embark on a trip around the world as you sample foods from San Francisco's top restaurants and taste California's finest wines, bid on the silent auction treasure vacations and dance to best bands at the hottest event of the year. . . .*

"Where were you, honey?" Frances asked again.

"I had to run an errand. For Willie. David Stimpson made a donation to the Archive."

17

"That's nice, dear."

I turned back to the invitation to the next gala. *Black tie. International chic. Yes, I plan to attend. Please send _____ tickets at $250.*

"What's that?" Frances stood at the kitchen table, running her hands through her caramel-colored hair, fine as silk. I moved toward that generous mouth, close enough to get her freckles in focus, when she danced away. "I saw raccoons out in the garden," she said. "We need a better lid on the compost."

"Yeah. This is for you." I picked up the box from Macy's. It had been a long time since I had given Frances a present. She looked surprised as she took the box from my hands.

"For me?"

"It's time to prune the roses." I took off the lid. "So they will bloom bigger and better next year."

Frances's fingers searched through the tissue paper. The sequined material winked and glittered. Drawing out the gown with a gasp, she held it up to the light, pressed it against her breasts and gathered it in at the waist. I looked at her face. She clearly loved the dress. But there was also something else. She was biting her lip. "I have to tell you something hard, honey."

"What is it?" I kept my voice even, while my eyes traveled to the open door of her office. The cold blue cap of her desk light illuminated her Rolodex.

"I got a call today from the president of the board of the Seattle Women's Health Clinic." Frances looked up, flushed with excitement. "The largest women's clinic in Seattle is going to be the target of a major right-wing demonstration tomorrow. The fundamentalists are demonstrating against abortion, and—" She took a deep breath. "They've threatened the lives of local physicians, in print. Last night one of the physicians came home to find his house burned to the ground. His family just escaped, Emma. I have to be there."

"We've been planning this—" The dress hung like a limp weed off my arm. "We've been talking about this gala; it's the only one I ever wanted to go to!"

"I'm sorry, I have to go to Seattle, Emma."

"You want to do it."

"I have to do it. The police aren't providing protection worth shit. The whole future of reproductive services—"

"Reproductive services," I echoed dully. I picked up the tissue paper, crumpled it into a ball and made a rim shot into the wastebasket from twelve feet. "Will you have some personal security? It sounds like a really dangerous situation. Why don't you let me go with you? I know the profiles, I can scan the crowds—"

"No, no, I'll be getting a lot of attention." Frances looked down and checked to make sure all her fingernails were still there. "Their keynote speaker canceled," she said quietly.

So that was it. Their keynote speaker had canceled. *Ipso facto* Frances was now their keynote speaker.

"Let me go with you."

"Emma, you have to go to the gala. That's *your* job."

I looked down at the box with Howard Blooming's journals. It was time to be noble and brave. Frances would do her job and I would do mine. An army of lovers could not fail. Or could we? "How long before your plane takes off?"

Frances was pouring coffee into a promotional car cup that had been dropped off by a pharmaceutical salesman at the clinic where she worked. *Chlamdryl,* the words on the cup read. *For Chlamydia and other vaginal infections.*

19

"Traffic at the airport is always a nightmare." She took a sip. "Have to leave extra early. I'll drop you off at the gala."

"Gala won't be so gala without you. Besides I hate these things. Look at this—" I waved the engraved invitation made to look like it was a solid gold passport on heavy cardboard.

"Oh, great! It's the Civil Rights—"

"Civil Rights Champagne Fund."

"It's an AIDS benefit."

"It's an excuse to have a party, Frances."

"What's wrong with that?"

"San Francisco Medici coming right up, but not *out.*"

"A lot of them *are* out. Listen, I need to know people on the A-list, Emma. I need money to do my research. I have things to accomplish. If you would just get that chip off your shoulder maybe you'd find out—"

"What?"

"Nothing, I don't know . . ." Frances's eyes drifted over to the box.

"That the end will justify the party? Anyway, I guess you'll have another chance to wear that dress. Now, where's my tux?"

The silence was deadly. "I forgot to rent your tuxedo." The postcard from the Virgin Islands suddenly caught her attention.

"You forgot to rent a tux?" I looked back at the sequined dress now draped over the kitchen chair. Just a slip of a thing, a tiny tube of tinsel it was. And there truly was not another fucking piece of evening wear in the house.

"I want to see you in that dress!" Frances's hazel eyes had returned from the sandy beach, the frozen palm trees. I stared at Frances in horror, that became mock horror, that became a way of trying to lessen the distance that

20

was growing between us. I pulled the garment toward me and pressed it against my chest. I stripped down to my bra and boxers, and, as if I were wrestling a boa constrictor, the dress eating me up alive, I pulled the taut elastic material up and over knees, thighs, buttocks, waist and breasts. Frances was laughing, crossing her legs.

The dress fit my body like a glove. Too bad I wasn't a hand. Frances was laughing so hard she almost choked, spilling coffee out of her *Chlamydia* mug.

My extra five inches of height over Frances put the hemline just on the decent side of venus, *mons* venus; I looked like a working girl with hairy legs and no haircut. The material gathered by the cleft between my breasts, the scales making a soft swishing sound as they brushed against each other, like a whispered message from my décolleté. And then Frances wasn't laughing anymore; she was arranging the shoulders, pulling at the neckline and stepping back from me.

"Emma, you look really gorgeous! Trashy! *Ordinaire!* I want you in sequins all the time!" Frances was on her feet, kissing me hard and fast. Her swift tongue found its way between my lips, surprising me as usual, and her hands roamed over my flesh, deciphering my ribs. It usually took less than that to make me wet. Especially since dry times had hit our marriage lately.

"Hey!" I was left kissing the air. Frances had disappeared into her office again, saying, "I have to get my papers together and pack my bag."

Despite Frances's approval of my costume, there was no way I was going to be bound by pantyhose and sequins all night. I might have been mugged for Frances's gown or I might have been mugged for Howard's journals. I just

21

didn't like going on an assignment without some decent shoes and my basic tool kit.

I got out my black canvas bag which had been water-proofed inside. I slipped my lightweight cotton black pants into it. A pair of tennis shoes, a decade old, the soles worn slick and treadless. A tight-fitting black turtleneck which could be rolled up to my eyes. And for good measure, I added a high-intensity flashlight and a tiny kit featuring several sizes of screwdrivers with various heads.

I put my hand up to the bump on my head. I added a can of Mace. The bag yawned as wide as it could go, Howard Blooming's box fitting perfectly between my clothes and the can of Mace.

"Just a sec, honey." What was Frances doing?

My eyes drifted over to the *Bay Times*. The paper's cover featured Executive Director of the Archive Tracy Port and senatorial hopeful Renquist Falkenberg, jogging in the Japanese Tea Garden, startling any number of tourists. Renquist was huffing and puffing, trying to slim down, and Tracy, as usual, looked straight ahead. A small insert on the front page claimed, "Gay Mural Spans Archive Heaven, an Interview with Larry Boznian, Postmodern Painter Extra-Ordinaire." Before I had time to flip to the page with working drawings of the mural, perhaps the most interesting highlight of the evening, Frances appeared in travel gear.

"C'mon, honey, we gotta go." Frances's hair, fresh from the brush, made a static halo around her head. I wanted nothing more than to ruin her lipstick. And I did. Frances may have changed styles, but her kiss was still the same, like waves of iambic pentameter, *this* and then *this* and then . . .

"By the way." Frances pulled back. "I have something for

you to bring for me to the gala tonight. A donation for the Archive."

Just what I needed. Something else to keep track of.

"Tracy called me tonight and said she wanted me to donate my original lab notes on *Lesbo-Parthenogenesis*."

Frances's original research. Of which I was so proud. *Lesbo-Parthenogenesis*—the combining of two ova to create a female child—was in reality far, far off. But Frances had had some limited success with female parthenogenesis in frogs. There were some exciting breakthroughs, but she had always kept her experiments relatively quiet; only parts of the lesbian community were aware of this work, although Frances's courting of the A-list signaled a dramatic change in attitude.

"I'm still working out the terms of access with the Archive," Frances went on. "The board is taking forever to come up with a policy." Frances handed over a thin pile of notebooks inside a manila envelope. Tiny grids and perfect little printed notes. Years worth of work. I tucked the notes carefully into the bag. She turned her back to pull the car keys off a hook on the wall. "By the way, Laura said that the garden is looking a little weedy."

"Yeah, she growled at me on the stairs. Well, sweetheart, rubber chicken time!" I could avoid unpleasant topics just as easily as Frances could. I looked again at my lover's face and features. Busy. Brilliant. Diligent. Driven and dedicated. I wanted to kiss her again, to suck the magenta color off the precious pillows that were her lips, to slide my tongue between her teeth, to kiss her and make her fly. Frances, however, was in a hurry to make her plane. She picked up her coffee cup for her last hit of caffeine. *Chlamdryl. For Chlamydia and other vaginal infections.* We walked down to the car in silence, each carrying our various burdens.

"Are you okay?" Frances was asking as she parked at the curb of the newly finished building.

"Yes," I lied. There was an air of liberal guilt, a disturbing wind that would determine the tone of the evening. All the women would be wearing lipstick. None of the men would be wearing dresses. I sighed. The A-list gays were, as always, gender predictable.

"What fresh hell is this?" I muttered, looking up at the finished building, remembering the angry letters from women in the *Bay Times*, complaining about the architecture. Each Ionic pillar, indeed, looked like a cross section of a penis and each one was lit up in a different color of the rainbow. Above the columns, a gracious figure of Sappho lounged, an architectural concession to the Lesbian Revengers.

"Well, this is it, babe." Frances's fingertips grazed the bumps along the steering wheel. "I'm really sorry I can't be here," she said.

"Yeah." I looked at the crowd which tripped up the stairs in evening clothes.

"I've got to be going." Frances slid her arms around me and pulled me close. "I love you, Emma."

"What time does your plane get in? Did you leave a phone number?"

"In case of emergency," she said, an unstated warning. Frances would be in professional mode. She wouldn't want me to call. "I'll be back on Tuesday."

I leaned forward slowly and planted a long kiss on her lipsticked lips, then clambered out of the car. The bulky canvas bag seemed to have a life of its own, as it bounced on my hip. The elasticized mini-dress crawled skyward as I struggled to get my legs out of the car, every inch of thigh exposed.

"Make my day, Emma."

Fate had found for me the perfect witness to this humiliation. Tracy Port. I clung to my bag and papers, praying I wouldn't drop anything, trying to stand up straight. The last thing I wanted to do was bend over in front of Tracy in this dress. My gaze traveled up Tracy's stone calves, those marvelous hamstrings and sturdy knees. What would Tracy be wearing to an event like this?

The same dress. She wore it much better than I did and from the look on her face we both knew it. Tracy turned around, looking me up and down, her eyes noting the unshaven legs, the inappropriate shoes, the barely decent way the dress clung to my fuller, taller figure. "Hi Frances!" Tracy said, and then she turned around to show me how it should be done.

She bent down to talk to Frances. The dress didn't ride up, it just seemed to hug the pair of pillows that were Tracy's buttocks and made her calves pull tighter above her slim ankles. A plastic pager sparkled off a thin satin belt which cinched Tracy's waist. My sequins were becoming a hairshirt now as Frances's attention glided over the slinky surface of the Executive Director of the Archive. Frances didn't seem in such a hurry to make the airport anymore.

"My God, Tracy, you're wearing my dress," Frances was saying. "Or the dress Emma's wearing. I had forgotten to pick up Emma's tux—" Tracy turned around momentarily to look at me again. They chuckled. "Well, well, Tracy, this is your big night," she burbled. "Congratulations!" They exchanged air kisses through the open car window.

"Aren't you coming tonight, Frances, dear?"

"I'm *so* sorry I can't be here, but Emma has my papers."

"I have an appointment with Allen Boone," I said to Tracy's back.

"Just go around the side of the building, Emma." Tracy pointed to a darkened corner far away from the crowd without turning around. A muted utility light marked a gray door set into the side of the building. "Delivery," she called back over her shoulder as if to underscore the point. The corners of the box were biting into my side through the bag. I felt the headache that was going to accompany me tonight. I needed to let go of the packages. I needed to let go of Frances.

"Bye, Frances," I called. She looked over Tracy's shoulder at me and smiled. I set off to find the office of Allen Boone.

CHAPTER THREE

GENRE

Vaults keep the secrets which can be ravaged in the present. I couldn't help but feel like Howard Carter, exhuming things better left buried, burying things which might be better off revealed as I walked down the sidewalk towards the gray metal door. The Archive would house letters, journals, photos, manuscripts and miscellaneous ephemera that was not miscellaneous to researchers. The shifting tides of attitudes, the moments of danger, passion, politics, friendship and love all behind the doorway I was looking at. A doorway marked STAFF. HAND DELIVERIES ONLY. LOADING DOCK BEHIND THE BUILDING OFF THE PARKING LOT.

I rang a doorbell and waited. A buzzer let me in and I stared down a linoleum-floored hallway. Fluorescent lit, it could have been any hospital or school basement. No windows, only a few unmarked doors, one of which opened at the end of the corridor. A small, rotund man in his early forties mopped his brow with a handkerchief. His pleated shirt was wriggling free of a pink cummerbund at his waist and a pager dangled dangerously from his belt. "Oh!

There you are!" An instant broad grin, framed by a manicured red goatee, just graying under his chin. Bald, possibly shaven, a well-developed torso carried on short legs.
His heavy reddish eyebrows were familiar. Cobalt eyes lit
up as he watched me pull the flowered box covered with
duct tape from the black canvas bag. "Emma Victor! Can
you wait for one second?" He held up his hand and disappeared behind an anonymous door. He returned moments later.

"Emma, Emma!" he said as if I were an old friend.

"That's right." I shook Allen's warm hand. Wet palms,
not exactly perfect for touching paper. A gold chain-link
bracelet glittered on top of his starched cuff. "I believe
you're expecting this." I opened up my canvas bag and
held out the box. Pansies and duct tape. "From David
Stimpson."

"The final journals and papers of Howard Blooming."
Allen's mouth became a quirky "v" of a smile. Blue eyes
gleamed. "To have them here in *our* Archive!" He took the
box into his arms and gazed at it lovingly.

"Allen, what kind of security arrangements do you
have?"

"Security arrangements?" Allen cocked his head, his
bald pate picking up the long glow of a fluorescent tube.
"You do know, the vault isn't finished." His smile wavered.
"In fact, a great deal of the Archive is hardly finished at all!
We're still trying to get donations."

"But, Allen, I'd like to get these locked up. Surely—"

"You don't understand. There's a closet where we've
been locking some of the items, but that's upstairs. We're
hardly equipped—"

The pager at Allen's side buzzed impatiently. He drew it
off his belt and peered at the numbers on the digital dis-

play. "Damn!" Tonight of all nights," he spluttered. "Everybody needs me! I'll be right back. Uh, do you mind, just waiting in my office for a minute?" Allen waved his hand toward the darkened room behind him. "I've got to go." He was a bit breathless, looking at the box with Howard Blooming's papers. "Actually, we do have a safe. An old safe that a banker gave us. All *their* money is on computer now. I suppose you could put—" The pager buzzed again. "Listen, I'll be right back. Please wait—my office—haven't really moved in—" He made a circular motion. I turned around looking into the dark doorway of Allen's office.

"Just wait inside, please! There's a light switch—" His pager beeped again.

I stepped inside. Allen closed the door. The dark, fetid room was full of musty smells that I couldn't quite place. My hand moved along the wall to the right. Building code. The light switch was supposed to be *there*.

Noise. The distant mumble of voices. A rumble and a clatter of metal which stopped after a high-pitched squeal. The voices louder now. My fingers stopped their search. I stood silently in the darkness. A multitude of aromas started to unwind. Moroccan leather and mold, saddle soap. A small cone-shaped desk lamp provided muted light; my eyes adjusted to dimness as I roamed the cubicle allotted to the little historian. Ghostly temples of papers topped pyramids of leather suitcases, brass corners winking. Behind the piles of papers a bubble glass window provided a rectangle of light. Something fully blocked half of the window, but the other half revealed shadows moving back and forth. Shadows that belonged to the loading dock. A solid entry door to the left of the window would be the front entrance to Allen's office.

29

The walls were puzzles, pictures with and without frames hanging from nails; the hasty configuration had a kind of logic. On one side of the wall were portraits, Lorena Hickok, Eleanor Roosevelt, Walt Whitman, Carson McCullers, Langston Hughes. Strips of newspaper articles, caught in cellophane envelope, were tacked to the wall in some dialectic that was only decipherable to Allen Boone.

The point of a desk jabbed my side; I turned to find stacks of LPs and 78's—T.C. Jones, Beverley Shaw at the Club Laurel, and on the back drinks were tipped up, thirty years ago. The Village People, Bronski Beat, Meg Christian. They say she belonged to a guru now.

A small clearing in the middle of his desk was a workspace. A tarnished silver milk pitcher functioned as a pencil holder. A Rolodex. A Navajo print coffee mug. I peered inside. Beige remnants with crystals. Allen took milk and sugar. A princess model phone in beige. I picked it up. Line dead. A magnifying glass, tweezers, a pair of white cotton gloves, an egg timer and an electric pencil sharpener. And overlooking the desk was a bronze framed portrait of a trio: Howard Blooming, Renquist Falkenberg and—who was that with the long thick red hair? Yes. Allen Boone. I suddenly remembered Allen from innumerable political events, schlepping fifty-gallon drums of melting ice, after the champagne had cooled and been drunk. Now he looked more like Yul Brynner than Jerry Garcia.

The photo was housed in an etched bronze frame, corralled by a black velvet mat. Allen and Renquist on either side of Howard. A pair of unlikely bookends, they leaned toward the lens like flowers reaching for the sun. Howard had that shining, triumphant smile. What made him smile like that? I reached out my hand toward the picture, changed my mind and drew it back. I didn't need to see Howard's face up close.

The far edge of the desk held an elongated box. An index card on the end promised "Napkins" in a sure hand of black ballpoint ink. Under the lid I found what must have been hundreds of cocktail napkins, delicate squares alphabetically sorted, each in their own cellophane envelope. Carefully I plucked out a napkin under "p." "The Paper Doll" in lightweight script, Union Street. On the other side, "To Dottie, love, Carmen" on the back and a lipstick autograph. A kiss from half a century ago. Someone had noted the date on the back in light pencil. Nineteen forty-four.

Howard had told me about San Francisco after the war. The return of troops from the Pacific Rim was the beginning of Gaylandia. Allen knew what to collect. The napkins charted the moment in history when San Francisco's Barbary Coast had become the Gay Coast of the world. Howard had begun his career as a chemist in the Army; he'd fallen in love while stationed in Hawaii. When the troops were deployed from the Pacific Theater, they were dropped off in San Francisco. Party time and Gaylandia was born.

I replaced the napkin carefully and sidled over to the door where voices were picking up. Allen had mentioned a safe. I pushed the front door of his office open a crack. To the right, the massive bulk of a black iron box, as big as a closet, let me know what had blocked the bubble glass. The top of a loading dock door was visible just above the hulking antique, the black enamel finish and double decal stripes in gold that spelled out "Wells Fargo, Inc. San Francisco and Sacramento."

If nothing else, the safe was a marvelous decoration. But

31

how safe is a safe? The six-inch door was slightly ajar, giving me a look at the bolt-retracting gears and movement dial, shiny and bright.

The ordinary safe is simply fire resistant and a deterrent to a thief. The key word is *deterrent.* That's what tools were made for. But it still looked like the best bet for Howard's papers. Dumped off by the loading dock door, it wasn't going anywhere soon. I put my fingers to the thick steel door and pushed. I felt the brass bolts noiselessly opening on greased hinges. Rows of glittering numbered safety deposit boxes waited inside. Out of the lock of each box hung two finely wrought keys. Howard's journals would fit into one of the larger boxes.

The sudden rumble of a metal door and the voices sharpened and became familiar. There was no way I could get into the safe now without attracting the attention of the people who were arguing just behind it. The people whose voices were very familiar.

"A receipt. I just want a receipt for my manuscripts!"

It was Helen Thomas, keynote speaker at the dinner, keynote speaker at many, many dinners that Frances had dragged me to. I peered around the corner of the safe. The prolific mystery writer had her hands on her hips. A black silk dress accented her small waist, bronze piping setting off a dramatic flange of a collar which framed a swan-like neck. The centerpiece of her dark décolleté was a gift from her patron, poet Berniece Able. A heart-shaped amber trinket, covered in a delicate platinum spider's web. The Amigreed Amulet. We all knew about it. When Helen fictionalized the story of the amulet in her book *Grandmother's Poison,* her career took off. It glowed with a sharp yellow glint against her chest; Helen wore it with a cunning sense of style.

Now, however, Helen was not looking stylish. Her face was turning purple and her body was twisted with fury. A towering column of white manuscript boxes balanced precariously on the foot of a hand truck next to her.

I saw the low spark of black sequins against the gray rolling door of the loading dock. It could only have been Tracy Port, squaring off opposite the mystery novelist. Tracy was sighing dramatically. "Look, Helen, I'm short of time here. I interrupted an important conversation with—"

She paused. An important conversation. Did she mean Frances?

"—someone to help you bring your manuscript into the Archives, but I had no idea—*no idea*—that you meant all this!"

From the side of the safe, I could easily make out the soaring manuscript boxes. How many pages were there? I figured that Helen had written twenty-seven books. In a pile that size there must be seven drafts of each book. The forests must have groaned when Helen started writing.

"We can't possibly take all this into the Archive, Helen. Think of the hours microfilming, the volunteer corps. Hunched over the photographic machines—"

"You mean you don't *want* my manuscripts?" Helen's voice was low and dull, dull like a knife. Her petticoats seemed to grow in volume under the black tulle. I moved back toward the chaotic darkness of Allen's office.

"Perhaps we could consider the *award-winning* ones? The first and last drafts of each?" Tracy suggested.

Helen narrowed her eyes. "They've *all* won awards, Tracy! This body of work charts the development of twenty-seven plots—which chronicles a parallel development of a new way of thinking about suspense—about *justice*! I have *struggled* and been *acknowledged*."

But Tracy had fifteen hundred guests to acknowledge. "I have no time to argue, Helen. Perhaps if you didn't change your *plots so often*." Tracy's voice had an edge of sarcasm, a cutting edge she didn't bother to control.

"Are you rejecting my manuscripts, Tracy?"

"That's exactly what I'm doing, Helen. Manuscripts? Potboilers have made you rich, but they're hardly artifactually significant."

Helen's face worked itself like a puzzle. There was an adjustment of an eyebrow, the tightening of a lip, a squaring off of the jaw into a new configuration. "If you have such contempt for my work," Helen asked quietly, "then why did you ask me to be the keynote speaker at your event?" The question hung in the air. It didn't need an answer. "It's because I'm black, that's why you needed me here, isn't it?" Helen's voice was flat. Tracy said nothing. She seemed to be waiting. As if on cue, Helen exploded.

"All those flattering phone calls!" The tendons in Helen's neck stood out. "You realize I passed up being on the panel at the BlackOUT Film Festival to add a little color to your podium?"

The BlackOUT Film Festival. No wonder Helen was pissed.

"Oh, now, Helen, don't you think you're being just a little *paranoid*?" I could feel Tracy's voice gathering strength for a final verbal slap. "Why don't you go back to your table? Back to your dear, darling, Lee?"

"Lee?" Helen murmured. The word began with a surprised whisper and ended in horrible, heartbreaking certainty.

"Think about it, Helen. You'll never know what really happened on that Olivia Cruise."

"The Olivia Cruise? But Tracy, I thought—I thought you were with *Deborah!*"

"Deborah! Don't be so naive, Helen. Lee is every dyke's dream. And there weren't a lot of pulled muscles on the Olivia Cruise, Helen. Everybody was too busy *swimming*. And let me tell you, if you think Lee is good on dry land, you should give her a try in deep, tropical waters. Then she *really* gets wet!"

"Tracy." Helen took a deep breath and a look of disbelief crossed her face. "You really know how to *hate*."

"Oh, Helen, go back to your table!" Tracy laughed. "Back to your darling Lee. Maybe if you're really sweet she'll give you another convertible! In the meantime, I'll find a way of disposing of these." Tracy punctuated her suggestion with a dismissive flick of her toe at the manuscripts.

"You know, Tracy." Helen Thomas clutched the amulet around her neck. "You just barely deserve to *live*."

"Another murder mystery, Helen? Good luck figuring out the plot!" Tracy laughed. "Try *outlining* first!" Tracy turned and strode away on taut little legs into the arena of the gala dinner. I wasn't sure she'd heard Helen's threat. But someone else had.

Allen Boone stood in the darkness of his office, pink cummerbund and pink face glimmering, satin and sweat. He was staring intently at the box in my hand as if he could see through it and read all that was inside. Helen moved slowly up the stairs, a stricken look upon her face, a woman sleepwalking in a nightmare.

"What's with Helen?" Allen asked.

"She's a little upset."

"Has there been another misunderstanding?" he asked

quickly. "It's really all the board's fault. The time they take to come up with policy decisions! We *still* don't have acceptance guidelines. They're so inept it is practically impossible for us to do our jobs!" Allen was talking a mile a minute as he eyed the box that held Howard Blooming's journals. "Poor Tracy. Still, she *can* be *difficult*!"

"If this safe checks out"—I indicated the safety deposit boxes—"I'd like to secure these papers."

Allen gazed up at the hulking antique quizzically. "I don't know anything about this thing. What were David's instructions exactly?" Behind Allen I could see through the back door of his office.

"Sealed," I said. "Sealed for sixty years."

"Oh." Allen's face fell by degrees. "Sixty years," he whispered. I could almost hear him counting. We'd all be dead in sixty years. "Well, let me think about it. Come inside," he beckoned, his head glowing as he flipped a switch in his office and the place lit up. From the walls, faces glared at us from inside frames and sheet protectors.

"When the donated materials have all been assembled at the Archive, then I'm going to donate *my* collection." We gazed at the paper pyramids, the boxes, bags and photos. "It *will* be a project." Allen sighed. "And the board just drags its feet. . . ." He seemed to slump over. "But let me show you my pride and joy."

He gestured grandly to a display case in the corner. "Come, come." His hand circled, pulling me through his collection. I looked past a gold ring on Allen's hand into a glass-covered display case where forty or fifty pens rested on green felt.

Three rows of happy soldiers were laid to rest, tiny hand-lettered labels numbered underneath each nib. Tortoiseshell fountain pens, metallic blue ballpoints, a glass spiral quill, and several real quills, their feathers matted and clumped together, the ends worn. Two chewed-off pencils were held together with a red satin ribbon next to a delicate maroon automatic pencil.

"It's my Queer Quill Collection." His eyes sparkled. "Walt Whitman, my most expensive acquisition yet, from a quill pen auction at Butterfield's."

"And those?"

"Carla Tomaso chewed those pencils herself." The metal ferrules were bent and dented. I thought about the paint that must have made its way into Tomaso's mouth as she was writing. "And Sandra Scoppettone's red fine-line, hardly used. And here is the pen of Foucault. Now that's verified." The philosopher of culture had used the most ordinary of French dime-store pens. What *papeterie* had sold him the baby blue ballpoint? Its transparent barrel showed an empty ink cartridge and spring mechanism.

"The Henry James glass dip pen is not authenticated, but fun to think about. I got it in Italy. Probably a tourist rip-off. But it's beautiful." A twisted Venetian shaft, golden glass ending in a transparent lavender bubble and a round-handed nib. "There's Carson's fountain—I also have a letter authenticating—and this rusty pen point was purported to have belonged to Lizzie Borden!" Allen ribbed me, a little too hard. "Who wants to collect just the good gays?"

"Whose pen is this?" I asked. A soft-nosed, bullet-edged, heavy aqua fountain pen, banded in silver. A suitable accessory for a ladies' lunch. A lesbian lunch. A woman who would raise her veil, pull the silver arrow clip out of a breast pocket of a tweed jacket and sign—

"It wasn't a man, it wasn't a woman, it was the sea—"

"What?"

"Daphne du Maurier." He smiled wryly. "A self-hating

37

lesbian if there ever was one. I have a letter. Nevertheless she was in love—in consummated love—with Gertrude Lawrence. *Sepia* ink."

"And this one?"

"Lorraine Hansberry," he murmured, looking at a smart silver dart of a ballpoint pen. Narrow as a needle, tiny stripes etched along the barrel, I imagined the fingers which held it. "Such an intelligence, died of cancer, so young . . . wrote in a hurry, ballpoint pens, ha! ha! ha! Here's something from a garage sale almost twenty years ago now. Janis Joplin's pen."

A peacock feather made a long arch bisecting the cabinet. Its iridescent blue eye glimmered, feathers ending in an ordinary Flair pen. Amongst the other understated writing implements, it looked like much ado about nothing.

"I'm not even sure she should be in the collection." Allen sighed. "But the pen looks so good in the cabinet and it's real San Francisiana. She slept with more men than women, from what I hear . . . a Lady Gillette . . ." His voice droned on. I found myself wanting to reach behind the glass, wanting to feel the tortoiseshell pen of Carson McCullers between my fingers. Or Walt Whitman's writing instrument. Could some words still be trapped in the cleft of a golden pen nib, in the cells of a quill? Needing only a living hand to bring them out?

"Carl Van Vechten's ink stopper," Allen continued, cummerbund riding up over his belly as he leaned forward, squinting at a dark rubber stopper with something that looked like tenderness in his eyes. A mother bending over a newborn baby. "Couldn't get Carl Van Vechten's *pen*." He sighed. "But I've heard Yale might be willing to part with one . . . I'll know next week." *Tap, tap, scrape.* A strange tapping, four canes rapping, was coming toward Allen's back door.

"Omigod! Omigod!" Allen pulled me quickly past the pen collection and steered me into the hallway. *Tap, tap, tap, tap, scrape.* Glancing at his watch. "Have to make sure the office door is locked." He popped back into the little room and I heard the closing of a door. Returning. Allen stood at attention, adjusting his bow tie and pulling on the tails of his coat.

Tap, tap, tap, tap, scrape. Coming closer. A familiar sound, as was the figure which accompanied it. The person who drove the walker down the hallway was none other than Pulitzer Prize-winning poet Berniece Able.

"What in the hell do I have to do to get into this totally inaccessible shit hole?" Berniece's large ivory teeth were yellow, with thin black stripes down the center of them. The pallid pink pouches of her cheeks filled and emptied with air as she bore down upon us, a large canvas bag hung off of each fleshy shoulder. Bejeweled fingers grasped the walker, as much a potential weapon as an aid to support. Her sharp gaze, encased in rubbery features, sought Allen's eyes. "And there has been *no one* to brief me!" she accused him.

"Ohmigod! Berniece!" Allen was so busy apologizing and helping her with her load that he had almost forgotten about Howard Blooming's journals. I saw his hands tremble as he took the cloth sacks from Berniece. She released them gladly. The red of rubies, a square-cut sapphire and a cluster of small diamonds winked from her long weathered fingers. "You said eight-fifteen on the dot."

"Berniece, I'm so sorry—"

"Well, Allen, you've been hounding me for my scrap-

39

books for years. Years. So here they are." She smiled suddenly, her eyes becoming little gleaming crescents. "Here they are, dear," she repeated, a softness creeping into her voice.

"Berniece." Allen's mouth fell open, and closed. "I don't know what to say." His voice soft as flannel, Allen leaned over the railing of her walker to give her a big hug. Berniece, for all her bluster, let go of the walker. Clutching Allen's arms, the weathered fingers sank into the material of his suit.

"It's been a long time since I was shown to the back door," Berniece fondly admonished him.

"Oh, Berniece, the scrapbooks!" Allen could hardly contain himself. He pulled out one of the older photo albums and dropped immediately to the floor. Sitting cross-legged, he fingered the soft black paper. I moved closer and squinted at the yellowed prints that Allen was scanning so closely, each print carefully affixed with black corner mounts. Sepia faces shaded with broad-brimmed hats, vacations of long ago, lived on those pages. "Yes, yes," Allen breathed. "Here's Djuna Barnes."

"I thought she was a recluse," I said.

Berniece Able looked up at me for the first time. She let go of her walker with one hand to wave away a white strand of hair. She squinted her watery blue eyes, the little round mouth with the sagging lower lip pulling together in some negative decision. "Put the books down before the acid in your skin eats away all the faces of my former friends," she barked.

"Thank you, Berniece." Allen bowed slightly and stood up. "We are so very grateful. I can't tell you, this kind of acquisition is exactly—"

"Stop bowing and scraping. I'm glad to get rid of them.

Goddamn ghost list! All dead now. I have Lee and Helen. I'm luckier than most poets, with or without a Pulitzer Prize."

Ah, yes, didn't I remember that Berniece Able had been responsible for the match between Lee Turgo, her neighbor and chiropractor for years, and Helen Thomas? Lee Turgo had Rolfed Berniece Able into a standing position when the elderly poet was in deep pain, permanently hunched over, it seemed. The romance with Helen had been completely orchestrated by the laureate. It was one of her most successful epics; the couple had remained together for decades.

"Here!" Berniece hauled out a photo album whose cover was a silk psychedelic quilt, embroidered with bright orange California poppies. Berniece seemed to feel the separateness of each stitch with her highly jeweled fingers as she turned it over. "Helen made the cover for me, when she was a student." Berniece still sounded proud. I imagined Helen, as a college student, spending hours over this sentimental handiwork, a tradition of hand-crafted offerings from female students to female teachers for thousands of years. Perfect for the Archive.

"Did she sign it?" Allen was asking as Berniece handed the precious book over and watched him open it.

"I don't think so. There's an inscription."

"Oh, no!" Allen whispered.

"What?" Berniece demanded.

"Nothing, Berniece, nothing."

"What?" Berniece stomped the feet of her walker.

Allen shrugged, pointing to the photos trapped between gummed cellophane pages and cardboard. "This gummed adhesive, the images—" Allen muttered under his breath.

"Aw, there's Mildred! Never could get the barbecue started that day," Berniece said. I imagined the photo was of Mildred Dickerman, the world-renowned anthropologist and Berniece's lover of thirty years. "She had a hard mind in a soft science." Berniece flipped the pages, leaving happy memories behind. "Look." She seemed pleased to find a living person between the pages. "There's that *vampire* Tracy Port." Berniece poked a finger at a younger Tracy Port with long, hippie hair. Tracy's legs, skinny before the fitness craze, were crossed under an Indian bedspread miniskirt.

"Please, Berniece, she's my boss." Allen was uncomfortable.

"I'll say what I like!" Berniece shrugged her shoulders. "And stop whining about glue! I wasn't recording history when I pasted those in, I was having a love affair!"

"Yes, of course. Sorry, Berniece."

"Take the scrapbooks and do what you will." Berniece picked up her walker and pounded all four feet upon the floor in unison. I wondered if she needed the walker at all. "And you, young lady"—Berniece aimed her sights at me sternly—"don't assume every biography you read is true. Djuna a recluse! There's a lot of trumped up, closeted garbage out there masquerading as history. That's what this Archive is for."

"Wait, Berniece!" Allen crowed. "I've got it—Emma, Berniece—it's just the thing. It's just going to make the evening." Allen clapped his hands together, his palms making a hollow echo. "I'm going to have you each personally make the presentation during the dinner."

"Allen, I don't think—" I started.

"To let everyone know the kind of material we're getting." He beamed. "It couldn't be better—not even if

Tracy had thought of it herself!" He pulled his office door closed behind him. "The donations will roll in tonight."

"Do you want me to sign—" Berniece began to ask.

"Later, dear!"

"I really think Howard's journals should be in the safe—" I protested.

"Too late!" Allen said, bustling us out the long hallway as quickly as Berniece's walker would allow. The canvas bags with Berniece's photos bumped against Allen's sides. *Tap, tap, tap, tap, scrape.* Berniece's jewels glimmered, red, white, blue as her fingers gripped the metal tubing of her walker. "I'm compiling history right now," he said. "I'm compiling the history of now, now." Allen was chanting like a child and the sequined dress was strangling my body. The box covered with sticky tape seemed to cling to me. It was beginning to feel impossible to get rid of.

CHAPTER FOUR

APPETIZERS

Above ground, Berniece was surrounded by acolytes show-ering her with compliments. Pretending to bear up under their attentions, her eyes scanned the crowd. I needed to find my table. The cavernous hall was filled with snowy white circles and laden with heavy-handled silverware and numbers prominently displayed. Odd centerpieces poked up from tables along with table numbers. I wanted fifty-three. I peered closer at the centerpieces. Bird-of-paradise blooms were stuck into cement blocks at steep angles and draped with ivy, reminding me of earthquakes.

"Wow!" Next to me a crowd of people peered at the ceil-ing, mouths agape. Above us stretched the twisting torsos of muscle-laden figures flying across the plastered heaven. Multiracial bodies in fresco showed off their pecs and abs as they seemingly threw books to the heavens.

A huge, diaphanously clad female, her dark maroon breasts just visible beneath an Isadora Duncan nightie, her arms rippling with biceps, attempted to touch the out-stretched hand of an effete gay male poet. God as a mas-

44

sive black lesbian with a heart-shaped face, a cloud of jet black curls and feet as big as a hotel lobby.

"Larry Boznian's idea of camp," someone said. "Did you ever see his portrait of Michael Jackson done in macaroni shells?"

"No, that was—"

"I heard there was a donation of three hundred grand for this, this, cartoon!" a purpling face above a tuxedo claimed.

"Check out the seraphim!" Someone chuckled. Indeed, a bouquet of angels featured faces of local celebrities.

"Five hundred bucks got you a place on the ceiling for eternity," a bespectacled woman in a long evening dress told us. "What a great fundraising idea—wish I'd come up with the money. I wouldn't mind being on that ceiling, looking *down*," she mused. I noticed that some donors had opted for hell, where a gaggle of leather-clad literati happily roasted hot dogs over burning hellfire and brimstone.

"Hey, Victor!" That sounded like good news. I spun around to see Rose Baynetta in high gear, coming through in her wheelchair. Rose is a friend and sometime colleague who runs a private security agency.

"Glad to see someone in drag here, Emma." Rose snorted, staring at my dress. "See! The only lipstick is on lesbians. No gender bending here. Go figure! What happened, your dress shrink or something?"

"Thanks, Rose." Rose's curly blond hair formed a golden frame around a face that was always brown, the result of many freckles crammed close together. Rose had worked hard, worried harder and charged handsomely for her services, providing surveillance, bodyguards and state-of-the-art techno-sleuthing. She paid her operatives well, and I'd had occasion to use several of the simian types

Rose employed. Rose herself had been visiting the gym a lot lately. She showed off her arms in a sleeveless silk T-shirt and I noticed a recent "Rose" tattoo. Few people knew that her entire back was wallpapered. A lot of people only saw that Rose was paralyzed from the waist down. "I need to consult with you on a security matter."

"Good. We're at the same table. Allen arranged it. Now *there's* a human being! Have you met him yet, Emma?"

"Yes. Tell me about him."

"He's been sort of weekend lovers with Renquist for I don't know how long. That's how I got seated at the VIP table. His birthday is coming up. Very, very hard to find the appropriate present for Allen."

"I can imagine."

"I'll have to hit fifteen garage sales, or fifty."

"Can't you just get him something practical?"

"We're talking major eccentricity, Emma. Speaking of which, what's with the carpetbag?" She indicated the canvas bag, bulky with the hatbox of Howard's journals, Frances's notes and a change of clothes.

"Rose, that's what I want to talk to you—"

"Hi, Rose, dear!" Allen came over and clutched her hand, curling it inside his own. "Last weeks's find—a handwritten journal by one C. Hope Chumball, secretary to Charles Laughton and Elsa Lanchester. A fifty-cent journal in a secondhand store. A little extra paper, but then I found the writing. *Highly* entertaining—"

We were interrupted by a lot of noise, a lot of political noise. Renquist Falkenberg, city supervisor, was making an entrance to applause.

"Did you hear about the BART extension, Emma? Finally approved!" Rose crowed.

"We did it! We did it together!" Renquist received hugs

and hands. "The Bay Area Rapid Transit will now extend to the airport. And I vow to you, the airport light rail will extend itself into a Bullet Train which will speed from San Francisco to Los Angeles and will liberate California from the car! Ha! Ha!"

Renquist, with the grace and ease that only large people, comfortable with their bulk, can have, extended his hand to a vast range of voters in turn. There were congratulations which continued. "Mixed-income housing," he was saying, "located at light rail stops. Hi there, Mathew! Yeah, Marin is next!" Renquist was victorious, his oversized tux glittering with a selection of mojos. "Yes, the wetlands will be protected," he was saying. Allen and Rose had melted away into the crowd and Renquist was coming toward me.

"Emma," he said softly, drawing me to him. We'd always camped out in the same camps when it came to Howard Blooming and public transportation.

"Renquist, I'm so glad about BART," I said. Why was it that so many people enjoyed hugging Renquist, myself included? I found myself smiling as I surfed along the rim of Renquist's belly. The silver mojos dangling from his neck pressed against my cheeks, leaving temporary tattoos on my face. Public transportation to the airport. Frances would have that extra twenty minutes before she left next time. Renquist released me as he noticed my large canvas bag.

"What do you have there, Emma?"

"A donation for the Archive." The journals seemed suddenly heavier as Renquist scanned the bag.

"Lovely! I thought maybe it was a Generation X accessory!"

"It's Howard Blooming's final journals."

"What?" The large jaw slackened and his eyes widened, dilating.

I opened the zipper of the canvas bag and gave him a glimpse of the box.

"Where did you get them?" he asked quietly. Very quietly.

"From David Stimpson."

"Why is all that tape wrapped—"

"Sealed for sixty years."

There was a brief silence. His face registered what might have been the tiniest degree of relief. "Well, Howard always knew what he was doing, didn't he? Now, if you'll excuse me, Emma." Renquist drifted away.

Howard Blooming had made it clear that he wished his successor to be Falkenberg. He had chosen well. After Howard's death Falkenberg had eagerly turned Howard's political capital into filling for his campaign coffers, liberal money from as far away as Hollywood. He helped closeted gay movie stars who wanted to assuage their guilt to become anonymous donors to various causes, groups that fought for the civil rights of people who *had* come out. Renquist brought the African-American community into some formerly lily-white organizations, the all-white groups always grateful for the diversity that Renquist's dark face brought. But Renquist brought a lot more than that. He brought sound judgment and an even hand to all disputes; he was an able deal maker who constructed win-win situations out of communication breakdown.

"Hey, Emma, look who else is at our table!" Rose was at my elbow again. As I looked up, Deborah Dunton, the couples counselor and author of the best-selling *Lesbians Who Love Too Much*, approached. Deborah Dunton was twenty-nine years old, medium weight, medium height and medium intelligence. She had dishwater blond hair, a southern accent which she tried to conceal and a brow that worked overtime to look earnest. She always wore expensive Italian shoes. I'd always looked at her feet when Frances and I had consulted with the famous couples counselor. *Her* unconscious had made us cut short our therapy. Deborah searched her handbag for a pen, then turned to Allen Boone.

"Deborah's such an understanding therapist—" Rose hissed sarcastically.

"Until you leave her," I finished.

"Wasn't a good experience, Emma?"

"There are hours that I spent in that Toys "R" Us office of hers I'd like to forget forever."

"What'd she do, Emma?"

"Nothing I could actually put my finger on." I watched Deborah accept a pen from another fan who had appeared with a book. "She liked to sit next to me on her couch. She gave Frances her therapeutic schedule so that Frances could call her during her free hours. She encouraged Frances to do so. Once, when Frances was out of town, Dunton called to make sure I was okay. I had been fine. Until she called. It was one of my lonely physician widow Saturday nights."

"Are we talking legal grounds? Malpractice, Emma?"

"No. Not that I'd ever bring a suit. But Dunton has the kind of movable boundaries that cause wars between countries."

"Between dykes it is disaster."

"Or worse. A number of former clients are disgruntled. I think she's cutting back on clients and trying to become a writer," I commented.

"I'll tell you, Deborah's status as relationship guru nearly floundered last year."

"How?"

"On a cruise," Rose confided. I remembered the conversation on the loading dock in the basement of the Archive, between Helen and Tracy Port.

"What's your hard information?" I asked, curious.

"The way I hear it," Rose explained, "Deborah had been running after Tracy for months. When Tracy had expressed some interest in one of the women-only cruises to the Bahamas, Dunton booked tickets for Tracy and herself as a birthday surprise. She'd reserved separate rooms and hoped for the best. That's the buzz.

"Once on the boat, however, Tracy avoided her. And worse, Tracy threw herself publicly at the cruise chiropractor, the smoldering Lee Turgo—"

"—and longtime mate of Helen Thomas," I murmured. That's why Helen had been so upset. And possibly why Berniece Able had called Tracy a vampire.

"We all know Helen is always going off on some book tour," Rose said. "Translations mean transatlantic trips. Lee might still be in love with the crime queen, but Helen wasn't there to keep the sheets warm."

"I know how she feels, but *Tracy Port*?"

"You don't know Tracy when she turns on the charm, Emma. She's almost *normal*. Anyway, no one ever knew if Lee Turgo succumbed to Tracy's advances. But Deborah Dunton was dumped and worse. Feature public humiliation on deck, Emma. At every bridge party, scuba diving expedition and shuffleboard contest, so I hear." Deborah took a sip of white wine. "There was even reference in the *BAR* gossip column. *Lesbians Who Laugh Too Little*. After

50

that, sales of *Lesbians Who Love Too Much* dropped like a lead balloon."

I looked over at Deborah Dunton making eye contact with old clients in the dining room, winking and waving. Someone had pulled a hardcover copy of *Lesbians Who Love Too Much* out of her handbag and Deborah was scribbling her signature on the title page. "But sales picked up again." Rose finished the saga. "*Lesbians Who Love Too Much* will always be a classic. It seems that lesbians, at least some lesbians, will always love too much."

"What's she doing here? She donated to Tracy's cause?"

"After a major donation—I think Daddy's trust fund came through—Deborah was elected president of the board of the Archive, a position in which she is essentially Tracy's boss!" Rose set her empty glass down on the table as she finished her story. She looked around for another bottle. "They really skimp at these galas, don't they?"

Deborah Dunton, president of the board. And here she comes, I thought, smelling Deborah's signature scent, onguard gardenia.

"Why hi there, Emma," Deborah purred. "Long ti-i-i-i-me, no see." The Southern cadence was still audible. Shiny ebony buttons held a thin silk blouse closed at the neck; Deborah played with them as if to make sure she was sufficiently covered. Rose wheeled away. Thanks a lot. "How ah things goin'?"

"Okay." I tried to guess where Deborah would place herself at the table so I could sit as far away as possible from her. There were still too many open chairs to be able to tell.

"Where's Frances tonight?" Deborah's tone was always neutral. I scanned the room desperately for Rose, for any-

51

one with a hardback copy of *Lesbians Who Love Too Much*. "Where *is* Frances, Emma?"

Those tones, always those supercilious, insinuating tones. Did they teach them that at therapy school? Was it supposed to sound empathic? I searched for an answer to her question that would require the least explanation. "Working," I said.

"And how are"—Dunton ventured closer—"things going with your relationship?"

"Okay."

"You have a lotta repressed anger, Emma." She waggled a finger, tempting me to bite it off.

"Only toward therapists with bad boundaries. Can I pour you another drink, Deborah?"

Deborah raised her thin brown eyebrows. "It seems like you still have some leftover issues—"

I was saved by the arrival of Carla Ribera.

"Blast from the past." Rose wheeled back as we all turned to watch the dramatic entrance of Rose's former heartthrob.

"Just back from Rome!" Carla announced, her lips a fierce slash of red; black silky curls brushed high off her forehead trickled down the middle of her back like the waving tail of a stallion. Carla Ribera was a fashion photographer who could wear the clothes as well as she could shoot them. Five foot ten, Carla had couture clothes custom cut to her hefty size. The result was always a success. An exquisitely cut Edwardian jacket of teal blue lay over a roughly textured rayon shirt with flounces at the cuff. The open neck gave Carla a kind of pirate look, perfect for the business she was in. Carla had been a hippie, but now she was a jet-setter. Unfortunately, that included the pungent smoke of the Gauloises Carla was waving around the room. A small dapper man was standing behind her.

"Just back from Rome!" Carla announced again.

"Where nobody minds breathing your second-hand smoke, Carla," Rose drawled. "Bought a new closet for your clothes and your life yet?"

"Oh, Roseanna, why don't you get an identity instead of identity politics," Carla Ribera shot back. A small, but grim, grin passed between them. Carla had pruned Rose from her life when her fashion career had taken off. Carla blew smoke high up into the air from that large red mouth, her black curls trailing over her shoulders. How had this image of trendiness ever bonded with the rough and ready Rose?

Easy. Carla used to be a documentary filmmaker. During the shooting of one of Carla's films she interviewed activists who were in wheelchairs. She didn't expect to fall in love with one of her subjects. But Roseanna Baynetta, known by most of us simply as Rose, had had the face of a state fair queen and a tongue like a razor. She had been a ballet dancer before a car accident had cut short her career. The dramatic story made good film footage. And Rose's hands had given Carla a few surprises, too.

Rose's father had been at the wheel when the accident occurred. The other driver had been drunk, but Rose's father had hardly been sober. He had pushed Rose away from him, sending her to boarding schools and showering her with expensive gifts. He was in the security business and worked for several large fashion houses. But Rose didn't want his money or the dresses. Rose wanted his equipment.

Slowly she learned the security trade and gathered his

cast-off supplies. She and Carla joined forces. Rose investigated and uncovered. Carla made documentary films from the results. They collaborated on any number of projects during their five-year relationship.

But then Carla got tired. Tired of applying for grants, tired of giving benefits for her films, tired of fighting the network system in the States, tired of being cast in a minority slot. Rose introduced Carla to her father, who helped her get an interview with a large fashion house in Paris. Carla's pictures stopped moving and her career took off.

Carla restyled her hair, her clothes and her sexuality to fit her new life and the fabulous new people in it. A femme top in bed, Carla Ribera jetted around the world and laid every runway model in a jet-set version of *Lesbians Who Love Too Little*. She never made another documentary. Rose pretended, with misplaced righteousness, to despise her. Rose couldn't forgive her. Carla couldn't forgive Rose for not forgiving her. It was tiresome. And it was not over.

"She's still in love with me," Rose confided.

"All those foreign locales and long-legged models must be just a pose," I agreed.

"Ahem!" A spoon found a glass and everyone stopped talking.

"I would like to present to you all," Carla bellowed formally, "the creator of the mural which spans above us, Larry Boznian!"

The small man behind her was ushered toward us. He was about fifty, with a square patch of fur under his lip and the largest ears I had seen since the Mickey Mouse Club. He was wearing a red-checked sportsjacket. Larry Boznian pressed his lips tightly together in what might pass for a smile.

"It's fabulous!" Allen cooed.

"What an accomplishment!" Renquist congratulated him.

Larry, eyes flickering at the ground, muttered, "Just a cartoon." His arm darted out sideways to a tray of drinks, torn fingernails evident around a glass of white wine curled instantly to his chest.

Carla Ribera came to the rescue. "I want you all to welcome Larry to San Francisco. He's here with—Larry, where is Fresca?"

"She's in the *loo*," Larry said, his voice a surprise. That clipped accent, the *loo*! I looked at the painter. He really didn't seem the creative type. Everything about him was exceedingly neat and kept up, like a well-tended garden. The little beard, bow tie, the suit with the pressed plaid pleated pants. Only his hands belied his profession.

His nails were torn from prying open paint lids, his fingertips stained with the mud color of mixed pigments. He hid his hands quickly when he saw me notice them. But his fingers were pressed down by another, new hand. A hand, it seemed, that didn't want him to pick up that glass.

It was a young hand, brown with strong fingers. Broad fingernails, cut short, with seashell pink nails. Bronze buffed arms that would have made Fabio jealous. A T-shirt, mostly worn away, revealed a gray athletic bra. Her breasts moved as she leaned forward. T-shirt flapped around generous hips where a pair of paisley-patterned jockey shorts were just visible through the holes. The jeans, of course, were ripped in long tears down the front and back. White ladders of thread tried to keep the knees together and, with the aid of a few safety pins, managed to succeed. A baseball cap was screwed backward on her head.

A large birthmark was laid like a ruby at the base of her throat. A heart-shaped face with pointed chin and broad cheekbones reflected the same determined expression as the Goddess on the ceiling. She was, in fact, the Goddess on the ceiling. I looked down and confirmed my suspicions. Submarine feet in black boots laced up mid-calf. She was Larry Boznian's model, and maybe, Carla Ribera's model, too. A little too fleshy for fashion, but a certain mysterious glamour clung to her like stardust. Just the stuff for Carla's lens.

Observant, taking everything in, she seemed to search the very corners of the room like a security guard. She couldn't possibly be as young as she looked. Or she wouldn't be here. She wouldn't have those searching eyes. Would she? Her eyes found mine and stayed there for a moment; careful flatness in those eyes. The only remaining empty chair was next to me. She was going to have to sit in it. I held my breath. This dinner was looking up. Deborah Dunton was far, far away, on the other side of the table.

"Please, can we all take our seats now?" Renquist was booming. "Allen, Deborah, let's see, we're still missing Helen Thomas and Lee, Lee Turgo. There's Larry, and yes, sorry, Francesca Alcazon, correct? Nice to meet you, Francesca."

"It's *Fresca* Alcazon." Her voice was honey.

"*I address my caress, my caresses to the one who blesses who blesses me—*" It was Larry Boznian and Larry Boznian was getting drunk. "Fresca is author of *Language Empiricism: Gertrude Stein and the Repudiation of Syntactical Causality,*" Larry said proudly, "which won the Modern Language—"

"Larry, please, you make it too important," Fresca said.

"I've got some Stein letters to Virgil Thomson if you'd like to see them," Allen piped up.

Fresca's eyebrows raised. "From Thomson's Paris period?"

Allen thought about it, playing with a little field of bread crumbs in front of him. A fountain pen gleamed from an inside breast pocket. I imagined ink leaking out onto the lining of his coat, staining the pink cummerbund. A pocket protector. Something silver for his birthday. An initial engraving would personalize it, perfect for an archivist. I would mention it to Rose and save her fifty garage sales. The bread crumbs had given him the answer. "No, the Thomson letters we have were written during the forties when he moved back to New York," he confirmed.

"Oh." Eyebrows descended, eyes dimming.

"Fresca's never interested with anybody's New York period!" Larry sneered. "There is no there *there*!"

"And this is Helen Thomas." Renquist's voice boomed above Larry's tinny whine. Helen Thomas drew Fresca's eyes like a magnet.

"The mystery novelist?" Fresca asked in a measured tone.

Helen nodded.

"I've read *all* your books. I can't tell you! I'm so glad to meet you." Fresca wasn't afraid of being a fan.

"Thank you." Helen's eyes blinked slowly, long lashes grazing her cheek, looking for all the world like Bambi. "That's always lovely to hear."

"And may I ask"—Fresca's eyes narrowed in on Helen's chest—"is that the Amigreed Amulet?"

"Yes!" Helen was always a little too delighted to tell the story. "Do you know about it?"

"I read *Grandmother's Poison* on a transatlantic flight."

Fresca's fingers wound themselves in a strand of hair by her shoulder. Twenty-five, I thought. Twenty-five and been through a lot. There's an old woman's wisdom inside that child, playing with her hair. "I didn't even notice that I was in an airplane seat for twelve hours!" Fresca continued, "Great story, and who could have ever guessed the ending!"

"*I* didn't read the book," Larry said, for no apparent reason at all.

"No, you just slept on my shoulder during the flight." Fresca patted his hand a little too quickly, trying to calm a cynical storm that was coming. A waiter approached with a hard drink. Fresca caught his eye, shaking her head. The waiter disappeared. Who was Fresca? The muralist's lover, model or *nurse*?

"The amulet is purported to have had poison in it." Helen seemed oblivious to Larry's cynicism. Or she liked bending over toward Fresca. "See the wax seal?" The amulet, poised in Helen's palm, had a silver stopper where the two curves of the heart met. The stopper was attached with a thin chain, and a tiny bit of sealing wax around the rim was still visible. "The amber isn't clear enough to see if there's anything inside. But allegedly it belonged to Rasputin—"

"The lover of the Empress of Russia," Larry mumbled.

"Made by one of the Fabergé brothers, as I recall." Fresca squinted. "And it ended up with an ancestor of Berniece Able. Wasn't that the story?"

"So, the old lady gave you a necklace and you wrote a book." Larry's bitter sarcasm was becoming too hard to ignore. He had somehow acquired another drink. "You must have a *nice life*."

"Oh, shut up Larry, and stop ruining yours." Fresca

pulled the drink away from the man and poured it into the centerpiece. Everyone pretended not to notice. There must have been a twenty-year age difference, but Fresca acted for the world just like Larry Boznian's *mother*. "Helen's novels are not just potboiler mysteries, Larry," Fresca said. "Helen makes her point by subverting the traditions which have kept our political agenda suppressed—"

"Doesn't matter who's elected." Larry, completely in his cups, was audible to the whole table. "The same government always gets in. Whoever said art makes politics *clean*—"

"*In vino veritas.*" Allen Boone was watching Renquist.

"Ahem, ahem, ladies and gentlemen, our table is nearly complete." Renquist continued the introductions. "I'd like to introduce Lee Turgo."

Lee Turgo, Helen's mate. Lee Turgo. Mid-thirties, five foot nine, medium build with a big swathe of auburn hair which fell boyishly over her left brow. A tall, quiet, woman, big hands, big heart, and big bedroom baby blue eyes. Big deal. Well, there was an indelible charm. I noticed Fresca perusing the object of romantic competition between Helen and Tracy. I looked over at Lee's hands, the broad palms, and the tiny, perfectly manicured white nails. There was something mysterious about Turgo. "Long, thick fingers, four clinics and forty employees on payroll," Rose muttered from across my sequined lap. "If you are lucky, very lucky," she advised Fresca, "you could maybe get an appointment with her someday. They say you are never the same afterward."

"I could use a little bit of that." Fresca sighed to herself, her eyes fluttering over the unfortunate muralist.

"Helen, honey, that's you!" The rumbling voice of the

laureate carried over the table. Berniece's scrapbook was being shown around. Helen was cooing over it, stroking Lee's neck as they hunched over the photographs. Lee Turgo put her arm around Helen's waist and peered closer, that shock of auburn hair falling into her eyes. She pushed it away to better see the picture.

"Sure is." Lee Turgo was a woman of few words and little sentimentality. She scratched the side of her neck as she viewed the pictures.

"It's that baptism, honey." Helen poked her in the ribs.

"Yeah, I remember."

"There you are—in bell-bottom pants! And look at all the babies!"

"Babies in arms, strollers and slings. Babes nursing, bottle feeding, sleeping, crying, fussing, laughing, in the morning of their life," Berniece mused. "Hey, that's you, Allen!" Her finger roamed over the page. "And Renquist!" Carla Ribera came over and bent low over the book. "Didn't you take those pictures, Carla?" Berniece enquired.

"No, I—" Carla gulped down some wine, squinting at the photos.

"Yes, you did," Berniece insisted. "Come on, Carla, you started out as a shutterbug just like everyone else."

"I'm sorry, I didn't catch your name." Fresca's velvet voice came into my ear, a question stated with the flat tones of a fact.

"Emma Victor." I held out my palm and received her eye beams.

"What are you doing here?"

"I might ask you the same thing."

"I asked you first."

"Okay, I'm a patron. How's that?" I said. "And you?"

"Friend of Larry and Carla's. They always like to bring a friend along to what they perceive as corporate events, not to mention the fact that I'm on the ceiling. That's the chip on *their* shoulder—the chip they always leave behind when it comes time to take a bow."

"Hey, I can understand that."

"It's that dysfunctional relationship between art and money," Fresca said. "Keeping your vision and paying the bills. Producing the work and moving the units of product. Carla's in *fashion*. That was her solution."

I looked over at Carla, who was interested in Berniece's jewelry. "But, Emma, you must be major A-gaylist to be at the VIP table?"

"Girlfriend of A-list," I admitted. "Well, wannabe-A-list."

"And you, Emma? Where do you see all this stuff heading, the galas—"

"The murals?" I said. Fresca winced. "I can see it," I intoned. "A few years from now, she'll be holding a cheese sandwich and they'll be calling this the Velveeta Lesbian and Gay Archive . . . The Baskin-Robbins Gay Men's Chorus will sing . . . everything's going corporate. But I won't."

"I wouldn't mind settling down." Fresca examined the moons on her nails, rising over carefully kept cuticles. Again I had that strange impression of her as someone timeless. And born yesterday. Twenty-year-old hands with an eighty-year-old history. "I could sure use staying in one place," she said. "Getting together a whole store of dried beans, peas, a pantry of preserves—"

"What, this from the author of *Language Empiricism*, what was it, *Gertrude Stein and the Renunciation*—"

"*Repudiation*, but I like 'Renunciation' better. Gertrude would have liked it, too. But before I completely renounce

61

my life, maybe you would tell me what you want? Just to be even."

"I want, I want. . . ." I looked around the room at all the milling and swilling. The canvas bag between my feet, the dress was squeezing me, an unhappy hide. "I want to change my clothes," I said.

Fresca's lip curled. "I certainly don't know why."

Flash! Blink! Whirr! Our table came under flashbulb attack. It was a photo opportunity for everyone, except Fresca Alcazon, who decided it was time to help Larry Boznian to the bathroom.

"Wait, photograph!" Milky white cleavage was escaping a bustier that had seen better days. Tattered stockings and garments had been pulled helter-skelter over her head. Polaroid camera poised, pierced and perforated in every visible spot on her body, Gurl Jesus, waitress at Red Dora's Cafe. And now, it seemed, gala photographer.

Gurl glittered just like the flashbulbs she was popping at the diners at our table. Swiped with black lipstick, chomping on a wad, taking photo after photo. The empty chairs of Fresca and Larry afforded her a good view of me.

"Hey, what you doin' here? Never expected to see you." Gurl popped a flash as I held up my hand.

"The coffee's better at Dora's, but the books and the bucks are going to be here," I said. "That's why you're here, isn't it?"

"Yeah." *Chomp, flash, chomp, flash.* Gurl changed batteries on the flash attachment, finding a new battery in the webbing of her dress and popping it into the Polaroid. "It's a gig," she said and turned around toward Tracy, taking the executive director by surprise. *Pop! Pop!* More photos of Tracy, moving behind Helen, of Renquist hugging

Deborah Dunton, Dunton pushing him away. *Photo, click, whirr.* Of Allen talking earnestly to Berniece Able, who couldn't stop turning the pages of memories in front of her, even as she was distracted by Carla Ribera, who kept poking her nose into the scrapbook, declaiming any responsibility for the photos. Gurl Jesus's camera was whirring and whining.

Flash! Flash!

Tracy managed a final grin and stood up. "I have to start this ceremony before the waiter *kills* me!" Tracy rose. The roomful of hungry diners looked her way. So did Deborah Dunton and Lee Turgo with mixed expressions on both their faces.

"We'll do a postmortem, sometime, okay, Emma?" Gurl Jesus hoisted a tattered bra strap which had slipped off her shoulder. "Prints will be available at Fox Photo on Eighteenth and Castro starting tomorrow! Look in the window!" She started aiming at other tuxedoed patrons, tilting her hips suggestively. In the distance diners smiled and beckoned. She took off, skinny twitchy legs, construction boots clattering on the marble.

One seat away, Larry Boznian, his face a little fresher from some cold water, took his seat. Fresca Alcazon's fingers grazed my arm, a surprising gesture, an invitation? I looked sideways at that profile. Ginger snap. Perfect posture, except for the invisible umbilical cord which kept pulling her in Larry's direction. The perfect caretaker for part of Carla Ribera's jet-setting set. Forget it, Emma. Fresca crossed her legs and leaned forward. I saw her breasts move under the raggedy T-shirt. Somehow, it made me think of St. Croix and palm trees.

Everyone looked toward the podium. I found myself looking at the tender juncture where Fresca's jeans struggled to cover her paisley boxer shorts. The silk stretched, like a patterned sealskin over her pubis, a long, long stretch of beach. Warm and endless.

"Any closer," Rose whispered, "and your face is going to be in her lap."

CHAPTER FIVE

SPEECH

Tracy mounted the podium carefully on her high heels, arranging some notes in front of her. *"If I may have your attention!"* We looked up. Tracy, in her black sequined armor, was so energetic, well informed, so politically correct. *"It is my great pleasure to welcome you to the Reading Room of the Howard Blooming Lesbian and Gay Memorial Archive of San Francisco!"*

Cheers shook the rafters; the painted Goddess above us seemed to soar, her filmy gown billowing in the waves of applause.

"Fuck San Francisco," I thought I heard Larry Boznian mumble. Fresca and Carla exchanged worried glances.

"Tonight, I want to welcome you all, to this momentous occasion. Our history—our lesbian and gay history—has been ignored, our books burned, our stories rewritten, our tongues silenced. But no more!"

More applause. Tracy beamed as the sound of three thousand hands clapping swelled and subsided.

"We must band together to fight for our right to exist! This li-

brary—this lesbian and gay library—will preserve our past, a past we have fought to uncover, a past we must fight to protect!"

"Get ready for revisionism," Rose whispered.

"When we started this project fifteen years ago, it was just a dream."

"Yeah, it was a nightmare for the public library staff," Rose hissed. "History shouldn't be in the hands of the government; the papers of the lesbian and gay community should be held by a community non-profit group. What if our history is destroyed by some evil reactionary turn of political climate?" Rose shrugged her shoulders.

"The Magnus Hirschfeld library in the Institute for Sex Research had been destroyed in Berlin in 1933 by the Nazis. Valuable papers lost to history forever! Twelve thousand books and thirty-five thousand photographs! It could happen here!" Fresca's voice cut in. A woman who loved books.

"Eight hundred grant applications later, we appealed to our community . . . " Tracy droned on, cataloging the late-night meetings, the endless fundraisers, the huge sacrifices of time and money that went into erecting the monumental edifice that housed our history. *"And tonight,"* Tracy said, *"I am proud to say that over nine hundred of you here have donated one thousand dollars!"*

"Nine hundred thousand dollars!" I whistled. *"Almost a million!"*

"Please, donors, raise your hands!" Tracy called into the throng. Hands shot up from all over the room.

"And now, I'd like to present Larry Boznian, creator of the mural which spans the ceiling of our archive, creating a homo heaven, in the style of Michelangelo, for our brothers and sisters to enjoy for eternity!"

Mumble, mumble. Larry Boznian was such a newcomer! But then, as the audience began to look up at the startling frescoed figures above our head, the occasional clap was repeated, until a thunderous roar filled the room.

Larry Boznian stood up too quickly and lost his footing. He grabbed on to his chair, and then his hand found Fresca's shoulder and he steadied himself. Her hand gripped his like a vise.

"Cheers!" He raised a glass to the crowd. Larry Boznian was a genius. Larry Boznian was a drunk. "Cmon, honey, stand up." Larry pulled Fresca out of her chair. "You owe it to the world to *smile*," he said and tilted her chin up. The crowd, recognizing the model for the Goddess, roared in approval. With a satisfied nod Larry settled back into his chair. "You owe it to the world to stay *seated*," she said, referring to his drunken condition.

"What is it like, the moment when you give your masterpiece to the public?" Allen asked.

"I'm more comfortable on my *back*." Larry crossed his legs, nearly falling off his chair. Fresca had problems not rolling her eyes across the table at Carla. Helpless.

"And you, Emma, how comfortable are you on your back?" Fresca asked me.

"What?"

"Yes, we celebrate our lesbian and gay heritage with pride, brothers, and sisters, pride!" The crowd burst into more applause, and Tracy gave them enough leash to cause whatever was waiting in the kitchen to congeal. The headwaiter was eating his knuckles by the kitchen door.

"After dinner, during dessert," Tracy continued, *"I understand that we will be accepting acquisitions for the library. We will be happy to house Frances Cohen's original research notes on* Lesbo-Parthenogenesis, *the memorabilia of Berniece Able, and*

the final papers"—she paused here for emphasis— *"of Howard Blooming!"*

I felt the big gummy ball of tape trapped in the canvas bag at my feet. The announcement resulted in shocked silence, then murmurs of delighted surprise. *"And now, for our main speaker of the evening, popular mystery novelist, Helen Thomas!"*

Across the room, Helen rose from her chair to applause. Her skirt swung in a perfect circle as she turned to make her way to the podium. But Tracy Port took this moment to nod to a frantic waiter. Helen was just mounting the pulpit as scores of servers emerged from the kitchen, long lines of black-suited men balancing tray upon tray of clanking dishes.

Clearing her throat, Helen had just adjusted the mike when Tracy arrived back at the table followed by a phalanx of obedient waiters pushing large covered platters in between the diners to the rhythm of her nod.

Service was family style, but the atmosphere wasn't. Nobody wanted to start passing large covered dishes, nor did anyone want to serve others while Helen was speaking. I heard Helen clear her throat loudly. The tall woman with the big voice usually had no trouble attracting the attention of a crowd. But the famished diners had been waiting too long for dinner.

"Well, I'm starving!" Tracy took the lid off one of the casseroles. She nearly dropped it, a noisy clatter which attracted the attention of several tables. Soon everyone was busy with food, lifting the lids to reveal mounds of potatoes ready for each plate—and no one was listening to what Helen Thomas was saying.

"When I was growing up in the projects," she began.

"Too bad." Fresca's mouth came close to my ear, whispering, as we eyed the potatoes. "There is such great produce in California . . ."

Lee Turgo was smoldering, watching her lover struggling to project over the noisy diners. But it was hard not to watch dinner being revealed in the middle of the table. "Fish, fish, fish," the crowd was muttering, passing platters and scraping serving spoons, making Helen's speech almost inaudible. "Shhh!" hissed Lee.

"*I remember my great-aunt . . .*" Helen was saying. Lee Turgo shot us all a warning glance but the situation was way out of control.

"I am a vegetarian!" Fresca confided, her warm breath and continued attention almost making me forget my loyalty to Helen. "So is Larry! Completely vegan!"

Completely smashed, I thought, eyeing the drunken painter with distaste. What *was* their relationship anyway? Bisexual?

"No one really expects anything from the food tonight," Deborah Dunton stated. I found myself patting Fresca's leg, the soft strings of her ragged Levi's tangling with my finger. "Shh, let's listen to *Helen*," I whispered, turning back to the podium, straining to hear Helen's words. What was she saying?

"*The bookmobile in our neighborhood . . . the projects . . . window on the world . . .*"

Helen was losing speed quickly. Her voice was crawling back into her throat. The sea of diners was groaning over the cod. Mounds of *Gratin Dauphinois* were exhausted and replenished by busy waiters; bar boys were filling requests for extra drinks from the discouraged diners. How could Helen compete?

She didn't. She gave up. She mumbled, she chanted, she raced angrily through her speech. And who would blame her? When Helen left the podium she was fuming. And she went straight to Tracy Port.

The *Gratin Dauphinois* had just been served up onto Tracy's plate. "Are the potatoes in a dairy sauce?" Tracy wondered aloud, ignoring Helen's arrival.

"You have quite a sense of timing!" Helen sputtered, looming like a dark malevolent shadow behind the executive director. Lee Turgo nervously knitted her talented hands under the table.

"Wonderful speech." Tracy forked a flaky morsel into her mouth, avoiding Helen's eyes.

"How would *you* know? How would *anyone* know? Could anyone even *hear* me up there?" The table fell quiet. Helen fell into a chair next to Lee, who put her hand over Helen's, but Helen shook it off.

"I'm sorry, Helen," Tracy explained in an offhand way. "The headwaiter was having trouble with the chef—the fish—"

"Fish! You think this floor-wax-covered flounder is *edible*? Pass me some potatoes!" Helen almost jerked the platter of potatoes out of Tracy's hands. I wondered for a horrible moment if she would hurl it at Tracy. But Helen was trying hard to get it together, concentrating on spooning potatoes onto her plate. Her hand was shaking badly.

"Are you sure this isn't a dairy sauce?" Tracy held a forkful of potatoes in front of her, looking at it strangely.

"No, there's no dairy, dear," Renquist consoled her.

"Did you hear what I said, Tracy?" demanded Helen.

"Please, Helen," Lee Turgo cautioned.

"Don't you *please, Helen* me!"

Lee gritted her teeth and looked into her lap, that swathe of hair covering her eyes, making it impossible to see her face. Poor Helen. I could see that she was close to tears.

"Excuse me," she muttered, and raced out of the dining room. The black skirt billowed behind her as she ran furiously out of the hall, toward the wheelchair-accessible restrooms, dissed beyond belief. I counted to ten, picked up my canvas bag, slung it over my shoulder and went after her. I found Helen Thomas repairing her lipstick in a quiet corner of the women's room. Her hand was shaking.

"It was nice of you to follow me out, Emma," she said. "But don't worry, I'll survive." I looked at her face. She was having trouble keeping within her lip line. She put down her lipstick and sighed. "Tracy's just a drama queen; she loves to make this kind of stupid trouble between couples. Her fling with Lee wasn't important. I know that." She moved a fingertip over her upper lip, removing an errant stroke of color. Her hand was fine now. "When push comes to shove, Tracy Port just ain't marriage material, Emma."

"Who is?" I watched Helen run her glossy, bronze lipstick over her lips again. The motion seemed to make her calmer. Back and forth. Blotting carefully. Getting everything under control. The warm metallic color just matched the piping of her collar. An alarm bell was ringing in my head. Something was terribly missing from Helen's outfit. Before I could attend to it, Helen said firmly, "Emma, do you mind, I just need to be alone for a moment."

"Helen—"

"Please." She screwed the lipstick back and snapped on the top. I gave her a quick hug. I left her there, smoking and thinking. I hoped it did her some good. She wouldn't be any happier later.

I returned to the table to find Fresca propping up Larry Boznian in his chair.

"Maybe you'd better send Larry home in a cab," I suggested.

"You know, maybe that isn't a bad idea." Fresca's hands rose off the tablecloth as if the tablecloth might keep her from doing something she wanted to. "Maybe that isn't a bad idea at all."

"I could show you a bit of San Francisco—" The words came out of my mouth before I knew I'd said them. San Francisco rolled up its streets at eleven o'clock.

"It's just that the artistic community here in San Francisco has not been at all supportive of Larry's work." Fresca's hands rested again on the tablecloth, her fingers knitting invisible socks and sweaters. All for Larry Boznian. "Larry's an outsider; people are like that everywhere," replied Fresca with resignation. "Everywhere we go."

"Sounds pretty grim."

"It does? Oh shit, Emma, I'm sorry. Am I complaining again? I'd better duck back into my Gertrude Stein. It's the only thing that gives me any perspective anymore. And Larry will shape up. Once he gets his due."

"Oh, San Francisco is so provincial!" Carla Ribera interjected. "It's a pretty town and nice to *look* at, but what is there to *do* here?"

"You used to like it, Carla," Rose said softly. Her voice held no rancor, only sadness. "You used to live here."

"Do you think the potatoes had any dairy?" Tracy repeated again. Something in her voice made everyone stop. Forks stopped in mid-air. Conversation ceased. "I think these potatoes have—" Her throat closed over the word "dairy," a sound that didn't make it past her wind-pipe.

"Tracy, what is it?" Deborah leaned toward the executive director.

"Tracy?" Renquist's voice went up a notch.

"Tracy!" Deborah breathed, watching her change be-fore our eyes. Tracy's face had paled to an unnatural, waxy white.

Slowly, silverware was lowered to plates of food. People looked at each other and at the remains of the dinner on their plates. Whatever was happening to Tracy wasn't hap-pening to anyone else. But it was awful.

"She's dreadfully allergic to dairy!" Deborah screeched. I noticed, for the first time, the medical bracelet on Tracy's wrist. She was starting to fold at the waist, a spasm suddenly jerking her body into a grotesque fetal position.

"Does she have a hypo?" I jumped up and, holding the canvas bag with one hand, I opened Tracy's purse with the other. I began rifling through her personal effects. People with deadly allergies often carried a hypodermic syringe and a drug in case of an allergic reaction. Too bad Frances wasn't here. But inside Tracy's purse were just Kleenexes, a wallet, Dramamine, two tubes of lipstick and the tinfoil of an after-dinner mint.

"Oh my God, Tracy!" Deborah shrieked, and we all watched as the executive director's face began to tell a nightmare of a story. Tracy's teeth clenched together and then her mouth flew open. A black snake of a tongue was released; her head jerked back, her neck folding like a hinge at an impossible angle. Claws that had once been Tracy's hands grabbed at her throat and scratched deeply, as if trying to rip open her own windpipe in the struggle for air.

A confused buzz filled the hall. People were pointing in our direction, craning their heads, rubbernecking, seeking the better view from neighbors who asked anxiously, "What's happening?"

Tracy fell to the floor.

"Honey, don't, don't—" Deborah was grabbing Tracy's wrists, trying to keep Tracy's nails from scratching the short neck from which a strange gurgling sound emanated. Tracy was trying to say something. Her eyes looked beyond Deborah, searching the table.

Lee Turgo was a frozen pillar of salt, terrified that Tracy was reaching out—to *her*! Larry Boznian, suddenly sober, stared at Tracy's stricken face. Renquist had his arms outstretched and for a moment Tracy's hands responded, moving toward him, as if he could catch her. Her fingernails clawed the air. They were turning blue. "Is there a doctor in here? A nurse?" Rose was shouting at the top of her voice. The other diners were putting down their knives and forks. Slowly, they started to stand and move over toward us. The horrible march of the curious toward the macabre had begun.

"A doctor, a doctor—a paramedic? A fucking *nurse*!" Rose cried, waving her arms up and down, a Morse code of mortality. "A doctor, a nurse—"

"I'm a doctor," said a small woman moving forward through the crowd. Her tiny hands found Tracy's neck and searched for pulse points, as some terrible force seemed to take Tracy over completely. She was a puppet with invisible strings being jerked without pity. The doctor stepped out of her way. "Call an ambulance!"

"I'll hold her down," Deborah cried.

"No, she's convulsing, you might dislocate her shoulder," the doctor ordered, leaning over Tracy's tortured body again. We all watched as Tracy's face turned ashen and her lips became a dark, teal blue, just like Carla Ribera's suit. Her jerking subsided, her eyes rolled back into her head and the sounds ceased.

"She has environmental illness. It must be something in the building!" Deborah looked up at the fresco as if the paint were responsible. "Do something!" Deborah screeched at the doctor, at all of us.

The doctor stopped her probing and looked into Tracy's face, pulling up each eyelid in turn and then closing it again. "She's dead."

"Dead?" Deborah repeated.

"Dead?" the crowd gasped. Tracy was dead?

"No dairy. I didn't think there was—" Renquist sounded defensive through his shocked tones. "No dairy, no dairy . . ."

"This was no allergic reaction," the little doctor said. Then she picked up Tracy's plate of potatoes and sniffed them carefully.

"Smells like almonds," she said.

"She's not allergic to *almonds*," breathed Deborah.

It would take a moment for the concept to take hold, but I knew what the doctor meant. Renquist didn't have to worry about his menu advice, and Tracy wasn't allergic to almonds, or to anything in the building. Environmentally sensitive or not, everyone is allergic to cyanide.

We all stood there, a silent guard of the woman who had created the Howard Blooming Lesbian and Gay Memorial Archive, the event becoming more historic than any of us would have liked.

Just then Helen returned from the bathroom, her lips freshly bronzed, her composure regained. She made an opening in the wall of tuxedos which stood over Tracy's body, the large skirt of her dress throwing a shadow over Tracy's black sequins. "What?" she said softly.

"Almonds," the doctor said. "Cyanide."

I remembered my conversation with Helen in the bathroom, and I watched as her hands traveled up to her neck and made the unhappy discovery. "No!" she cried, "What? Oh no!" She was almost laughing. But there wasn't anything funny to laugh about. The Amigreed Amulet was gone. Quietly Helen Thomas let go of Lee Turgo's hand and faded into the crowd.

CHAPTER
SIX

POTATOES, OR
GRATIN DAUPHINOIS

Cyanide poisoning has been called "internal asphyxia." The victim is strangled from within, as the body's red blood cells are prevented from absorbing oxygen. Tracy Port, whose every cell had been instantly starved of air, now lay inert at the feet of the dressed-up diners, the shocked participants in what was supposed to be one of the brightest moments in our community's development. Tracy's heart was stilled, and Deborah Dunton let out a wail which would put all previous primal therapy to shame.

"Tracy, Tracy." Renquist Falkenberg knelt down beside her still body, a dark shape that no longer shuddered. A person we knew, who we couldn't believe was dead. Renquist reached out tentatively to touch Tracy and then pulled his hand quickly away. David Sing, the crime scene inspector, was approaching at a brisk, professional trot.

What luck, a queer cop on the scene of the biggest murder in the lesbian and gay community since Howard Blooming had been shot.

77

Mary Wings

I knew Renquist and David would quickly take control of the situation. David Sing was already busy securing the area: pushing back the tuxedos, leaving Tracy on the floor, like the Wicked Witch of the West; a house just landed on her and there was nothing the doctor could do.

"What happened?" David asked the physician.

"My guess? Poisoning," the woman said. "Cyanide."

"All right, clear the area, step back."

"Let the officer do his work," Renquist intoned to those of us too shocked to fully comprehend what was happening. "The proper authorities are here on the scene and will take care of everything. They will tell us what to do."

"It's over now," David called out, informing the crowd. His back was turned away from the table. I looked around for Helen. She was in a corner with Lee Turgo. I knew what she was looking for. Her pendant was gone. She hadn't noticed it, but the pendant was missing during my conversation with her in the bathroom. Helen had been too firm about being alone for me to tell her what was missing from her outfit.

Helen's fingers couldn't find it, even as they desperately searched. Her fingers, underneath the film of black silk, explored the space between her breasts, in case, just in case, the chain had broken and it had fallen and gotten trapped between bosom and brassiere. She was sputtering. I had a very bad taste in my mouth. Helen, I was sure, had been framed.

I dropped to the floor, looking for anything, any clue that might get Helen off the hook. With one hand I clutched Howard's memorabilia close to my chest; with the other I turned over dropped napkins and combed through crumbs.

There wasn't a pendant, but there was something else.

A brown rectangle. A leather lump. A thick wallet. I picked it up, the worn leather still warm, describing the shape of some ass which had sat on it for years and years. I flipped it open and my fingers snaked through the contents. A folded receipt from Streetlight Records, Classical CDs. Four credit cards, three condoms, two hundred dollars in cash. It could have been the wallet of any of the thousands of gay men in San Francisco. Except that the embossed name on the credit cards read "Renquist Falkenberg." Renquist's wallet, complete with just-in-case condoms, had nearly been donated to a crime scene investigator. I heard the distant whine of an ambulance and put the wallet in my pocket.

David Sing was waiting for me as I emerged from under the table. "What are you doing, Emma?"

"Lost my earring."

"Just keep the fuck outta here, do you mind?" The young officer was getting angry, and I had no interest in pushing him over the edge. I stepped back into the clot of people and faded backward out of the room. I took the opportunity to change clothes in the bathroom.

In the cold light of the white tiled chamber, the sequined dress was ejected in favor of baggy cotton pants. I pulled the turtleneck on, opening up the zipper around the neck. Things were too hot at the gala dinner. And I had a hot moment or two ahead to get some vital things done. I left the cubicle and returned to find Deborah Dunton, holding the dead Tracy Port in her arms.

Tracy's face was achieving bright pink color, as red blood cells rushed to the surface of her skin. Even dead, her body mounted a last-ditch attempt to find air.

"Salmon bisque," slurred the voice next to me. Larry Boznian.

"What?"

"Jussa color."

"I've heard light patter from the coroner," I said, the words falling on deaf ears.

One could expect a lot of strange behavior at the scene of a murder. The most devastated person could crack the worst jokes, and the murderer could do a wailing aria that would please the best crime scene conductor. Innocent women were frequently fingered for not being emotional enough. Dunton was covering her tracks there with copious wailing. Allen was stroking his beard, over and over again as if he could pull it off his face with enough effort. His own eyes were wide open, not able to look away from the horror in front of him.

"Get back! Get back!" David Sing was calling out with practiced authority, his hands waving in front of him as the crowd receded from the pink-hued horror in the black sequined dress. Someone screamed. Someone sobbed. A flashbulb popped.

I was still holding the black canvas bag when I heard Berniece cry out, "The scrapbook! The scrapbook!"

Searching frantically around their chairs, Allen and Berniece looked for the large, embroidered photo book with photos trapped behind the adhesive-backed cellophane. "The scrapbook—you were holding it, right?" Allen was trembling.

Berniece's voice acquired a certainty and a volume that made us all turn around. "Carla, *you stole my scrapbook!*" Berniece was leaning over her walker, pointing at the fashion photographer in her Edwardian-cut coat.

"Don't be ridiculous!" Carla was returning from the washroom. The fresh lipstick on her mouth glistened as she smiled quizzically at the poet. "What *are* you talking about, Berniece?" Carla's hands were stuffed deeply in the pockets of her long-tailed coat.

"I said, Carla, that my scrapbook is gone. When Tracy— and we all were watching—" Berniece spluttered, but the blank look on Carla's face confused her for a moment. "I distinctly remember you coming over to my chair and— and—"

"Berniece, I'm sorry. I don't know what you're talking about. Did you lose something?"

"Carla," she said firmly, "I'm certain you took it!"

Carla sighed and rolled her eyes. Lee Turgo tightened her mouth. "C'mon, Berniece. Let's go home. Where's Helen?"

Then the city supervisor appeared, back from the rest room. "Here's your wallet, Renquist." I handed it over.

"Oh my God, *here* it is!" He didn't check for credit cards or theft, just put it quickly in the inside breast pocket of his jacket.

"Now if the rest of you will please give your name and address to the officer at the door." David Sing was trying to clear the room. "Emma, that means you. *Move it!*"

The whining of a far-distant ambulance began. As it grew louder, my task became clearer. Whatever had or hadn't happened to Berniece's scrapbook, I realized what I must do. Soon the place would be crawling with cops. Everyone and everything would be under scrutiny. If Howard had wanted the journals sealed for sixty years, I certainly didn't want the cops taking custody of them. The old safe stood in the basement. A nineteenth-century safe donated by a gay banker, full of metal boxes, each of which could only be opened or locked by two finely wrought keys used in unison. Howard would have loved it.

I rushed through the dining room, past the tables with

plates of battered, gray cod lying limp on the trays, eyes gazing at Larry Boznian's ceiling as if his postmodern treatise would provide a visual clue. Tracy dead! I held the canvas bag tightly. The concrete corridors stretched endlessly under my feet.

I ran down the internal stairs into the basement, three steps at a time. I found the double doors which would lead me into the reception area of the vault. The lock on the double door was easy to foil. Too many hinges and too much play where the doors met, it was quick work with a plastic credit card. I was still breathless when I entered the vault.

There were all of Helen's manuscripts still on the loading dock. Her fight with Tracy flashed into my mind. So did Allen staring at the box containing Howard's final papers. I walked over to the safe, its foot-thick door open, inviting. The keys were waiting in deposit box locks. I had only to choose.

I gazed over the metal containers and chose one large enough for the tape-covered package. I opened my canvas bag and pulled it out. I looked at it mournfully. How could I put Howard's journals away for sixty whole years? But it had to be done.

I turned one of the keys and pulled. A large metal drawer slid toward me. I took one last look at the tape-covered box; I got a ballpoint pen and wrote my initials on the surface, over the joins of the tape. Now there would be no way someone could unwrap the tape and rewrap it without my knowing.

I placed the box in the drawer and watched it disappear as I slid the drawer closed. I turned the key to lock once and turned the second key in the other direction to complete the procedure. Then I put the keys into my bra, metal cold against my nipple, and zipped up the neck of my sweater. Mission accomplished.

Then I remembered Frances's notes on *Lesbo-Parthenogenesis*. What had happened to them? A feeling of dread crept over me.

I hadn't seen the collection of notebooks since I'd first sat down to dinner. Frances's careful observations on grid paper were gone. My hands felt around inside the canvas bag. The bag had been zipped up all evening. The bag had been between my feet. The *Lesbo-Parthenogenesis* manila folder was gone.

Dunton would say it was hidden aggression. Frances had gone off without me and left me with her notes. So I lost them. As hundreds of others have lost significant artifacts belonging to their lovers. Manuscripts. Paintings. All through time, lovers have lost things entrusted to their care by the beloved. Hemingway and Hadley. Hidden aggression? Hidden or obvious, the notes were gone.

Then I smelled cloves and leather. Fresca Alcazon was right behind me, panting. "Where did you go, Emma?"

"Just getting a breath of fresh air."

"In a vault?" she said sardonically, raising an eyebrow.

"I'm a donor, remember?"

"Oh Emma, I've never seen anyone die like that." Fresca's eyes lowered, the child again. "Right in front of me, I wanted to find you. It sort of spooked me, you know." Fresca was breathing more quietly. "I can't believe Tracy's dead." There was a quizzical look of disbelief that flashed across her face and was buried suddenly. She bent her head and, before I knew it, my fingers had found their way into her mass of dark brown hair. She leaned toward me, or did I pull her to me? Somehow we were holding each other.

"Did you know Tracy?" My voice was soft. There was a sweet scent from her hair. Gentle layers, tangles of hair, wound rings around my fingers. Gently, she pushed me away. I peered into her face.

"Except for what Larry told me, I didn't know her at all," Fresca mused, her eyes grazing the security boxes. "I have an original copy of Gertrude Stein's *The Making of Americans*. Signed copy. First edition." She smiled. I watched her big eyes glisten for a moment. This woman loved books. "It's really nice and I guess it must be worth a lot. Larry invited me to the gala and I thought I would donate it to the Archive. I called Tracy, left a message with Allen Boone."

"A very nice gesture."

Fresca shrugged her shoulders. "It seemed like the right thing to do. I travel a lot. What do I need with a first edition?"

"You like Gertrude Stein."

"She's wonderful. Some people find her tough going, but that's because they don't listen to her words. They don't take the time to linger. You almost have to go into a trance, read passages out loud to understand them."

"Okay." I still had the smell of Fresca's hair on my hands. "Recite something. Something pertinent to the situation here."

Fresca looked at me. "No, really, I—"

"Come on." Howard Blooming's notes were safely locked away, the keys cold against my heart. Frances was in Seattle. I smiled at Fresca. "Don't be shy. I want to hear Stein's words. Give me another image, tonight. Help us both out."

"Okay." Fresca's hazel eyes rested on the old safe. She seemed to be gathering inspiration, not counting keys.

Her mouth went slack, her eyelids closed slowly, stretching over the brilliant whites, the deep blacks of her eyes.

When the words came, I saw why she had been irritated with Larry Boznian. Larry Boznian's clipped accent and whiny voice had nothing on the deep, sonorous tones of Fresca Alcazon. She touched the mole at the base of her neck for a second, put her hand in the pocket of what was left of her jeans and began to recite.

" *'History there = is no disaster = Those who make history = Cannot be overtaken = as they will make = History which they do = because it is necessary = That every one will = Begin to know that = They must know that = History is what it is = Which it is as they do ='* "

She stopped mid-sentence and looked at me. I knew we were going to kiss. All the tumblers and teasers of combination in all the safes in the world couldn't compete with Fresca. She reached out for me. Her arms long, her hands confident. I felt those hands behind my back, her fingertips knitting naturally behind my waist. She pulled me toward her and I could feel the warmth of her belly. I wouldn't be able to get away easily. Her breath was hot on my neck.

" *'Not and now, now and not, not and now, by and by not and now, as not, as soon as not, not and now, now as soon now, now as soon, now as soon as soon as now.'* " Pulling me closer, Fresca's legs were hard, her body thin and sharp as a knife. I twisted away.

"C'mon." I took her hands and pulled her away from the safe. I put my hands on the metal door and pushed. It slipped neatly and quietly on its oiled hinges into its stainless steel frame. I pulled up the big handle, heard the bolts slide into place, spun the combination lock around. A roulette wheel that no one could beat. At least not without a lot of tools. We left the basement vault. I held open one of the double doors and listened to it relocking behind us.

The room upstairs was now an official crime scene, roped off by yellow caution tape and crawling with cops taking notes and photographs. In the distance, the popping of flashbulbs illuminated the pink bubble that had been Tracy's face. David Sing strolled back and forth talking to his colleagues. I scanned the room and saw Helen Thomas, huddled confusedly in the corner of the room. Berniece Able and Lee Turgo were giving their names to an officer.

"Hey, look." A big voice boomed over those gathered by the table. I drew closer, Fresca sticking closely by my side. "What's this?" It was Renquist's voice cutting through the din. He was looking aghast at the dining room table where Tracy's potatoes were being picked over by a cop putting samples from the table into little glass tubes. But that was not what Renquist was referring to.

An officer had lifted a napkin on the table and everyone pressed around to see what lay underneath. It was a split shard of amber and a piece of filigree work as lovely as a Fabergé egg. The strands of silver spider web had been violated, the amber heart split like a piece of rock candy. *Grandmother's Poison.*

David Sing picked up a fragment of amber with a pair of tweezers. He peered at it closely, then sniffed. He inspected the plate of potatoes, bringing his face close to the dish, and then returned his gaze to the pendant.

"Whose necklace is this?" he asked loudly. No one needed to answer. We all looked at Helen. She seemed suddenly very alone; a tall frightened figure in funeral black.

"Come here, please," David beckoned at her. From across the room Helen came toward us with long, confident strides. But she was shaken.

"This is your necklace?" David asked her.

"Yes." Helen breathed the word as if this were a bad dream. "I just noticed it was missing."

"Are you aware that this necklace seems somehow to have been contaminated with a poisonous substance?"

"Well, there's sort of a myth about this piece of jewelry."

"I'm going to have to ask you to come downtown for questioning," David informed her. He was all business now. I moved in closer.

"Helen, don't say anything!" I advised. David turned to me with a furious look. A cop took Helen's arm and held on to her tight.

"We are arresting you for the murder of Tracy Port," the homicide inspector intoned. *"You have the right to remain silent . . ."*

Lee Turgo was at my side. "Emma." Her hand clamped onto my shoulder. The auburn bangs were sticking out in all directions as she nervously stroked the top of her head. "Emma, I *have* to talk to you."

". . . anything you say from this point on can and will be used against you . . ."

"You work for Willie Rossini," Lee sputtered. "Tell her, you just tell her, I'll hire you to prove Helen innocent. Anything, anything . . ."

I put my hand on Lee's arm. "Don't worry. I'll get a call in to Willie immediately. I'm sure she'll represent Helen." I looked over again at Helen, surrounded now by a circle of cops. Her entire face and body were stiff. "Don't worry, Lee. We'll get her out on bail, within twenty-four hours. She can talk to Willie in the morning."

"*. . . will be used against you in a court of law . . .*"

The sheriffs were deciding which one of them would handcuff her. Helen's eyes widened as two women came closer, the shining cuffs snapping around the delicate silk tulle gathered at Helen's wrists.

It was too neat. Too tidy. And the whole romantic mess of the Olivia Cruise had been too public, too easily exploited. I remembered my conversation with Helen in the bathroom after her fiasco of a speech. The amulet was gone by then. It could have been eased off her neck at any time, by anyone, during one of those many hugs and kisses that the evening had afforded.

I watched Carla Ribera helping to escort a drunken Larry Boznian into the night. Fresca Alcazon had disappeared, maybe to find her own life. Rose was wheeling her chair into an elevator at the far end of the Reading Room. The doors slid quietly closed behind her.

Lee Turgo, her hands stuffed in her pockets, was staring at the toes of her wing tips. Berniece Able stood next to her, an icon, now thoroughly distraught and confused.

I would find out who had killed Tracy Port, I thought. And I had a good hunch that it wouldn't be Helen Thomas.

CHAPTER SEVEN

DIET
FRESCA

I met Rose out on the pavement. She was in her van, leaning out of the window. She wasn't exactly broken up by Tracy's death.

"Who will be executive director now?" she mused, pale blond eyebrows raised in insinuation. "Deborah Dunton? She's the president of the board. The natural successor. I wonder if she murdered Tracy?"

"Rose, much as Deborah would be a pleasing candidate, the murderer could have been any one of us at that table. Or a dozen other people for that matter."

The nasty tones of a drunken argument wafted over to us in the evening air. In the distance I saw Fresca Alcazon, Carla Ribera and Larry Boznian huddling together.

"The überbabe's got a thing for you, Emma."

"Chill, girlfriend, I'm a married woman."

"Fresca looks like one of Carla's creations." Rose reached for the ignition, paused.

"Too fleshy for the rag trade," I disagreed.

"Fresca looks like she takes care of herself pretty well."

89

"As well as taking care of Larry Boznian. And the latest thing is *heterodykes*, Emma."

The voices picked up again and I found myself staring at the sidewalk drama. Fresca towering over Larry and Carla, putting her hands on her hips, proclaiming something. From time to time her head twisted in my direction. The silhouettes of Larry Boznian's ears stood out like two big fins. He was having a hard time getting the words out and what he did wasn't worth listening to. Carla Ribera was alternately admonishing and pleading with him. At one point, he grabbed Fresca's arm violently. She shook it off even more violently. She looked strong in the streetlight, looked strong fighting off Larry Boznian. The drunken, clipped British reached us. "I don't want you to go off and lie in any *guttahs*."

I hoped he wasn't talking about me.

But he was. Fresca was on her way over. The rags on her arms were covered in a very expensive black leather jacket. Extra styling, heavy hardware and a yellow silk lining. Rags indeed. Something heavy bumped against her hip.

"Bully for you and chilly for me!" Larry Boznian's bitter words sounded worse for their British accent. Carla threw up her arms and walked away from him, her long black curls tossing on her back as she strode swiftly up the hill to her car. Larry Boznian stood alone, turning back and forth, screaming after the two women in the darkness.

"Carla's cute crowd," Rose murmured. *"What you get is no tomorrow."*

"There's something about Fresca. Twenty going on eighty."

"Don't fool yourself, Emma. Heterodykes, who needs

them, babe? After all"—I stepped out of the car. —"many are called, but few are chosen." She drove off.

I watched Rose's taillights become smaller as she drove down Market Street until they disappeared. Fresca stepped into a circle of light. I could tell she had been crying. There was a red ring around her mouth and she looked beaten. And angry. And beautiful.

"Can I take you home, Emma?" Fresca Alcazon was breaking through my defenses like a burglar.

It was a cold and lonely night. It wasn't a night to spend alone. Fresca caught something in my eye that I couldn't hide fast enough. As she saw her chances improve, she smiled. It wasn't a made-for-consumption politician smile. It wasn't an approval-seeking or slippery, butter smile, either. It was a young, and even innocent, smile. It hit me like a curveball I couldn't avoid.

Fresca's transport was a 500cc BMW bike. I had clung to her back on the way home, the fringe from her jacket brushing my lips, a leathery French kiss. "This is your place?" Fresca looked up at the flat-faced Victorian duplex. Darkened windows.

"Yeah. My place. Thanks for the ride." No place like home.

"Could I—do you think I could use your phone?"

"Sure," I said lightly, but I knew I should have said no. If I let Fresca Alcazon into my house on a night like this, feeling the way I did about my marriage, it would be a miracle if I saw the dawn alone. So I took Fresca inside and pointed out the phone, then I wandered outside and sat on the stairs and looked at the garden.

Laura was right. The pot plants were too obvious. I could even smell them from the porch. Leggy, purple delphiniums, stalks folding under the weight of flowers, had hit the ground. A waste. Purple petals the nighttime meal of snails.

Helen was probably just getting booked. Someone would be grabbing her beautiful fingers, roughly pressing her fingertips onto a police blotter. It was a Friday night and Friday night could be busy down at the jail. I wondered what kind of cell mates Helen would get. It would be early. Maybe she'd get lucky.

I remembered the scene in the library vault. All those manuscript pages. And the condescension of Tracy Port. How could anyone ever have been in love with her?

I wondered what the lab analysis of Helen's pendant would reveal. I should get one of Rose's researchers to look into everything that had been written about that amulet. Perhaps an appraiser had indicated something about the contents that could help Helen? Perhaps I should read *Grandmother's Poison* again. I should definitely pole up those delphs. And take in the pot.

I looked up at the sky, the same sky which stretched above us all. Me, Fresca, Frances. Frances, up in Seattle. Frances whose notes I'd lost. Frances, somewhere in Seattle, with all those eager, fertile lesbians. They'd be hopeful; single. Some, no doubt, dying to bed the doctor who might give women the power of independent creation, if not the orgasm of their rainy, lonely Seattle lives.

Once, Frances had mentioned something about "opening up our relationship." "Opening." Like opening a can of worms, only these worms would have serpent heads, spiked fangs that could cut to the quick and eyes that only flashed yellow. Frances the Amazon doctor, potential miracle worker, would have a lot of amorous opportunity on the road. I said I'd think about it. That was what was said.

We'd been interrupted by a phone call and the issue was never brought up again.

I shook myself. Frances and I were fine, just fine. It was good to have Fresca here. But only because she was a suspect for the murder of Tracy Port, just like everyone else who'd been at the VIP table at the gala dinner. There was a lot about Fresca that didn't add up. I would ask her some questions and that was all.

I sat up straight and tried to clear my head of lustful thoughts before I went inside. The rolltop secretary offered a cardboard envelope, the kind used to mail computer disks. I took out a label and addressed it to myself. Then I slipped my hand into my bra and drew out one of the now-warm keys, leaving the other one pressed against my skin. I sealed the envelope, slid it under a number of other envelopes that were ready to be mailed, and returned to the kitchen.

I found Fresca with the receiver pressed hard to her ear. How long was she going to be on the phone? Her eyes were quiet under the cloud of dark brown hair. Her hands fingered the threads on her jeans into complicated patterns. Did she *know* how beautiful she was?

Fresca's face registered something painful. "I'm really sorry about that," she said. "But I can't help it. You'll have to work it out by yourself this time, *Cara.*" She hung up and dialed another number quickly.

I shook myself again. Fresca and Frances now appearing on your telephone, in the boom-boom room of your mind. I needed distraction. Besides, there was Laura Deleuse to appease. The plants had reached their blooming potential. They had probably already been pollinated, generating seeds and becoming bisexual. Everyone was growing pot in the Mission these days.

I went down the back stairs with a machete and cut the plants down, then dragged the thick stems with their star-shaped leaves and aromatic flowers back up to the apartment. There were not as many seeds as I had feared. Fresca was still listening to whoever it was on the other end of the phone. She mumbled something. In Italian.

Engrossing myself happily in the dusky, cloying-scented blooms, I clipped off the larger fan leaves and threw them away in the kitchen garbage. Finding the brown paper grocery bags which would allow the buds to cure without molding, I slipped the long aromatic skewers inside.

Fresca had wandered as far as the static would allow her on the cordless phone. She was in Frances's office. I crept behind her into the doorway.

Tap, tap, tap. Those long, broad-tipped fingers tapped on the hardened plastic of the phone as her eyes flickered over Frances's bulletin board. There, more notes on the latest developments in ovum division were displayed in scientific hieroglyphics. Surely Fresca could not understand them—but she was nodding, perhaps in agreement with the voice on the phone. I saw her hand reach out, toward Frances's Rolodex. Before her fingers could walk further, I interrupted her.

"Can I help you?"

The jeans jumped high enough to clear a low hurdle. Fresca's face hid surprise. And something else, something I caught before she composed her face. Something like fear. She pressed the button cutting off the connection. Whoever it was, she hadn't said good-bye.

"Is this your office?"

"No, it's not my office, and you know it."

"Huh?"

"I'm hardly the scientific type."

"What type are you?"

"The type that doesn't like strangers wandering through my house."

"Am I a stranger?"

"Yes."

She looked at me in silence.

"What exactly is your business in San Francisco, Fresca?"

"I've told you what my business is. I've come to give the Stein book to the Archive. Christ, Emma! What is this? The third degree? I came here because I thought you liked me. Now you say I'm a stranger and bark questions at me like a district attorney!"

"Just checking out the scene."

Then just to cap the evening of murder and marital mayhem, Fresca started crying hard. Tears crawled down her buttery cheeks. She took hold of my hand and brought it up to her face, like it was something precious. Like I was someone she knew. Someone who would look after her and make everything all right.

"Listen, Emma. I need a place to stay. Just for tonight. Please—could I sleep on your couch?"

There was a sinking feeling in my stomach. We both knew what would happen next. I would say, "Yes."

"I just need a place to sleep. I really need a place to sleep."

"I'll put you in the guest room."

"Hey, what's that—*smell*?" She pulled back, staring at my fingers. I knew which aroma was clinging to my nails; the potent pollen of my backyard crop was infusing my hands with a heady post-harvest scent.

"It's pot," I explained.

"What?"

"I grow it."

"You're a *grower*?"

"A few plants in the garden. I just brought them up. They were females that looked ready to develop seeds." I stopped at the look of concern on Fresca's face. "Don't worry," I explained. "I give it away, smoke it myself and make sure sick friends have what they need. I've got three full bags on the counter in the kitchen. Five months of careful cultivation. I don't sell. So don't worry. You're not going to go all twelve-step on me, are you?"

" *'A year of grass is a year alas. When grass grows that is all that grows but grass is grass and alas and alas is alas.'* "

"When in doubt, quote Gertrude Stein."

"Dope is for dopes, Emma."

"I'll put you in the guest room," I said.

The guest room was filled with all the Day of the Dead artifacts from the Mexican vacations Frances and I took annually. I left Fresca standing there, looking at the bed while I went to bring her a clean towel. When I came back, she was sitting on the edge of the bed, murmuring, " *'When she shuts her eyes - she sees the green things - among which she has been working - and then as she falls asleep - she sees them a little different. The green things then have black roots - and the black roots - have red stems and then she is exhausted -'* "

She stopped reciting when she saw me. Her eyes were calm now. She took a deep breath, then let it out. She had spent some time composing herself. Because she had been terribly shaken. Now I lay me down to sleep. She didn't take her eyes off mine. There was a question there.

"Here's your towel," I said. "And a washcloth." I even had a bar of soap from one of Frances's hotel excursions. Frances used to fold all the towels carefully; the linen closet was a Mondrian of colors. Now she didn't even make the bed.

"Good night, Fresca." I returned to my bedroom, collapsing onto the queen size conjugal bed with the extra firm mattress. I fell instantly asleep, my own clothes my only covers.

I went back to the gala dinner in my dream. It was a different dinner. It was a better dinner. According to the dream version, I never quite arrived. Berniece was writing poems with Allen's pens and all was right with the world.

"Yawww!" A banshee sound straight out of hell and propelled by terror interrupted my dream of slight frustration. A sound that cracked the air. I got out of bed, and ran down the hallway.

Wide awake, bolt upright, with eyes wide open but seeing nothing, Fresca Alcazon, this woman, this stranger, was screaming in the darkness. I turned on the light, and she covered her eyes quickly and started hyperventilating. I turned the light off, turned the hallway light on and opened the door. I sat down next to her and spoke gently. Her T-shirt smelled of soap and bleach.

"Fresca, it's okay."

Fresca looked around.

"Do you want the light—"

"No!" A breathless word. Could Fresca be asthmatic? "No, I'm really okay now. Heh! Heh!" I stood up and went over to the desk where skeletal candles made an impromptu altar in our guest room. I struck a kitchen match.

"Larry!" she cried, looking straight in front of her, staring into the flame of the match and seeing, not the room, but chaos once again, instantly terrifying her. I blew out the candle and turned on the overhead light. Every corner was flooded with unrelenting brightness as I said, "Hey, take it easy." I held Fresca by her shoulders and pushed a fuzzy mat of hair out of her face, finding her eyes and looking into them.

"Oh, so it's *you.* Okay." She breathed quietly.

"I thought you'd come to. You didn't want me to turn on the light—"

"Oh shit, I'm like, sleepwalking, sleeptalking again, aren't I?" An uncertain laugh. "Can I have a glass of water?" A child's voice.

"Sure." I went to the bathroom and filled a tumbler full. When I returned, Fresca was almost composed, and embarrassed, just like any stranger who'd spent the night and revealed their worst nightmare to a stranger.

"What'd I say, anyway?"

"Oh, you just called out Larry's name."

"Oh, Emma, you're sweet. Thanks. Thanks for providing me with shelter, and not freaking about my freak-out. Hey, you're still dressed," she commented.

"Yeah, I kind of collapsed."

"Let's try and do something about that."

Fresca drew my hand to her cheek. My hand dove deep into a nest of fuzz at the nape of her neck.

"Well, I'm kinda—" I started.

"You know"—Fresca ignored me—"I've noticed that, in the worst moments, there's *always* somebody there. Maybe it's not the person you expect it to be. Maybe it's not even the person you want it to be. But there's always someone, and sometimes—" Fresca said, pulling me down onto the bed. My lucky lips found the delicate jawbone, the softly moving mouth. "—it's a lucky surprise. Oh, Emma." We were really kissing now. Fresca's kisses were slow motion, refracted with feelings and questions and echoes, infused with longing and maybe even desperation. Desperate sex could be great.

"I have to ask you something, Fresca." The apartment of my marriage floated away from us. There was only Fresca and myself and the skeletons, carved from coconut husks, cast out of sugar, winking with glitter-filled eyes at the way our hands found each other. Delightful surprises in hard thighs, soft belly, long sculpted feet, lengthy arms and a sometimes gentle, sometimes demanding touch. "I have to ask you the sex history questions."

"Okay, Emma." Fresca's hands were nearing the dangerous centers of my breasts, where I had left one key to the locked box in the safe in the Archive.

"This will be perfectly safe sex, Emma; your arms are so beautiful," Fresca mumbled, pulling at my clothes. In the candlelight, her birthmark glowed like a ruby, pulsing with the quickening beat of her heart. "I'm not lovers with Larry, I'm not an I.V. drug user—"

Fresca's soft, panther skin rippled over her ribs. That strong back which I'd clung onto while riding her bike moved under me. She took her T-shirt off quickly, very, very helpful. "In fact, Emma Victor, I couldn't be safer."

"Howzo?" My hands found their way through the sieve of denim to the gentle flesh of her hips.

"I've never done it with *anybody* before." A laughing skeleton whizzed by on a bicycle. Fresca's mouth was watering; her hands had moved safely away from my breasts. Oh, oh.

Her fingers winding around my neck, finding the roughness of a tiny scab.

"Were you hurt?" she asked, breath stopping, a moment of concern.

"It's nothing—I—fell down the stairs—"

"Are you okay?"

"Yes. I mean, don't I look okay?"

99

"Falling down the stairs," Fresca clucked. "Emma." A grave silence. "Are you in an abusive relationship?"

"No! Are you?"

"No. And don't ask me any more questions." Her tongue flickered across my cheeks, she kissed my eyelids, tickling my lashes with hers, a butterfly kiss.

Adultery was just as I remembered it. It was wonderful. I heard the chuckling of a mask, saw the wink of eye sockets which were only holes. Dead ancestors, like Tracy Port, like Howard Blooming. I was losing my concentration. I drank in another Fresca kiss. But I couldn't help thinking about all that had gone on before, earlier this evening. The gala dinner for the Lesbian and Gay Memorial Archive. The night that Tracy Port was poisoned, Helen was arrested, and the first night that I stepped out of my marriage. Concentrate, Emma.

" *'You like this best,'* " Fresca murmured. " *'Lock me in nearly. Unlock me sweetly, I love my baby with a rush rushingly.'* "

I was rushing. A fast rushing of fingers, the obstacles, metal buttons with thin, sharp edges. What was left of her Levi's. She slid them off. Belly and thighs as soft as the California hills, lovely down shaved in a racing stripe. I held her hips and I dove into the copper canyons of her thighs and as I searched and sucked, my arms traveled down to her legs, that delicate spot behind the knees where I meant to say a special hello. Fingers, muscles and flesh and something that didn't feel like a leg at all. My fingers stopped.

Sex history aside, etiquette demanded that I not ask questions, but I pulled away slightly and looked. Something horrible had happened to Fresca. Something had eaten away at the lower half of her calf. A quilted series of patches covered it, brown skin, pink skin. A mottled mess that was none of my business. Fresca pulled her leg up underneath her, suddenly self-conscious. Something about that leg set off a bell. But I had no idea why. My next kiss was off. I pushed her, as gently as I could, away from me. "Not now, okay?"

But Fresca reached out for me like a child, a strong child, pulling me down. Her hands were velvet, my skin was silk, her skin was satin. "We can just cuddle, you know." Fresca curled into my arms and I found myself holding her hand, squeezing the tips of her long broad fingers.

"I really like you, Emma. I really like you a lot, a lot, a lot," Fresca murmured in resigned disappointment. "God, I would love to live here in San Francisco. Have a garden. The light is magic, the air is clean."

"San Francisco isn't what it was. Nothing is made here anymore. Those who don't come for a visit struggle to pay some of the highest mortgages and rents in the world. You can walk all over railroad tracks down in the Mission. Tracks that used to take cargo from the shipyard to the factories. The factories are gone now. High rises and hotels lining the Bay. It may be Gaylandia, but it's far from fairyland. Don't get me wrong. I love the coffee."

"Will you make me coffee tomorrow? Maybe you can let me pretend, for a moment, that I share this life, this flat, this sunlight with you, this wonderful San Francisco."

"Boutique City, USA."

"You're such an American." Fresca was smiling, a Mona Lisa job. "What makes you think the world was ever a good place?" She yawned. No fillings. Teeth as solid and white as pearls. "Besides," she murmured, "I'm very good at pretending." I stared into the cloudy chaos of her dark and honey-colored hair, as I felt her fall into dreams. She still smelled of cloves and clean, sun-dried cotton. And now she was sleeping, leaving me to the privacy of my own thoughts. I had a lot of them. Delphiniums and Helen Thomas locked in a jail cell. Fresca who hustled herself off to the *loo* just as Gurl Jesus appeared to take photos. Fresca's body jerked into the deeper fall of sleep.

My foot reached down for the nest of disintegrated blue jeans and pulled them slowly toward me. I reached into the back pocket. I found a wallet and flipped it open. The driver's license of Eleanor DeWade, who, if I was to believe the picture pasted there, was sleeping next to me.

That's when the thought hit me. *Me.*

Could it be that the poisoner had been confused? Perhaps a professional killer, posing as a waiter, had instructions to kill the woman in the black sequined dress. The woman who was holding Howard Blooming's notes. Maybe Tracy's death was a *mistake.* Hubris?

I pushed myself up off the bed. Fresca was sleeping on her stomach, sprawled diagonally, as if she was used to having a bed to herself all the time. As if she didn't have a care in the world. She snored. Okay.

Her leather jacket was on the floor in the corner. I remembered how I had eased it off her shoulders, how she had helped me take it off and flung it far out of reach. I dove down to retrieve it. Inside I found what I had suspected was there. Something I had noticed while clinging to Fresca on the bike ride home.

A little gun.

A .22, nothing to get too worked up about. Better than a BB, but you couldn't kill anybody with it. Not right off. If you were a good aim, you could take them out at the knees, though. A nice little gun, if you knew exactly how to use it.

I rotated the cylinder. It was empty. I put the unloaded gun deep under the bed. Then I sat on the carpet and looked out the window, far away from Fresca. Had Helen hugged Fresca? No, Fresca was in the *loo*, I remembered.

Thump! Thump! I froze. Someone was on the eave roof.

A noise above our heads. Chicken Little. The sky was falling and Fresca was instantly awake. Poised above me, frozen, her lips parted, as if she knew the moment was coming. "Quiet!" she hissed at me, as if this were her house.

Thunk! Thunk!

There was no doubt about it. Somebody *was* walking on the little eave of the building. Fresca leapt off the bed and tore into the kitchen. I heard paper bags being torn open, and the toilet flushing; gurgling over and over.

"Wait!" I cried, but it was too late. I heard the jiggle of the handle, metal and porcelain, again and again, and I knew what had happened. Fresca had contributed my latest crop to the sewage system of San Francisco.

"Cool it, will you? That's my crop! Stop!" I watched her bending over the toilet, intent on her task. "It could be anything on that roof. It could be my cat!"

"Yeah, a hundred eighty pound cat. I'm not staying here and getting busted!"

"Stopping up the plumbing with hemp stem isn't going to help. They raise that stuff for *ropes* you know." I went over to the bathroom sill and leaned outside. The garden behind the house was quiet, free of lurking shadows. I went back to the bedroom, peered up, over the gable, to the upstairs apartment.

Laura was home. I saw the triangle of light spilling down

103

the pitch of the roof. I went downstairs and walked outside around the entire house. I took a flashlight and examined the hard dry lawn for something, I don't know what.

Then I walked back up to my apartment through the decimated garden. Fresca was ready to leave. Somehow everything that had started out nicely between us had soured. "Thanks for ridding me of my crop."

"You have an exciting life, Emma."

"Yours doesn't seem so peaceful, either." I wondered how she would do without her .22. We locked eyes for a moment, lust, anger and frustration a high-octane fuel that was getting us nowhere fast.

"I'm sorry, Emma. If you have to be cruel to be kind, then I'll take it as it comes."

"I thought you said you weren't in an abusive relationship."

"I'm not. But—let's talk later." Fresca threw on her leather jacket, gave me a quick kiss and, without checking her pockets, was gone.

WRONG
NUMBER

Dawn. The big orange ball was cracking, breaking open like a rotten egg on the sharp edge of Mount Diablo. I followed the glowing sphere as it split the darkness, its pink message whispering something obscene. I hadn't slept at all.

I'd spent the rest of the night trying to rescue my plants after Fresca's disposal operation. I managed to save one bud from the top of one plant. I would start a new crop.

Marijuana seeds are not easy to sprout. I'd originally tried keeping them in damp soil, and they thumbed their shells at me and never opened. I remembered the paper-towel-and-jar method of seed sprouting from elementary school: soften them for days in the paper towel, and fool them with a moist yogurt container in a cupboard right over the refrigerator where it's warm. The folded cloth on the sides of the container draws moisture up like a wick. Hot and wet, just like Fresca Alcazon.

Sometimes the summer-like Octobers would fool the otherwise annual plants and I could squeeze in two crops a year. And working with the plants gave me a contact high that was conducive to, if not deductive abilities, then flashbacks, and a whole lot of information based on intuition.

I forced my thoughts back to the previous evening. To the moments before I'd met Helen in the bathroom when her amulet had been clearly missing from her neck. Had she been wearing it during her speech? That would be easy enough to find out. At the table, Helen was placed uncomfortably between Lee Turgo and Tracy Port. Renquist Falkenberg hugged everyone and lost his wallet. Larry Boznian acted as if he was very drunk. Fresca carried a .22 and someone had mugged me earlier that evening.

I walked into the bathroom and took off all my clothes. The sneak and creep clothes I'd slept in, if you could call it sleeping. The turtleneck was stale, and the pants needed a brushing. The bra was empty.

The second key was gone.

I ran to the basket where the mail was waiting. The self-addressed computer disk mailer waited patiently under the utility bill. I squeezed the cardboard together between my fingers. The first key was still inside.

I ran back to the guest room and searched the floor inch by inch. I came up with Fresca's .22 and a lot of cat hair. I went down the stairs to the garden, through the weeds and back upstairs, examining each tread. Each stepping stone. No key.

The phone rang. Willie Rossini was on the line. "Listen, I'm sorry to ring so early, but I've managed to get bail for Helen. She's entered a plea of not guilty. Pick her up, will you, Emma?"

I put the outgoing mail into a plastic sack and dropped it off at the Bryant Street Post Office on my way to the Hall of Justice. The letters would reach their destination on Monday. Then I went to the Hall of Justice and found a disheveled Helen, her black shirtwaist crushed and wilted, signing a receipt for the manila envelope which contained her personal belongings. She barely nodded to me as she signed the receipt.

"Lee's waiting for you at home."

"Okay."

Helen looked like many people look after their first night in jail. Reduced to a number, reduced to a series of functions, food tubes which must be locked up. A black star who had burnt out: Helen's face looked gray and grim.

"How'd you do in there?"

"Fine. I got more dialogue in a night than I could ever want." Helen managed a smile. "Two women were sobbing, three women were screaming and televisions were blasting until they turned the lights off." Helen had deep blue lines under her eyes. "They made us polish the handles of our cells in the morning." An ironic twist took over her lips.

"Don't worry, Helen. Willie feels confident she can get you off."

"Then why do I feel like I'm going to be crushed by the wheels of white justice, Emma? I already have the tire tracks across my back."

"Willie will make sure you never go in there again, Helen."

"I hope so. My dialogue is good enough already."

"Let's get you home."

I put my arm around Helen. She seemed to lean into me for support. She was trembling, deeply, all over.

Jail doesn't do good things for people. It makes some

107

people angry, some people crazy, some people despairing. Despite her bantering about dialogue, jail had simply and completely terrified Helen Thomas.

Lee Turgo was ready with tea, and Berniece Able was pacing as fast and as impatiently as her walker would let her when we arrived. "Helen should have sold the amulet! Instead, she wrote a book about it! I *told* her it was bad luck." Berniece's knuckles turned white on stainless steel rods.

I looked around at Helen and Lee's duplex. Built in the late 1920's, the cozy apartment featured a keyhole-shaped proscenium between the living room and dining room, a cheery kitchen with a hand-built breakfast nook, and other amenities thought necessary at the time, such as built-in telephone grottos and laundry chutes.

"Oh, Lee," Helen cried. Lee's alpine complexion flushed as Helen rushed toward her. The two clung together for what seemed like an eternity, Lee in a flannel bathrobe, Helen in last night's evening gown. Helen seemed to gather strength from Lee's embrace. "Just let me get out of these clothes and have a shower, would you?" She danced into the bedroom. After a moment's hesitation, Lee dashed after her.

I sat alone with Berniece Able. We listened to the clock for a while before I asked her, "What made you think Carla stole your scrapbook?"

"I felt her take it out of my hand."

I smiled. That's just what we like from a witness. Absolute certainty.

Berniece continued, "After she became the house pho-tographer for that ricket rag she got ruthless. Who does she give press coverage to? Waif lesbians under thirty!"

Just what we don't like from a witness. Lots of motive to believe the worst.

"Willie will be arriving any minute," I said, and we sat in an exhausted silence until the doorbell rang.

Willie Rossini was a large, hunched-over woman of sixty. She wore a gray flannel suit with a very pale pink silk blouse and bookish trifocals. She had a lot of lenses. She had seen a lot. And she had heard a lot of stories. But Willie Rossini was still willing to hear a lot more. She wore a big, black pearl in a modern setting on hands that were shockingly young and graceful.

Lee emerged from the bedroom in jogging pants and a sweatshirt. Helen, her wet ebony ringlets dampening the shoulders of a T-shirt, plopped herself down on the couch, curling her long legs in their heavy, black tights all the way up to her chest. I did the introductions. It was time to try and get all the facts straight. And to try to keep Helen out of jail. Those accused by the legal system need some kind of iron bridge over their back that will let the machine roll over them. Willie would construct that bridge out of wobbly facts and incorrect legal moves on the part of the law enforcement and justice system.

Helen went over the events of the evening. I prompted her to begin with the donation of her manuscripts to the Archive. Allen Boone had made an appointment to accept them shortly before the dinner. We went over the dinner and Helen's speech.

Helen supplied other facts about her literary background, the university classes she'd been teaching when she moved to town. She also volunteered that she had been arrested once before, but that the charges had been dropped. She'd been accused of assault with a deadly weapon—a Swiss Army knife, in fact, which Helen alleged she had been cleaning her nails with when a psycho ex-girlfriend came at her.

Willie probed gently with questions, and then finally asked the hard one. Had there been any romantic animosity between Tracy and Helen?

"I think Tracy fell in love with Lee," Helen explained quietly. I saw Willie's pencil pause over the paper. Nothing on her face changed. It wasn't the fact that Helen knew of the affair, it was the deliberately neutral way that Helen had said it. "On an Olivia cruise."

"Right." Willie looked over at her. "I want to be absolutely clear with both of you. This is a murder charge. The DA's office will stop at nothing to make their charge stick. They are going to interview every person about what happened on the Olivia Cruise. So Lee, I have to ask you some hard questions. Do you want to answer them here in this room? Or should we talk privately?"

Lee looked into Helen's face. She took hold of her hand. "I don't want any secrets from Helen, if that's what you mean."

"Okay, Lee." Willie paused imperceptibly. "What happened on that cruise? Think very, very carefully."

We listened to the clock tick. Lee was choosing her words.

"I was on the cruise, partly as a freebie. I had been taken on as the cruise chiropractor, but I was really just supervising three masseuses and a shiatsu therapist. Every now and then, if someone was in pain, I would make a diagnosis, perhaps start a course of treatment. It wasn't exactly heavy work. I had a lot of time on my hands. And, well, Tracy Port came on to me pretty flagrantly."

"Flagrantly?"

"Yes. She would move really close to me. At first I didn't

understand what was happening. I thought—I thought she was having some—some balance problems."

"What did you do?"

"Nothing—at first."

"Nothing?"

"Well, you know, I just sort of hoped it would go away."

"When did this start?"

"In the beginning. Right at the start of the cruise."

"And then?"

"She just seemed to keep making these passes in public. It was odd. I never felt her come on to me in private. Nothing ever happened."

"You're sure about that, Lee?" Willie was leaning forward in her chair. "Everyone on that cruise will be questioned. If someone saw something you say never happened, it's not going to look good for Helen."

"Lee, honey." Helen was smiling. "I'd been out on that endless book tour. If something happened, it happened. We've been together a long time, before and after that cruise. Whatever you did, it's not going to cause problems now. You'd better tell us everything." Lee took a deep breath.

"Okay. About mid-cruise, after a snorkeling trip, where, I have to say, I got quite a good view of Tracy's swimming talents, a whole underwater, uh, performance and, well, that night, I found her alone on the deck."

"And?"

"I tried to kiss her."

"What happened?"

"That's the hell of it. She wasn't interested. She wasn't interested at all! After all that flirting, she just laughed and blew me off. After that I just thought, shit, the woman is schizo or something. I stayed *out of her way*." Lee shook her head and ran her fingers through her hair. "I never thought much about it again."

"Okay. Thanks for that. Helen, I'll get back to you to discuss what happens next when I've had a chance to think things through. You won't be arraigned until Thursday. Keep your nose clean. Stay home. Don't talk to the press. Not the gay press. Not anybody. Change your phone number, if necessary. Relax as much as possible. It's going to get worse before it gets better."

"Do you think you can get Helen off?"

"There's a lot of things that add up too neatly and a lot of things that don't add up at all." Willie looked through her trifocals at Helen. "Helen." The author sat up, returning a gaze of six pairs of blue eyes. "Did you do it?"

"No," Helen said. "I didn't."

"You see, Helen's innocent." Willie stood up. "And that's a real plus." The lawyer stretched out her hand with the black pearl and gave them all each a warm handshake. "I am just beginning to build a case. I'll let you know when I come up with something significant."

Helen nodded. Lee got up to show Willie out, her face a mass of worry. The boyish brow was getting its first crease. It would probably never go away.

"C'mon, Emma." Willie gestured to me. "Walk me to my car."

Once we got outside, Willie slipped into her car, unrolling the window. "Okay, Emma, I'm on the case and so are you. See as many people as you can, and let's collect as many motives for murdering Tracy from as many people as possible."

"I'd like to put some of Rose Baynetta's techno-sleuths on to researching Helen's necklace, the appraisals."

"The Lee Turgo angle?"

"I'll check that out too." I started making a mental list.

"I think you'll find out a lot about Tracy Port that you might not have suspected," Willie said. "In any event, I don't believe for a second that our young chiropractor thought Miss Port was losing her balance."

Willie started the engine. "Oh, and one more thing, Emma. The anonymous bidder on Howard's place. You do know who that is? It was Renquist Falkenberg."

I buzzed by home for coffee and left a message on Rose's personal machine. Rose, it seemed, was still in bed. I went to Frances's office to look for old copies of the *Bay Times*. All these public figures. Suddenly, I hoped Frances was okay in Seattle. Didn't she need protection, too? I looked at the desktop that might or might not have interested Fresca. There was the telephone number written on the pad, the telephone number she always left, where I could reach her, in case of emergency.

It was too early in the day to call. But Tracy, after all, had been Frances's friend. Shouldn't I call Frances now? I picked up the phone and dialed.

After the ringing stopped, I heard a synthetic voice: *"The number you have called is not in service. Please make sure you are dialing the correct number and try again. Thank you."* I looked at the numbers inscribed precisely upon the pad. Engraved upon paper. The wrong number.

I pulled on jeans, a T-shirt and a windbreaker against the stiff early morning wind that came in from the Bay. I was going to take a long walk this morning. To Red Dora's Cafe. Red Dora's was always open. There were wild raves that ended at dawn, and a whole new theme party would begin around poached egg time.

113

Mary Wings

I wanted to find a little punky girl, a woman who was pierced in all the most interesting places, and didn't mind showing you where. A freelance young lady who called herself Jesus and made a living with a Polaroid camera. A woman who had been at the table, but not as a guest. I clattered down the stairs.

"I don't want to know if you have an affair!" Frances had cried once, during our lovemaking. "Promise me you won't do it with anyone from around here!"

Now I realized why Frances didn't want to know if I had an affair. Because she didn't want to tell me about *hers*.

CHAPTER NINE

RED DORA'S BEARDED LADY CAFE

Somewhere it must be written that the children of capitalists will revolt by inventing a fashion which will terrify their elders. Every succeeding generation thinks they have discovered the final boundary of transgression, only to be horrified by the next wave of revolution in youthful appearance. Certain elements, particularly the twenty-nothings found at Red Dora's, discovered that multiple piercing easily did the trick as time marched toward the second millennium.

Horrifying many a parent and passerby, they perforated their young bodies, dangling metal and jewels from every eyebrow, nostril, ear curve. They tattooed their necks, arms, wrists and feet. Bracelets and rings were inscribed on skin by artists whose craft was evolving to a high level of refinement. There was no shortage of living canvases available; tattoos were the latest thing on young dyke hides in San Francisco.

Albert Camus said everyone is responsible for their own face by the time they are twenty-five. The girls at Dora's

115

took this to heart and got busy at eighteen. It was a world away from the stockbrokers and dentists who had attended the Howard Blooming Lesbian and Gay Memorial Archive Gala Dinner. Thank God.

These girls hopped on their spray-painted, and probably stolen, mountain bikes and lounged around Red Dora's all day long, creating new poetry with their leather tongues and complicated affairs of the heart, which they referred to as "the lesbian hairball." It was in such a nest that I sought the multi-pierced Polaroid photographer who had taken the name Gurl Jesus.

All this piercing and permanent painting certainly put the women at Red Dora's out of the running for straight day jobs and mortgages. Having grown up watching the country being gutted by three Republican administrations, these girls didn't look at the future too closely. It was never meant for them. They placed themselves outside the running and went on a rampage from time to time.

There were those lesbians with briefcases who dabbled in the occasional body adventure and hid a pierced nipple underneath the power suit at the board meeting. There were also those who removed their nose rings at dawn, before they went to the office. But these were not the women of Red Dora's.

At Red Dora's, all the current conventions of beauty faded away and were replaced by outlandish acts of intention. Faces accented with silver, gold and tiny diamonds: Red Dora girls wore their wealth on their faces, in your face, and not stored in a lockbox or stock portfolio. The women at Red Dora's had become beautiful to me.

Surrounded by a war zone, Red Dora's was in a neighborhood of stray bullets. The walk across the street from the federal housing project, where drive-by shootings were a monthly event, promised an adrenaline rush. I stayed on the far corner, and crossed twice, one more time than I needed to, even though it was far too early for gangsters.

Nevertheless, I thought about hitting the ground. I waited for the screams. Because I'd heard them before, on this street, at this intersection. I had seen the people running. Mushrooms, the gangsters call them, people who just popped up at the wrong time.

Bullets took out the occasional passerby, but gangsters kept the rent low enough for a group of women as opposed to profit, and as unafraid of bullets, as the women of Red Dora's undoubtedly were.

I walked inside. Dora was busy steaming milk and pouring coffees. Dora did not have any piercings that I could see, but she did have a beard, a dark smudge underneath her chin. I headed for the counter to the complaints of a cluster of people whose clothes had seen much wear, who were lounging in line, waiting for their cappuccinos, café lattés, peanut butter and jelly sandwiches, Crunchberries, bagels and beer. Precious metals and gems flashed on them, like dewdrops on sleepy children. Children who slept in the gutter.

"Dora, remember me—Emma Victor? You know Gurl Jesus?"

"What's this about?"

"Does she work here?"

"Could've."

"Let's go outside."

"Well—" The people in line shifted about uncomfortably. They were waiting for their caffeine fix.

"Brenda, will you take care of these folks?"

A listless blonde managed to disentangle herself from a

117

rebar chair and sauntered behind the bar. Dora jerked her head toward what might be called a garden outside.

An illegal dog leaned against a group of stolen bicycles and twitched its ears.

Dora showed me to a vinyl car seat which had been mended with duct tape. I balanced myself on the springs, which were barely contained behind the plastic material, and sent up a silent prayer against impalement.

"So Girl Jesus—"

"That's Gurl, actually. *G-u-r-l.*"

"Whatever. Works here?"

"Who wants to know?"

"Listen, Dora, if Gurl had made a sudden disappearance—"

"I didn't say that."

"But you're wondering why she didn't show up for work. The place looks a little short-handed today. Brenda looks like she could barely handle a damp sponge."

"Maybe Gurl got sick."

"You don't want to tell me, okay. But your friend with the Polaroid may be in trouble."

"That's news?"

I heard something which could have been a car backfiring, a cherry bomb, a gunshot. It didn't matter to Dora.

"Where can I find her?'

"Emma, what's this all about?"

"I'm looking into the death—the murder—of Tracy Port."

"That bitch!"

"Well, well! What's she done to you, Dora?"

"She owns a condo down the street. In the Victorian Mews. The neighborhood is poised for redevelopment. And they want us out. They started a petition once. But they failed miserably. We're doing our best to be ugly and in their faces."

"There was a lot of animosity?"

"Oh, yeah. Tracy Port, but it was that—that vile friend of hers—the southern destroyer."

"You mean Deborah Dunton?"

"Yeah. She owns a unit up there, and a seat on every board in town. Live and let live is not her motto. She came before three separate neighborhood commissions to protest our liquor license. You know, the only parties worth attending are her two-hundred-dollar benefits."

"She was on the library board. The board that hired Tracy."

"And now Tracy's dead," Dora mused. "Who did us the favor?"

"I don't know. That's what I'm trying to find out. Gurl Jesus was there."

"She's no murderer."

"But people with cameras at the scene of the crime are always of interest."

Dora whistled. "So they might be," she said slowly.

"So where is Gurl Jesus?"

Dora looked at me, shut her lips firmly and said nothing.

"I'm not working for the cops. I'm working to clear Helen Thomas."

"So?"

"So, maybe in the spirit of misplaced sisterhood—"

"Sorry, I have no idea where I left it."

"How about saving Gurl Jesus's ass?"

"You really think she's in danger?"

"I'm starting to think that. Especially as her friends are being a little too cagey about where she's at. There is a

119

murderer on the loose. And Gurl Jesus had a camera at the scene of the crime."

"Hmm." Dora thought about it.

"Where does she live, Dora?"

"That doesn't matter anymore."

"Why?"

"She called this morning. Said she was quitting."

"Short notice."

Dora shrugged. The concept of *notice* was far beyond the realm of Red Dora's existence.

"So why? What reason did she give you?"

"A lot of people here like to take off suddenly. Maybe Gurl is one of them."

"Only the day after a murder, it looks a little funny."

"Everything looks funny to me here."

"You won't be laughing if she turns up dead."

Dora had the grace to look faintly wounded.

"So what did she say? Called this morning, said she's quitting work, splitting town . . ."

"Something like that. Said she'd stumbled onto something good, was going to split the country for a while. She was pretty excited."

"And so where can I find her?"

Dora was silent.

"Did she have a last errand or two, before she left, or anything?"

"Had to pick up her paycheck. Came by earlier."

"And then where'd she go?"

Silence.

And then it struck me. What do girls of Red Dora's, girls with a big life change coming up, girls with a little extra cash and the road on their minds *do*?

"Is she at the Gambit, Dora?"

Dora said nothing. "I didn't tell you that."

"Give me a name, Dora."

Dora thought about it. We both thought about it. Gurl Jesus had been at the scene of a murder. Gurl Jesus had a camera. Suddenly being onto something good could also mean big trouble for an overly confident twenty-nothing.

"Thad," Dora said.

That was all she needed to say. Within minutes I was out the door, walking quickly out of shooting range of the projects, and watching the property values go up and up as I walked the long incline toward the Castro.

Garbage gave way to gardenias. Shiny brass knobs and mailbox plates twinkled in the morning sunlight. Ah, the Castro, where the Gambit, the premier piercing palace of San Francisco, was located; where one Thad worked and had probably worked on Gurl Jesus more than once. Piercing was a highly personal, ritualized experience, and I knew that people like to return to their original operators.

Being Sunday, there was a huge line in front of the place. Getting pierced was a Saturday morning kind of thing to do, I realized as I made my way upstairs into the lobby.

Picture posters of pierced genitalia, stretched and pulled in various directions like strange, fleshy parachutes, lined the walls. I avoided looking at them, and perused the personnel who inflicted such pain upon their clients in the name of beauty. Dressed entirely in black, wearing a turtleneck and velvet slippers, a piercer was showing a customer the latest in Prince Alberts. There was no way I was going to stand in line.

Of the three salespeople, only one was male. A trimmed goatee was accented by two silver studs threaded through his lower lip. Both eyebrows had been penetrated and the series of loops looked like curtain hardware, over water blue eyes. The salesman was busy helping another customer.

"A zircon can look just as good."

"Are you sure?" *She* was not sure.

"Well, nobody could tell unless—"

"My boyfriend's a jeweler."

"Well, honey, what are you doing in here?"

"He has to get used to the idea first. Then I'll get him to do a diamond for me."

"So you'll take the zircon?"

"Yes."

"Okay, you just sign this release form—"

"Excuse me," I cut in.

The blue eyes didn't look my way, but his voice said, "You'll have to wait your turn."

"But I just need some information."

"Like I said, you'll have to wait your turn."

"Does someone named Thad work here?"

"He's busy." The man's lips clamped shut.

"Does he have a client named Gurl Jesus?"

"I can't divulge the names of *clients*." Irritated.

"What if they are in grave danger?"

"I only do body work here, dear, nothing lethal. I'm really busy, now if *you'll just wait your turn*."

"Can I get this inserted now?" The woman elbowed her way in front of me. She was holding the zircon up to her dark skin, the fold between flesh and nose. It sparkled in anticipation and she smiled.

"Yes, just go into, let's see, booth number three." He directed her quickly away. "I'll send Georgia in to see you."

That done, the young man, ignoring the whole line of impatient customers, hissed at me, *"Who are you?"*

"A friend of Gurl Jesus. Emma Victor. I need—"

"Well we're terribly busy, and I can't divulge the names of other customers."

"Did Gurl Jesus give Thad a large tip for quick service?"

"I can't spend my time talking to you. I've got business to—" Then what I'd said sank in. I could see his mind working, mentally leafing through my wallet. In a sudden stage shout he said, *"If you want your nose pierced—"*

"Okay."

"What?"

"You'll tell me about Gurl Jesus," I whispered.

"Two hundred dollars."

"One."

"One-fifty."

"One."

Pause. "Okay. One." His stage whisper returned. "That will be, let's see, the piercing, the stone, and would you like some cleanser? We recommend the cleanser. It's very soothing. Helps you protect against infection."

"You better tell me about Gurl Jesus."

He nodded at me.

"You will tell me about Gurl Jesus?"

"Yes."

"By the way, no zirconium. I want this, *this* stud inserted." I pointed to a diamond glittering on a black velvet backdrop. "And the dish on Gurl."

He brought out a pair of needle-nose pliers. "I have to bend the wire so that it curls a little bit on the end. Like these." He pointed to the black velvet case where gems on the end of corkscrew wires glittered. "The curling end keeps it in your nose; you don't want a backing inside your nose. This is the way nose studs are always inserted." He held it up for my inspection and I nodded. "That's one hundred and thirty-five dollars. Will that be cash or credit card?"

I brought out the plastic.

"Right this way, miss." He glided on the silent pads of velvet slippers along the tiled floor into the back. "By the way, I'm Thad."

"Oh, *you're* Thad." But he had stopped in front of a series of booths separated by purple velvet curtains which did not fall quite to the floor. I dropped a quarter on the carpet and looked quickly under the curtains. I did not see the construction boots or tattered tights of Gurl Jesus anywhere. There was a pair of high heels and Bass Weejuns opposite to one pair of velvet slippers. The cubicle next to me had only slippers. The other feet were not visible at all.

There was chamber music playing, maybe Mozart, and the interior was medical. The instrument sterilizer was burbling away, the leather examining table had white paper rolled out over it in a big sterile strip. All this was meant to inspire confidence. All I wanted was Gurl Jesus's whereabouts; I didn't really care if I had my nose pierced or not. But I guessed it was good that I was in a sterile environment.

Everywhere was white. The white walls had built-in white cupboards and drawers. I thought about all the people being pierced in the building at this moment. What did they pierce penises with? Thad opened the door of one of the cupboards. I knew when he looked inside, I wouldn't want to see what was in there.

"Is it going to hurt this time?" A gruff but nervous voice rose from the cubicle next door.

"Only the prick."

Prick. Lidocaine. I imagined the procedure that was taking place behind the velvet curtain next door, where someone was lying down.

"So can you tell me, did Gurl Jesus visit here this morning?" I asked him quietly.

"Ouch! Fuck, that hurt!" A cry came from next door. Thad ignored it.

"I always pierce Gurl Jesus when she comes in," he said. "Except when we're very busy, like today."

"Do you know where she's living now?"

"No. Now just hold still." He held my chin in his hand, turned a dentist's floodlight onto my face and examined the shape of my nose, the crevice where nose met cheek, the shape of my nostrils. There certainly was a lot of space to a face. He adjusted the lamp above him and a spear of light penetrated my eyes.

"That's bright!"

"All the better to pierce you by, my dear." Then he brought out a ballpoint pen and touched it to my nose. He held up a silver hand mirror so I could see the little blue spot where the diamond would come permanently to rest.

"No, back farther."

"There."

"Okay."

Thad was coming toward me with what looked like a Flash Gordon radar gun. Excerpt that there was a needle-sharp bayonet on the end of it. In his other hand, he held what looked like a plastic drinking straw, a half inch in diameter.

"Wait a second. I'm not going through with this unless you give me some kind of lead," I said. Thad held his fire. The diamond waited patiently on the sterile tray.

"Did you feel that?" from across the curtain.

"No."

"Good, I'm going to do another one now."

"Okay. Hurry, will you?"

125

"Two down, four more to go—" I heard from over the curtain.

"Gurl Jesus, she must have a studio or something, somewhere."

"Yeah, that's what I hear."

"Okay, before you shoot me with that thing, tell me where—"

"Only one more left," said the voice on the other side.

"Good! I gotta get—"

And then I recognized that voice, the voice from the body that was getting one, two, three, no six holes pierced somewhere through it. But before I could get off the table, Thad's silicone tube was up my nostril and his piercing gun was aimed at the side of my nose.

"Don't move," he instructed.

"Okay, Gurl, get outta here," he called over the curtain. *"Run!"*

He pushed the piercing gun next to my nose. "Just hold still. Your eye isn't very far from here, you know."

As far as I could remember, I had not seen anyone with a pierced eye. I didn't think I wanted to be the first.

So I sat there while I heard who I was sure was Gurl Jesus get off the table, pull on her tattered tights and zip herself into a satin sheath. I heard the sound of construction boots running out the back door of the Gambit and clattering down a San Francisco wooden back stairway. Gurl Jesus, running away from information that just might save her. If my hunch was right. But my hunches, I thought, were not always right.

My next feeling was but a nanosecond of pain, a minor moment of discomfort as a diamond was permanently inserted in the side of my nose.

CHAPTER TEN

DARK
NATIVITY

I grabbed the beauty weapon out of Thad's hand as it re-tracted from my face, and ran out of the cubicle, past all the other purple curtains behind which other patrons were being pierced. At the back of the building, I could hear the heavy construction boots of Gurl Jesus still running down what sounded like a very rickety wooden stairway. I followed the sound which led to a small deck overlooking a maze of gardens and fences, my hand heavy with the piercing gun.

Gurl Jesus was scrambling over redwood dividers, trampling orchid gardens, bearded iris beds, hybrid hydrangeas and all the things that gay boys grow in San Francisco. I followed the tattered back of the photographer as she ran an obstacle course of Florentine birdbaths, Gargoyle Grottos and Notre Dame knock-offs.

Gurl moved fast. Good thing, too. It would be but seconds before irate gardeners would be outside, shaking their fists and clucking at the state of their gladiolus beds. Then they would shrug their shoulders and work off their frustration by building giant biceps at the gym. Ah, white gay male middle-class culture in San Francisco. I could see Gurl Jesus's biceps as she vaulted over a bed of bearded irises. A different kind of bicep, a different kind of culture altogether.

"Gurl—wait!" I called. But the only reply was the muted sound of Gurl Jesus's combat boots, torpedoing through pale pink tulips. She leapfrogged a stone lion, getting her tights caught in a page fence. They tore, leaving a black flag twisted in the wire, but she never looked up. She gave no indication that she heard me. The kind of girl that never takes advice. Jesus.

"Gurl—stop! Please!"

She just kept going.

"Gurl, you're messing with rough trade. Gurl, don't deal with a—" But I knew she wouldn't listen. She disappeared over a final fence and I never got to finish my sentence. I aimed the piercing gun and took a dry shot at the fence over which the young photographer had vaulted. She would come out somewhere on 18th Street, I figured. But I wasn't going to chase her.

I wasn't going to trample the things that gay boys grow. I was going to go out the front door with Gurl Jesus's address and save myself a lot of trouble. After all, I thought, holding the piercing gun in my hand, I could get it easily, by nailing Thad's balls to the wall.

He was right behind me, thinking he was being sneaky. I turned without warning and soon had the gun firmly lodged in the hollows between his thigh and crotch. There was a big artery there. He knew it and I knew it.

"This won't be a piercing, Thad. I could pull the trigger, but nothing would come out the other side. It'd be a one-way hole. And it would hurt."

"Look—"

"Give me the address of her studio, Thad."

"Your nose! Let me take a look at that piercing—"

"My vanity will get you nowhere. I'm pissed off, Thad, very pissed."

"I'm shaking in my shoes," he sneered.

"Good," I said, pushing the gun deeper into his thigh. It wasn't the kind of body contact I longed for on a Sunday morning. The barrel of the gun was pressed deeply into Thad's groin now. It made an indentation in the coarse material of his dungarees. His thigh was hard and I had to keep up a steady pressure to keep the gun in place. "Don't think I wouldn't, Thad. You've got enough medical equipment in there to do a quick suture, or tourniquet, when I pop the artery in your groin. I know it wouldn't do any lasting damage. Just leave you very weak, with a little unexpected scarification. I just had the gun held to *my* nose, Thad. Now I'm returning the favor. It's *your* turn."

"I was just helping a friend—"

"Yeah, get herself in trouble."

"What do you know?"

"I know I'm just about out of patience with you. And I wouldn't mind pulling the trigger. I wouldn't mind one bit. You going to tell me where she lives or shall we just make a few holes first, for practice?" I had his back up against the wall.

Thad's head was tipped back affording me a look at his five o'clock shadow and more arteries I could stick my gun into. His chin was up high in the air and he was licking his lips. Christ, he was enjoying this! Just my luck. A masochist.

"Talk to me, Thad," I crooned, bringing the gun up to his neck.

129

"Be my guest."

"Tough guy, eh?"

"I've felt a lot of pain."

"Not like you're going to feel when I call the police and tell them that you're shielding an accessory to murder."

"You don't have anything on me."

"But you could have an interesting time cooling your heels at the Hall of Justice, Thad. I heard piercings don't go over so well behind bars. I heard something about someone getting—"

"Yeah, okay, I heard that story, too. You don't need to repeat it. If you want to find Gurl, go talk to her. Go to her studio. South of Market."

"Where?"

"Somewhere."

"Where, Thad?" I pushed the gun near the carotid artery of his neck. Would I pull the trigger? Actually, I wasn't sure. It was nice not being sure. It gave an edge to my voice.

"Talk." I pressed the barrel of the gun into his neck. The little black prickles of his beard seemed to push out of his skin. I could see his vein throbbing.

"Somewhere near that wino park."

"Street name, Thad. Number. You're on your way to jail if I don't find her."

"Sumner Street. Five-forty."

"Keep your hand steady for the next customer, Thad." I pulled the gun away from his neck.

He stood still for a moment. "Well, I've got to hand it to you," he murmured, massaging his neck. "I've never seen anyone get up and run like that after a piercing—you and Gurl Jesus both." Thad's eyebrow rings twitched in what passed for genuine admiration. I remembered the hole in my nose. Looking down over the curve of my cheek, I could see the twinkle of a diamond, obscured by something darker, like blood. What was Thad saying? About my nose piercing?

"Sorry, you still have a little blood on your—" He reached out a hand which I pushed away. "Usually people need to lie down after being pierced; they see stars, or get all hot."

Suddenly I *was* hot, and stars were burning bright white holes in my vision of Thad and the back deck of the Gambit. The ground. I could fall on the ground, I thought, and just in time I remembered what kind of thought that was. It was all I could do to repeat, "Five-forty. Sumner. South of market. Next to the wino park."

I gave the boy his gun back and tore out through the front of the building past all the patient customers waiting to be pierced. "Nice nose," someone called out as I ran down the stairs. I touched the tiny diamond when I got on the street. I hailed a taxi and gave the Sumner address. I would beat Gurl Jesus back to her pad, I thought, confidently: I would talk her out of doing what I thought she was going to do. But I would have had better luck raising Tracy Port from the dead.

The taxi let me off. South of Market, or SOMA, is San Francisco's SoHo where you can get cappuccino and a panhandler on every corner. Watch where you step; it's a public toilet down here, ever since the city decided to stop building them. Don't let your gaze linger on the outlandish signs hanging over the streets. Plaster cows, rainbows, discreet eateries with menus in Italian; this is the intersection of Ripple and Thunderbird. Don't look up, you could take a slide on something nasty.

131

Or you could move in and have a several-thousand-dollar monthly mortgage on some wanky designer hut that is just big enough to turn around in. But hip, very hip.

Sumner Alley had a few designer huts and a row of ancient flat-faced wooden buildings—storefronts turned into living spaces. Down the street, the wino park featured a big mural of Mexican revolutionaries and provided homeless campers with a colorful backdrop of a revolution that would never happen here.

A group of men, down on their luck, were warming their hands over a morning bonfire in a fifty-gallon oil barrel. A few pieces of pizza rested on a curling section of sheet metal. Everybody looked sleepy, rubbing their eyes. It was still only nine-thirty.

Gurl Jesus's studio was in the Victorian Row house. I walked up a wooden staircase and was stopped by the wire cage guarding the entryway. Someone had welded a metal plate on the grill where seven doorbells had been installed. A cat's cradle of wires hung out the back of the panel and extended into one of the door frames, held in place by what else? Duct tape.

I looked at the lack of names on the doorbells. You had to know who was here to come calling. Maybe you even had to have a secret password. Or a pierced nose. A row of shiny bells connecting to tenuous, but tenacious, lives through a thin two-gauge wire. Seven bells. And one of them had a cross on it. Must be Gurl Jesus.

I rang the bell but no one answered. So Gurl Jesus wasn't home yet. Any minute now, I thought. Any minute I would see her, have a little polite conversation and perhaps save her life. I sat on a nearby stoop.

I waited and waited. I thought about Frances and where she might be and how she might or might not have left the wrong number by mistake. I thought about mistakes in general, mistakes that I had made in this relationship, ways I could have been a better person. Then I gave up on this fruitless line of rumination. I couldn't have been a better person; I was only the person that I was. I'd almost had a one-night stand with someone, that's all. I didn't know if adultery would have been wonderful or a major disappointment. I didn't want to find out. But did Frances already know?

I didn't want to think about what it might have been like with Fresca's fingers inside me, when all I really wanted was Frances anywhere in the vicinity. My mate who was not dyslexic, a researcher who had always gotten her numbers straight. I wished to hell I hadn't lost her research notes.

I sat down on the stoop and watched the bums make brunch. The Dumpster pizza was sizzling now, and someone had their finger inside a peanut butter jar, wiping the edge of the glass. A broken bottle of what might have been port was passed around. I could see Salvation Army forks and some cracked china with silver edges from where I was sitting. One man stood and did the honors, cutting what was left of the pizza into equal slices, arranging it on a piece of chimney flashing and holding it over the fire to warm it up. The other men drank and stared in front of them, waiting for breakfast.

I looked up and down at the houses, jammed together, no spaces between them for the rain to fall and the weeds to grow. Where people lived in them, the wooden fronts were blinded by shades, Levolors squeezed tight. There were no cars. No action. It was Saturday morning. San Francisco was sleeping in.

I looked again at the bells and counted the windows on the front of the building. The windows and apartments must extend far back into the lot to hold the population that the number of bells indicated. Had Gurl Jesus come and gone? Or was she at home hiding? Waiting for some secret signal? I buzzed her bell twice, stopped and buzzed again. I sat down some more until I was tired of sitting. I kept looking for Gurl Jesus to come around the corner. Down the street, past the bum brunch, waving hello, in her tattered tights. She'd be scared when she saw me, but she'd stop. She'd stop and she'd listen and she wouldn't do what she was going to do.

But Gurl Jesus never walked down that alley. I crossed the street and took a longer look at the flaking paint on the front of her block. On the right, down three stairs another cross was scratched over the top of the door. Let the Inquisition pass this house. Gurl Jesus, born on the third wave, was no pagan. Just in case, she'd provided a sticker saying, "I'm pro-choice, and I *riot*!" on her door.

The basement apartment. It was so quiet on Sumner Alley. Not a happy, contented quiet. Or maybe that was my head playing interference. Frances was in Seattle, and I had almost committed adultery. By my fault, my most grievous fault.

That's when I decided to break into Gurl's house. And it was a good thing I did. After that things would not be quiet on Sumner Alley for long.

There was a small window with textured glass next to the door. It was small, but still bigger than my hips. I put my fingertips under the top of the frame. Dried chips of putty rained onto my fingers. If the window wasn't open, I could probably dismantle it.

I turned around. The bums were burning their fingers on the flashing, trying to get to their pizza slices. They didn't notice me. They had never looked my way.

134

With a quick push, I had the window open, had jumped over the sill and was inside the dark cavern that was Gurl Jesus's studio. I shut the window carefully, the rotten edge of the wood meeting the sill quiet as a cat's paw. There was a moment when I wished I were a cat.

Gurl Jesus's studio was dark as the jungle, damp and moldy smelling, crowded with creatures and an odor that started a cold stream of sweat that ran from my armpits to my waist. I stepped into the chilled room. No heater in sight. Permanently cold.

The long, narrow room was a dank tunnel with not much light at the end of it. Between the light and myself was something evil, something I didn't want to find. My nose twitched involuntarily and I held onto my stomach. The hairs slowly began to raise on the back of my neck. There were overflowing ashtrays everywhere, brown Camel butts decisively tamped out over and over again. Ashtrays and the smell of cordite. Between here and the light, Gurl Jesus had the place packed. Broken bicycles were hanging from the ceiling and thousands of tiny Polaroid photographs lined the walls, signatures, or graffiti all over them. She'd mounted three old Underwood typewriters on plywood and stuck them on the ceiling. A line of hubcaps, shiny shields from vehicles that Gurl had never driven, punctuated the corner. A file drawer stood open, two hangers jutting out of it. A Rolodex spine lay on the floor, an empty Ferris wheel, every single card torn out and thrown all around. Business cards of clients, of photography studios were scattered over the concrete floor.

Two old Samsonite suitcases, satin linings torn out, lay open, belching more of the favorite ancient clothes that Gurl Jesus, and many others, had worn for years. Stacks of unmolested CDs were piled into plastic towers, and I saw that tiny, expensive Bose speakers had been mounted in all the corners.

A group of gloomy, still figures congregated in the middle of the mess. They were stooped over, as if avoiding the bicycle which might crash into them in the next earthquake. I came closer. There were animals—sheep, a camel—and men with presents. They were made of plaster and so was the straw-filled cradle around which they gathered.

Gurl had somehow ripped off an entire life-size nativity display. I could just see her approaching the lawn of a church around Christmas time. It would have been in the middle of the night with the help of a borrowed truck, and a few other Dora dykes. They'd have driven up to the church lawn and made off with the holy family in the dead of the night, then installed them gleefully in Gurl's basement studio.

Three wise men held out offerings in plaster hands. Smack, crank, cocaine. Gurl Jesus had made her own gift suggestion in graffiti, across boxes meant to contain frankincense and myrrh.

A life-size Virgin Mary looked adoringly at a Barbie doll perched jauntily in her arms.

A sheep huddled by an empty cradle. Someone had put a brassiere on the top of its head. The little pointy, plaster ears were sticking out from either side of the circle-stitched cups. Cross your heart, I thought, noticing that the cloven feet of the animal were wet with something black and sticky. And it wasn't some joke of Gurl's.

I was the only person around to witness the smell of the cordite. Gurl's plaster family stared with plaster eyes at what could only have been blood. I walked through the statuary holding my breath, past a particularly thick-looking wise man, a camel hunkered down on the studio floor, something like a cow bell around its neck.

There, huddled by the hoofs of the humped beast, was Gurl Jesus. The young photographer was still holding her Polaroid camera. She'd just had her final piercing. In the back.

Gurl Jesus's shrunken cardigan had been bought secondhand, after someone had mistakenly washed it in the washing machine. Tight and furry, it clung to Gurl's back where in the middle, there had been a small explosion of flesh and blood. The knitting and purling were coming undone around the hole where the gunpowder burns left edges of the yarn charred. The lower half of the sweater had soaked up a lot of blood. But most of what had been inside of Gurl Jesus had leaked all over the floor.

Her legs flopped out from under her dress, a broken doll in tattered tights, the soles of her construction boots never to touch the floor again. Gurl was turned toward the camel, one arm outstretched, as if to reach up and pet its muzzle. The flowered dress was joined together at the sides by safety pins, which, in some poignant irony, still held.

I didn't think she'd been assaulted. Just cold-bloodedly shot in the back. The outstretched arm, the camera in her hands. Had she been meaning to take a picture?

I came closer, avoiding the sticky mess, a field for footprints on the floor.

I put my finger on her pulse. Oh yes, Gurl Jesus was dead. Freshly dead. She was still warm. She'd died, perhaps just moments before I'd arrived.

A back window looked out onto a garden of trash and calla lilies. It was open. The murderer gone.

I looked over her dress, at the legs that would no longer run, the pudgy fingers that wouldn't push the camera release, wouldn't light a Camel or curl up next to one. I didn't need to look at her face. I didn't want to look at her face. The creamy décolleté, the biceps.

I bent over and peered at the camera. One of those fancy Polaroids. I took out a handkerchief and opened the back cover. Empty of course. I clicked the latch shut and slid it back into her hand where a snake tattoo writhed, just to make me nervous.

Gurl Jesus had lived on the margins all her life. She was only at home out there. But the one time she ignored that and tried to make a profit, she forgot to look behind her. Where someone had a gun.

I looked around the dark studio. Without turning on the lights, despite the scattered Rolodex, the tattered Samsonite lining, I knew the place hadn't been ransacked. No, Gurl Jesus had gone quite easily to her crucifixion. She had handed over the photo, counted the cash, turned around and the photo enthusiast had plugged her in the back.

By *my* fault? Gurl Jesus, why didn't you listen? Emma Victor, why weren't you smarter or faster? My grievous fault. Gurl Jesus was dead, and I was no nearer to keeping Helen Thomas out of jail. I peered around the apartment again.

Gurl Jesus's filing system appeared to be old briefcases and purses piled up along the wall, but not all of them had been turned over. Papers and rags, stuffed animals and oil-stained doilies littered the floor. I tripped over a bicycle chain and peered into the bathroom. Someone had trashed that, too—the semblance of a search, a swipe of the hand through the medicine cabinet.

There was a broken bottle of bath oil on the floor leaving the scent of jasmine which made me want to cry. A hypodermic needle and an empty glass bottle with a few meth crystals left in it lay on the tiles, too. Gurl Jesus had been into speed. Meth-head. Crankcase.

Gurl Jesus was the kind of victim the cops loved to overlook. The half-hearted turnover of the apartment would convince them. Especially after they found the speed in the bathroom.

I went to the sink. An electrical water heating coil was neatly wound around itself. There had been no ceremonial tea drinking. No cookies. Just a bullet in the back.

I walked through the religious crowd and stared at the young woman on the floor in front of them, the brown stains on her fingers, the tattoo of a rose climbing up her neck. Why didn't you stop, Gurl Jesus? There were so many things I wanted to tell you.

Don't deal with those who've dished out death, Gurl Jesus; you can't get credit with a murderer. You just get yourself a little closer to death. Blackmailing a murderer is about the silliest thing you could ever do. But then, giving advice to dead people wasn't so high on the smart list either.

I lifted the hem of her skirt, my eyes traveling up the threadbare tights which bound her thighs. Gurl Jesus had been pierced six final times, through her labia.

The inanimate group was silent. They seemed to lean over the unfortunate girl, worried parents, a plaster family that couldn't figure out where they'd failed. I stepped over Gurl's body, making sure not to leave any tracks. I went over to the window and wiped my prints off the sill. The bums were singing now. Had they seen anything? Would they tell if they had?

The murderer had been confident, with the Polaroids in one hand and a gun in the other. I wondered if they'd thought of negatives. You couldn't make prints off the Polaroid negatives. They were throw-away pieces of chemical transference paper. But you might be able to read faces from them. And discover moments. I started searching through Gurl's garbage.

Eventually, underneath a discarded T-shirt and a pair of sandals with every strap broken were piles of Polaroid negative images. The curling, chemically treated paper teased me with vague reverse prints that recorded a gala evening with hundreds, almost thousands of faces.

It was the Archive dinner, but in reverse. I searched through the faces, looking for the table that might have been us. For the moment the murderer did not want me to see.

What would be on the picture? I could hardly recognize anything. Allen's shirt would be green. And his face would be black. Renquist would be creamy white, with chocolate teeth. Everybody had chocolate teeth. Thousands of teeth. Ripping into cod which even in the negative was colorless and gray.

It would take me forever to go through these negs. I picked up the curling leaves of coated paper and pushed them into a plastic bag. I turned and said a silent good-bye to the unfortunate thrill jockey. I crossed myself in some silly gesture that I thought Gurl might like, then I slipped out the window and was outside, behind the glass that hid the horrible nativity that spelled Gurl's end. I wiped the woodwork and the doorknob and even the little bell that I'd pressed. No one was looking.

I walked away from the bums and under the freeway underpass to Bryant Street. I found a pay phone, looked for some dimes and cried. It only took a couple of minutes.

I was four blocks from the Hall of Justice when I made the call. A pay phone was the only way to communicate with the police. They tape calls now. It's a good idea to put something over the mouthpiece.

The 911 emergency number rang and rang. No emergencies mattered *that* much in this city. Finally, someone came on the other side of the line, and I heard the beeping noises which meant we were being recorded. I spoke quickly.

I said there was a young woman who was dead in her apartment, on 540 Sumner, a young woman had been shot in the back. I said it was a good thing she was already dead, she could have bled to death waiting for 911 to answer. My beeper went off. I returned the page.

It was Rose Baynetta. She wanted me to come right away to the Howard Blooming Lesbian and Gay Memorial Archive.

CHAPTER ELEVEN

PRESERVATION

The playful parody that was the Howard Blooming Lesbian and Gay Memorial Archive stuttered in the daylight. Without the rainbow lights, the backdrop of the stars, both in the sky and on the ground, our Archive looked like any other mausoleum. A cold and dead repository, available for anyone who wanted to hold up a distant mirror, raising facts and feelings from the artifacts of time gone by.

I would have preferred to have gone home to examine the negatives filling the plastic bag which bumped at my side. But, coming from the scene of a murder, it seemed like a good idea to show up somewhere very public where I would be noticed. I walked into the big Reading Room, clear now of the gala tables.

There was a logbook at the doorway next to a smiling security guard. I signed the registry with the time. The last person before me had come in a half hour ago, so I fudged by a quarter hour, saying a silent Hail Mary for

Gurl Jesus's funky soul, and a few prayers that my presence at that dank, dark den of murder would never be known.

"Who are you here to see?" asked the guard.

"Rose Baynetta."

"I'm sorry . . . "

"She's a volunteer."

"Oh, we'll have to get you clearance."

I looked around a room as busy as Santa's workshop. Howard Blooming would have been proud. I thought about his papers safely locked up down in the vault. Secure in a box in a safe which required two keys. And no one had them both.

"Emma! Is that you?" Allen Boone's voice echoed through the hall. He was speaking to a group of people. I walked through the mahogany tables and could begin to make out his words. "Paper cloth, animal skins, adhesives—archival collections contain a wide range of organic materials." Allen's voice was instructional, but with a nervous edge. His audience contained at least five gray suits and a skirt. Funding possibilities. Perhaps this task had fallen to him in the wake of Tracy's demise. He certainly wasn't cut out for it. His shirt was hanging out of his pants. He waved me over to be included in his lecture.

"Volunteers—trained volunteers—are saving original source material, that is, actual photographs, prints, letters and books, that document some aspect of gay or lesbian life. It's not any easy job. The natural aging process means that molecular chains break down, or depolymerize. It's impossible to halt aging, but much can be done to control external factors that hasten the deterioration of papers and other materials. Temperature, humidity, light, pollution, biological agents, we've taken all factors into account within this building. Ha, ha, ha." He clapped his hands to-

143

gether a little too enthusiastically. "We're the *ultimate* control queens here!"

Bemused smiles; the group gazed around the room, at the ceiling, at Fresca Alcazon's face and body flying above them.

"Now," Allen continued, "in case, *just* in case, after this tour of the totally glamorous world of the archivist, you want to consider volunteering, you can give your name to Connie over there. Ha, ha, ha." Connie, a biker dyke in black leather, grinned warmly at the suits. "And, of course, donations, uh, the president of the board, Deborah Dunton"—he wiped his brow—"envelopes right over here on the desk."

When the group had been leafletted and safely shown out the door, Allen returned. "I'll give you a bit more of a personal tour, Emma. Ha, ha, ha." Allen took hold of my elbow and drew me away.

"But—"

Allen had stopped with dramatic relish behind the bony back of an elderly woman in a fuchsia jogging suit, her white hair twisted into a rigid French roll at the back of her head. Shriveled fingers with magenta nails twisted a band of linen tape from around a scrapbook. The outer boards fell open and revealed pages of yellowing photographs within frames of black paper.

"This is the collection of Marlene Higgins, the journalist," he whispered. "The estate turned over all her papers to us. She was a lesbian who won medals as an ambulance driver in World War II before she started writing for the *San Francisco Call*. Unfortunately, the medals were stored with her papers and have caused a great deal of distortion to some of the documents. And the adhesives."

"What about them?"

"Oh, Emma, scrapbooks seem to be virtual catalogues of every known adhesive. They break down over time, lose their tackiness, permanently stain documents and initiate dreadful chemical reactions. They say"—he eyed the album covetously—"they say that Marlene was good friends with *Eleanor*," he whispered suggestively.

"*Eleanor?* You mean Eleanor *Roosevelt?*"

"Yes! And *Lorena.* This is her scrapbook." He pulled back and pointed.

The elderly woman, her skin as frail as the onion paper which rested between the photos, was examining the ancient album.

Within one of the frames was a typical vacation picture with middle-aged women in 1940's bathing suits, the heavy elastic fabric, like girdles, pulled well down over their thighs. Their expressions carefree, these laughing, middle-aged people knew how to have a good time. Vacation photos. Water and sand, rocks and women with their arms slung casually about each other's shoulders. Four stocky women and one very thin woman with straight hair and thin, determined lips. A photo that could be anywhere, in any photograph album in the United States. Almost.

"Is that—?"

Allen nodded. "Yes," he hissed gleefully, "that's *Greta Garbo*! With Mercedes D'Acosta on their Silver Lake honeymoon! And Marlene Higgins and her girlfriend, Jo Hoffman, the oil heiress. Her name pops up everywhere. Marlene and Jo knew all the movie stars and the politicians."

"Is there really a photo of Eleanor Roosevelt in the book?"

"I don't know! She won't let me look." Allen lowered his voice even more. "She can't hear very well, but I have to be careful." The woman sat transfixed, staring at each photo for long moments, taking in the past, the photos a world more real than the present.

"So, who is she?"

"That's Jo! Marlene Higgins's girlfriend. She didn't want anyone else touching her pictures. She's considering having them sealed. Look at her, over ninety, walks two miles a day and is determinedly in the closet. I can't complain, I mean, she *is* donating the materials. She has some sense of posterity, of the importance of our history. I mean, how could you live in San Francisco and *not*?"

"Oh, you could, you could. By the way, Allen, do you have many sealed documents?"

"Well, funny you should ask. There's already something in the vault that *we* don't even know about. Or even who has the keys!" He raised his eyebrows conspiratorially. I kept my face carefully blank.

"You did—" he said. "You did take the Howard Blooming journals home with you, didn't you, Emma?"

"They're safe."

"Well, good. We're all in a state of shock here, as you can *imagine*," he continued. "Tracy's death is the only topic this morning. And, of course, we've already started on the Tracy Port collection." He led me to what was apparently the temporary Tracy Port Memorial, or at least, a sketch of what it was to be. I shuddered as I looked at a long table loaded with flowers and messages and a large picture of Tracy, who had unfortunately chosen a garish shade of blue eye shadow for the photo session. A lot of lilies stood guard on either side of the silver-plated frame.

Tracy Port grinned from ear to ear behind a thin sheet of glass, as if no one had poisoned her potatoes, or done a bad makeup job on her. Tracy grinned the way she had grinned at Frances. Grinned as if it were still her Archive.

I looked at that heart-shaped face, the chin that was nothing more than a little dab of fat below her lower lip. Weak chin. Strong eyes. Sculptured features, tight as the chiseled edges of a perfume bottle stopper.

But there was something different about Tracy Port. What was it? Just my imagination, probably. Tracy was just a photo of a dead person with a big smile and bad makeup now.

I glanced down at the scraps of paper, tender messages to accompany Tracy on her journey to the other side. "Tracy, we will miss you. Harold." "For Tracy, with love, Arthur." "I hope they catch the sucker that did this to you. Love, Frank." Most of the messages were from men. "Tracy, you made the Dewey Decimal System look simple, Ginger." Now *there* was a comment.

"Who's Ginger?"

"A volunteer in the microfiche department."

"Working today?"

"No, we don't have a full staff on Saturday—even the volunteers like a day of rest, Emma. We're going to miss Tracy. She was a marvelous book and paper conservator. And that's a rare thing these days."

"What do you mean?"

"Well, Emma, every year the educational system in this country creates thousands of attorneys, doctors, architects—I mean, *thousands*—and on the average, about *thirty* new art, book and paper conservators. While the *other* professionals are litigating, cutting, suturing, and building, there aren't enough professionals to conserve the artifactually significant properties of our culture! Tracy wasn't an easy person, but she sure knew how to preserve paper!"

"How were staff relations?"

"Oh, ha, ha, ha!" Allen's face drew into wry wrinkles. "Tracy wasn't easy, as I said. You know, she issued a lot of orders through me. 'Tracy believes this,' I'd have to say. Tell them, 'That's Tracy's view.' When Tracy spoke, it was ex cathedra."

"Would you say she enjoyed being executive director?"

"This Archive was her life. She saw the Archive as the unique and extraordinary opportunity it is. But at the same time, she wasn't great at community relations. She was always saying, 'Don't do anything to embarrass the Archive.' She wasn't always kind to biker dykes who volunteered. She was a real *jerk* to Connie, the volunteer coordinator."

"Would you say she made enemies?"

"But of course! In a non-profit organization this size? With the amount of work she had to do? Fundraising, administration, archival work. She wasn't always the *nicest* person. I'm *sure* she made enemies. But she got the job done. And, *she knew how to preserve paper.*" Allen was sweating.

"Emma! Where have you *been?*" Our conversation was interrupted by Rose Baynetta. "Girl, you got pierced!" she said.

"Real flash," I admitted.

"Hey, Allen, warn me when my friends show up with new diamonds in their noses." Rose led me back to a number of booths which bore an unsettling resemblance to the piercing cubicles at the Gambit, except that these had real doors. Thin stripes of light went off and on and on and off in a steady flickering rhythm as a myriad of documents were photographed.

"So, how's it looking for Helen?" she hissed.

"Willie's agreed to defend her. There's a lot of work to do. Some of which I wanted to talk to you about. There's an opportunity for some sub-contracting here. We're talk-ing print research, a few interviews. Historical stuff."

"Hmm, esoteric." Rose snorted. "But I'll be glad to do what I can. You can tell Willie I'll keep the cost down. Helen Thomas is no killer."

"What makes you say that?"

"I just know that she isn't."

"Look, Rose, I have to talk to you."

I told Rose about finding Gurl Jesus dead. Her face didn't move. I told her about the people on the roof of my house. I mentioned Fresca, but not her .22. Some things weren't relevant. Yet. I told her I might have a special as-signment for her.

"Emma, look here," Rose said quietly. "I want you to see something." She went over to the microfiche machine and put a picture into focus. "I'm here putting in my volunteer hours at the Archive and I've chanced—"

"Chanced?"

"Chance is always my friend, Emma. You know that." Hoisting herself on her arms, she twisted into a more com-fortable position in her chair. "I've got *all* the papers of Rudolph Sharpe here."

I looked around the cubicle.

In its center, a planetary camera towered over a news-paper column. Non-reflective dividers eliminated prob-lems with ambient and stray light sources. Carefully lining up for the photographic process were a series of folders, books and acid-free boxes. The complete papers of Rudolph Sharpe, no doubt. Rose rolled in front of the camera and adjusted the lens. "This system is capable of high resolution; we can shrink everything way, way down. How many articles can be written on the head of a pin, Emma? Let's find out." She reached down and cleaned the lens with a soft optical cloth. "We got the microfiche equipment from a whole range of businesses that are no longer using that system. They're all going digital now. We don't have access to that kind of equipment, but frankly, I prefer microfiche. If you get the proper focus it's just as good as digital. Thirty-five millimeter, first generation, silver gelatin, polyester-based negative roll microfilm. Just as good as any scanner, stored properly, of course. Rudolph Sharpe's papers saved for eternity. Or close enough."

Rudolph Sharpe had been one of the first openly gay reporters in San Francisco and in the United States. He followed in Marlene Higgins's footsteps, but with the closet door wide open. He was also the person who covered the Howard Blooming assassination and the subsequent arrest, conviction and the staggeringly light sentencing of Jeb Flynne. I saw that on the top of the pile of papers were yellowed news clippings of the riot after Flynne's light sentence had been announced.

As I stared into the half-tone dots of the photo, I was transported into that night of rage. I heard the angry chants, the bonfires, the gasoline tanks of cop cars exploding like cherry bombs. Windows popping like corks out of the frames of government buildings. The beaux art sugar tarts, gilded with gold, from which the city government, if you could call it that, ruled.

I remembered the community with a broken heart. Rudolph Sharpe had covered the riot well, even though his bosses were initially worried that his reporting would be biased, as if they would be objective.

"These must be one of the most important acquisitions next to the final papers of Howard Blooming. By the way, Emma, where are *those* papers?"

"Safe. Sealed. And not to be photographed."

"Oh, come on, Emma. Those documents belong to all of us."

"But that wasn't what Howard wanted, Rose."

"Tragic." Rose directed my attention to the camera. "I have to keep working, Emma. This is incredibly time-consuming. But worth it. Really worth it. Look—" She lowered the lens of the camera and focused on a piece of newsprint. "Did you know that Jeb Flynne made three trips to Washington before he shot Howard?"

"So?"

"And that he was active in college in the Students for Freedom movement before he was in the Army?"

"So?"

"Everyone knows that Students for Freedom was full of CIA. Half the people involved were there to spy on the other half."

"Back in the days of narcs and Nixon paranoia, Rose."

"Okay, sure. But, Emma, look at this."

I looked through the lens. I saw a picture of Jeb Flynne being arrested. There were any number of white male faces surrounding him in the hallway of a Sacramento County Courthouse.

"Yeah, okay I'm looking. A lotta guys taking a prisoner."

"Look at the guy two paces behind Flynne."

"The one without the necktie?"

"That's the one."

"Yeah, I'm looking."

"This." Rose reached into her large leather handbag and pulled out a file which contained an old *Ramparts* magazine. I looked at the cover of the folded left-wing journal. A feature article on South America pointed out a number of CIA agents who were responsible for the overthrow of Salvador Allende in Chile.

"See!"

"See what?"

"It's the same guy."

"Maybe."

"What do you mean, *maybe?*"

"All these middle-aged law enforcement guys look alike to me. They're genetically determined."

"Emma, it's the *same guy.*"

"Still isn't pushing any buttons for me, Rose. Sorry."

"Listen, Emma," Rose said. "San Francisco isn't some little isolated *Tales of the City,* you know. There *are* international conspiracies. There are people that go undercover. *Here.* Moles! People who need to *disappear.* And Jeb Flynne was a CIA operative. I'm sure he was. First, while he was in college. He did demolition work for the Army. He was set up to do the Blooming assassination. Then they whisked him off to some new location, with some new identity."

"And then bought him a ticket to the Archive dinner. Aw, Rose, I just don't believe conspiracy theories."

"But—"

"Rose, Howard's assassination was twenty years ago. Jeb Flynne killed himself six years ago. There's a coroner's report. Do you know how many people would have to be in on a conspiracy that size? Do you know how unlikely it is that somebody, somewhere, hasn't gotten drunk, bragged to a friend, in the intervening twenty years? How do you think most murderers are caught? They *brag* about it, Rose. It's just human nature. Somebody has a hot story or an itchy conscience. Somebody talks eventually."

"And I want them to talk to me."

"Rose—"

"Don't say it can't happen here, Emma. Lesbians and gays are the biggest political threat to the right wing that has ever existed. We are transforming gender culture in America. And it's the gender culture that keeps the patriarchy in place. When women and gays rise, beyond this backlash, we will rule!"

"Rose, listen to yourself!"

"I think there's been a spy in the movement. I think Tracy might have been it."

I looked at my friend carefully. Her hand rested casually on the counter. She looked calm and collected. She had access to any number of documents. After five years in the security business as a professional, Rose was interested in facts. Not fantasy.

Our little cubicle was silent.

"You don't believe me, do you?"

"It's just that I don't think that the world is that organized."

"Just look at this, Emma." Rose bent her head under the machine. I held my breath as I saw the image coming into focus over her shoulder. A meeting of an old Socialist Worker's Union party meeting. Tired people sat around a wooden table with a lot of paper on it. They looked into the lens and they didn't bother to smile.

"There, see that face?"

I moved my finger through the light. "Tracy Port, right?"

"Yes, but look back there—"

"This smudge with two dark holes?"

Rose grumbled and played with the focus. It helped. There was a face I would never forget.

"It's Laurie Leiss!"

Laurie Leiss, who built bombs and killed people. The face of Howard Blooming's cousin. Laurie Leiss.

"So what was Tracy doing there?" Rose's finger pointed

at the tiny image. "Tracy's not exactly your Molotov moll, would you say? I say she was killed by Jeb Flynne, Emma. The *disappeared* Jeb Flynne."

But I was still focused on Laurie Leiss. Now, she *had* disappeared. Except for once. A day I would never tell anyone about. Not even Rose Baynetta.

"Socialist Workers' cell," Rose murmured. "The revolution was different in the seventies."

"Yeah, now it's run by right-wing nuts," I said.

Laurie Leiss, well known as a political cartoonist, had been a leading revolutionary in what some had thought was a revolution in 1972. At the height of the Vietnam War, any number of radicals had taken up the gun in the United States.

They'd built bombs. Robbed banks. And the violence in Laurie Leiss's cartoons had moved out of her strips and onto the streets.

Laurie Leiss was under investigation for a number of these acts when a bomb tore up a brownstone in New York in 1973. Her fingerprints had been found all over the detonator fragments. Four counts of murder were added when the bodies of the upstairs tenants were dug out of the rubble.

A year later Laurie Leiss had contacted Howard. Asking for money. That was something only Howard and I knew. And Laurie Leiss.

A phone call came in on Howard's personal line. We never knew how she'd found the number. But I delivered the cash immediately. As Howard's press secretary, I knew the value of getting Laurie Leiss out of his hair quickly and quietly. And without asking questions.

Howard had me deliver the twenty thousand dollars in cash in El Cerrito. Twenty-dollar bills banded together;

they filled a small suitcase. It was a hot day. And the person who was Laurie Leiss, or Laurie Leiss's agent, approached me in the middle of a supermarket parking lot to pick it up. She wore a hat with a large brim and dark glasses. A shapeless nylon dress had billowed below her knees. She had walked quickly across the asphalt in flat shoes. A little woman with a big problem.

"Tracy was a mole, Emma. Let's face it, there was always something strange about Tracy—" Rose was saying.

"A queer sort of queer?"

"Yeah! The scene on the cruise with Lee Turgo was much too public—"

"I know, I know—"

"Think of all the damage she could have done here at the Archive! Think of all the things she could have destroyed."

I thought about it. I thought about pictures of Eleanor Roosevelt with Lorena Hickok, the one person who had ever loved her. And Greta Garbo. "Come on, Rose. Is this stuff dangerous enough for the CIA to destroy it? Even if Eleanor *had* been first lady, that was fifty-some years ago!" I tried to put the Howard Blooming papers out of my mind. How I'd almost handed them directly over to Tracy. No. Get a grip, Emma. Conspiracies are for nuts.

"I get it. Tracy was a secret agent and Frances was her consort! After all, Frances has disappeared."

"Disappeared! What are you talking about?"

"She left me an incorrect contact number in Seattle. I don't believe it was a mistake."

"What do you mean?" Rose's attention had been deflected from conspiracy theories. "Frances adores you!"

Mary Wings

"Yeah. And I'm starting to wonder if she doesn't adore somebody else, too."

"You're paranoid, Emma."

"And so are you. The CIA and Jeb Flynne. Tracy a mole? *Nobody* liked her, Rose. There are more than a few motives lying around."

"It's true." Rose sniffed. "Then there's Renquist Falkenberg."

"I thought they were big buddies?"

"I've detected animosity on occasions. I heard there was a time they weren't speaking."

"What about?"

"Politics, maybe. Renquist isn't exactly your radical fairy, you know."

"Tracy Port wasn't, either."

"I don't even want to think about the potential infighting in their field. Anyway, they became allies. Then there's that funky Fresca of yours."

"Well, for a start, she isn't called Fresca Alcazon," I said. "Get ready for a document search. She has a driver's license in the name of Eleanor DeWade. Born May nineteenth, 1968." I gave Rose the number that I had found on Fresca's driver's license. Rose was already shuffling papers, eager to get out and on the case. But before she called the office, I told her I would need more, a lot more, than a document search. Rose could handle all kinds of firearms. And, if necessary, she'd be willing to use them.

I walked home, letting the occasional bus pass me by. Crowds of people came out of churches, happy couples drifted through garage sales. I'd forgotten to tell Rose about my birthday tip for Allen. Happy birthday.

I imagined the crime scene investigators going over Gurl Jesus's apartment. Going over Gurl Jesus. I shud-

156

dered. I'd sat in on enough coroner's conversations to know their sense of humor. I wouldn't want to be present at the examination of the pierced and engraved body of Gurl Jesus. She deserved a better end. She deserved no end at all.

BAD
HOUSEKEEPING

I grimaced up at the house, clutching the bag of negatives under my arm. The nuptial manor just didn't look the same. Would it be changed forever by the moment I desired another woman, held her in my arms, heard her say, "I really like you, Emma. I really like you a lot, a lot, a lot." The light would look a little colder, the shadows a little sharper, the curios and souvenirs mocking, revealing love for shallow sentimentality. The fog was rolling in early and I wasn't human today.

The third step up to the apartment squeaked in exactly the same spot with exactly the same tinny groan. Laura's lights were off upstairs, but her car was in the driveway as it always was when she spent the night in. In the three years that we had been neighbors, she'd spent the night out twice. It was hard not to notice. It was impossible to ask Laura about it. I looked forward to the day when her car was not so frequently in the driveway; it might do something for her humor.

I opened the door with the key which fit the lock as it always did, tumblers rolling over like an obedient puppy.

As the door opened, the cats mewed and waved their tails, gray boas, feathers in the wind; they then turned and showed me the tight pink buds of their assholes. Mink was never as hygienic as one would have liked. Friend split to the garden; who knows where she was living these days.

The rest, of course, was more different than I could imagine. And I would never have to imagine again, because there it was in front of me. Everybody's worst nightmare. And now it was mine. Our apartment was trashed.

An earthquake, a tornado, a hurricane, a poltergeist could not have more thoroughly wrecked our home. It was as if some evil wind had come through and turned the contents of our lives inside out; had searched out, with angry hands, every corner and crevice of the life Frances and I shared together. Dirty hands. And disappointed ones.

The upholstery of the couch had been slashed, stuffing and feathers released. The room was filled with drifting clumps of white cotton batting, which Mink and Friend had no doubt made use of. Our books, all our many, many books, had been leafed through. It could happen here. It had.

I strolled from room to room surveying the damage, feeling a strange laughter caught in my breast. In the kitchen someone had made a bigger mess than Frances could have created making a fifteen-course meal. Our *cucina* had been completely destroyed.

I felt dizzy looking at the kitchen. Its center had not held. It was a storm-tossed ship, with all the wrong hardware. Every cabinet door flapped open and had regurgitated its insides on the floor. Cups, saucers, teapots and

159

tureens were shards on the linoleum. The cupboard was bare, its furthest corners searched and found wanting.

The back door drifted open. There were jimmy marks where they'd forced the lock. I ran my fingers over the raw place where the wood had been violated. Splinters. A few pieces on the floor. That door had been an easy piece of work.

I stuck my head outside and looked at the maze of gardens, at cats balancing on three paws, washing their faces, at my neighbor, flashlight in hand, checking for slugs amongst her tomatoes.

"*Buenos noches!*" I called.

"*Noches!*"

"Anything strange? *Raro?*"

"Huh? No, no! Everything *tranquillo.*"

"Great." I smiled. Just great. What were these people? Invisible intruders? Ghosts? I remembered Rose's words and shuddered.

I surveyed a bigger mess than Frances had ever thought of making, and wondered about the mess our marriage might have become. I was alone with it. And with picking up the pieces. There was no phone number for Frances.

A gauzy wisp of fog floated over the moon and wrapped itself around me. You're just feeling sorry for yourself, Emma Victor. Sit down for a moment and think better thoughts.

The lesbian and gay Stonewall riot, the Lesbian and Gay Civil Rights Act, the lesbian and gay media, the lesbian and gay telephone company, the lesbian and gay *Time* magazine. In the end, was it all going to be the same? Would community just be replaced by capitalism? Replicated in lavender. Would queer matter then? Would my marriage? Wasn't that why we had to preserve our history? Would anyone bother to read it? Would anyone ever read again? These were not the kind of thoughts that would spur me to action.

Back in the kitchen, the refrigerator motor tried to keep up, its doors flung wide open, cooling the entire kitchen, my entire world. The refrigerator and the freezer had been emptied and a new stew made, unlike any other, spiced with glass and combined on the floor. Frozen yogurt, split pea soup, the strange green tea diet ice cream Frances had bought and, of course, had never eaten. The strange foods she was always bringing home! The phyllo dough for some baking project that she'd never gotten around to. Was that apple season two years ago? Three? Would there be another? I was melting into a sentimental puddle as sweet and sticky as the mess on the floor. I was also crying, another hormonal trick. My adrenaline should have been pumping, vaulting over those fences, after Gurl Jesus, after the intruder that had ruined our home. Who was I kidding? The home was already wrecked. I suddenly felt that I was looking at the physical manifestation of what had been happening between Frances and me over the last months. Why hadn't I realized it before?

Sweet potatoes and leftover lasagna. A ribbon of yellow honey mustard dressing winding its way over a sesame bagel and combined with a quart of milk on the floor. A container of french vanilla non-fat yogurt had been opened and dumped on top of the mess; it held its shape and wobbled there like a fez. Every cereal box, spice jar and tea tin explored. Everywhere small enough for a key.

I stepped high over piles of trash that used to be books, food and furniture, the stuff of two lives. As I surveyed the

161

Mary Wings

damage from room to room, it was small comfort that they had not found what they were looking for.

I heard footsteps upstairs. Familiar footsteps. Laura's footsteps. Time to call Laura. Almost. I didn't relish the interview. But there was no way around it now.

I went to the bathroom where the last plant of my harvest reclined, a fine female plant that Fresca hadn't quite managed to get down the toilet. She still had buds. THC, the active ingredient in marijuana, is not water soluble. Someone could still get stoned from this baby bud.

I put the damp plant on the slanted back of the tub, rinsed her off, wrapped her in newspapers and found a plastic bag to put her in. Then I put the plastic bag underneath the bed in the guest room.

I picked up the phone in our time-honored neighborly tradition. We never rang the doorbell. Doorbells make cops nervous. They made us all nervous. We used the phone instead. We thought of it as polite. That's what the world was coming to. I called my neighbor.

"Hello?" The voice came from the bottom of a well where fifty thousand cigarettes had been punched out on a pair of battered vocal cords. "Who is it?"

"Emma."

"It better be good."

"My place has been tossed."

There was a long silence. I watched Mink chase a fly, trapping it between the window and her claws. Impaled, its wings droned helplessly on the end of one of her long, curved nails.

"I'll be right down," Laura said. But she wasn't happy about it.

*   *   *

I spent the rest of the time looking for clues and not touching anything. As far as I could tell, there *were* no clues. All the debris, from the finest toothbrush bristle to the broken spine of Frances's *Lavoisier* was indelibly, personally, ours. Except for the bag of Gurl Jesus's negatives.

And there probably wouldn't be any fingerprints, either. Then I noticed the final detail of the search that really made my blood run cold. They had removed the electrical sockets from all the walls in the apartment. The electrical guts hung out of each little square hole in the gypsum board. Laura was going to love this.

Laura trudged downstairs in her white cotton bathrobe with a monogrammed initial on her pocket and a narrow, mean look in her eyes, spending Saturday night *in*. Laura's shoulder-length, chestnut brown hair was tangled, a state I'd never seen it in. Usually she brushed a hundred strokes, but my phone call had interrupted her bedtime ritual.

Smoking had given Laura a lot of fine wrinkles around her eyes with which she could do the blinkless fuck-you stare for a remarkably long time. There would never be smile lines beside those lips on that face. Laura had a grim line of chatter and she didn't give much away. I would have to offer something first. That wasn't a problem. You don't lie to the cops. You just don't tell them everything. And if you're lucky, they won't arrest you.

"You've got five minutes." A fresh cigarette dangled from trembling fingers, and every now and then, Laura brought it up to her mouth, sucked at it and blew a long thin line of smoke at me. I saw the look in her eye as she surveyed the apartment. "I'm listening," she said.

"Trashed." I started with the understatements.

Laura looked at me, narrowed those hazel eyes into little slits, like my face was leaving a bad impression on her retinas. She looked around at the kitchen, sniffed and coughed. "Bad housekeeping, Emma." Laura hadn't brushed her teeth.

"You could say that." I almost smiled. Laura moved closer into my face.

"Nose piercing." She squinted at the diamond. "Very boho, Emma. Maybe you'll get lucky and they'll invent nose putty someday."

"About my apartment—"

"Okay, Emma, what's the story?" There was no fooling around with cops. Even if they were your neighbors. But that didn't make me want to recite any epics.

"I took an early walk this morning. I came home and found the kitchen looking like this. You hear anything?"

"Nope." Laura wasn't looking at the mess in the middle of the kitchen floor. She was looking out the window. At my garden with the three big holes in it.

"Garden looks empty, Emma."

"Yeah, well, that's beside the point. That's not what they were after. The plants were gone before they broke into the house."

"I'm going upstairs to my herbal tea, Emma. I suggest you take up the habit. It's easier on the kitchen." She turned around, the stocky form in the white mono-grammed bathrobe ready to haul herself up the stairs.

"Laura, there's more here than meets the eye," I started, but Laura had already begun her rant.

"I'm just glad it wasn't my place," she was reciting. "I'm glad someone didn't decide that *I* had a green thumb and decided to break into *my* apartment"—puff, puff—"find *my* gun. Some criminal running around with my Walther because my fucking house partner decided to grow weed on my property. That would really be fun to explain to my lieutenant. Yeah, there's a lot more here than meets the eye, Emma. Like why I ever—"

"Stop worrying about your fucking *gun* for a second, would you?"

Laura was always worried about her gun. Cop houses frequently get burglarized for weapons. I knew just where Laura stashed hers, in her dirty laundry. The last place anyone would look. Except me when I'd been searching for a rag to clean up some spilt red wine at our last dinner party.

"I want to get a security system, okay?" Laura drawled. I could smell the house meeting coming on. It smelled like burning hemp. And no AIDS patients were going to breathe the smoke. Laura was sucking in her cheeks as she dragged extra tobacco into her lungs and turned her back.

"Laura, it wasn't about the plants," I said to her back. "I don't think any security system would have stopped this crowd. And I've never heard of anyone expecting to find several pounds of dried herb behind a wall socket, have you?"

That stopped her. Smoke drifted over the head of untamed hair. She turned around slowly, feet first, then swiveled her hefty torso until those green eyes made a direct hit. Interrogation technique.

"Tell me what's going on, Emma."

"They were looking for something small, Laura."

"Okay. You going to tell me what they were looking for, Emma? I don't have time to play games."

"When I came home, I heard footsteps on the roof. Then they stopped. You came home. I went out for a walk. At dawn."

"From which we deduce—"

"Someone was watching the house, Laura. They started when your lights were still out, after I left the house. They finished the job fast. There must have been a number of them. They must have been pros."

Laura thought it over. "I'm listening, Emma."

"How could they have done this without alerting you?"

"You said that. Okay. They were looking for something small. Small enough to fit behind a wall socket. What were they looking for, Emma?"

"I had been given the errand of taking Howard Blooming's final papers to the Archive. I was mugged after I picked them up from David Stimpson. It may or may not have been an attempt to steal Howard's papers. I went to the Archive dinner with the notes, sealed them in the vault myself and—" I thought fast. I didn't feel like telling Laura about Fresca. "I took the key. This morning, I put the key in an envelope, took a long walk and mailed it to myself. The mail comes between nine and ten on Monday. I think that's what somebody wanted, Laura. That key."

"And now they know you don't have it. Fine. All you have to do is clean up this mess and wait until Monday. You want a police escort to your mailbox?"

"Or do I want to turn the Howard Blooming memorial papers over to the police?" I asked Laura and myself. She thought it over.

"They need to be in a safe place. Safer than where they are now."

"I don't want the Feds in on this, Laura."

"The Feds? What are you talking about?"

"Laura, do you think the CIA is in town?"

"You're pushing fantasy land here, Emma. You were mugged. You grow dope in your backyard and your house got tossed. That's all. You're making me nervous, Emma. I don't want to be nervous. I need my beauty sleep." She stubbed her cigarette out in a broken saucer.

"Laura, I'm really serious about the CIA. There are rumors that Jeb Flynne—"

That stopped her. Now she was going to laugh at me. She did, but it wasn't a funny, ha-ha kind of laugh. It had the derisive, hardened tone of someone who found human nature, notably mine, amusing. "I've heard enough conspiracy theories to write fifteen novels, Emma. All fiction. The human mind likes to organize things into patterns. That's ninety percent of conspiracy theories. Twenty years and no hard witnesses that have talked about Jeb Flynne. Somebody, on their deathbed, on their way to the top, or the bottom, would spill it. It's just a conspiracy theory to fit into all your nice conceptions about who's running the world. *Nobody's* running the world, Emma, and that's the sad truth. I know. It's my job every day to steer a little piece of it. And every urban city in America is way out of alignment. I'm sorry your house got trashed, but don't let it feed your imagination."

"The CIA spy unit Flynne was supposed to be a part of—"

"Rumor, Emma. He was just in a weekend officer's training college."

"This looks like a professional job." I waved my hands at the mess in front of me.

"So? Crooks are pros, too. Jeb Flynne was an idiot with an agenda and an assault rifle. You grew illegal substances in the backyard, of which I hope you have not a trace left, by the way. Crooks, Emma. Crooks are very, very busy people. Especially when it comes to illegal substances. That's the simple and boring truth. I just wish you'd stop growing pot in our backyard. Emma, when your plants get that big, your delphiniums just don't cover them up. While you're trying to make a lot of chemotherapy clients happy, I've got a profession on the line."

It was time for Laura to have another cigarette. Her fingers were twitching.

She bent down to pet Mink. She wasn't usually a cat-petting person. "You know what they say about the difference between cats and dogs, Emma?"

"I'm not up for riddles today, Laura."

"Cats don't visit you in jail, Emma." Laura laughed. She was really tough this morning. And, as ever, observant. "You have a message." She had noticed the button flashing on my answering machine.

I reached through the litter to the light, and saw the illuminated number one. I pressed the button and heard a message rewind. Laura hung around, just to make my morning. She lit another cigarette and leaned on the woodwork.

I listened to the screech of the backward voice. Frances, Frances, I hardly minded if Laura heard a message from Frances. It would probably make us all feel better. But when the tape clicked, it started to play back a voice I didn't need to hear.

Beep. *"Hi, Emma, this is Fresca. I just wanted to say that I had a really nice time last night. And I'm really, really sorry about your plants."* Fresca Alcazon's voice blatted into the silence between Sergeant Deleuse and myself. Christ, where was the volume knob? Over the horizon of her cheek, I saw Laura's lips curve into a rare smile, and I had a hard time not shoving her out the door. But it was way too late. For that and a lot of other things.

"A really, really nice time," Fresca continued. *"And I just want to say something—"*

Oh, fabulous. I could see Laura's back shaking with silent laughter as she gave Mink a long stroke. She didn't even *like* our cats.

Fresca was huskily burbling away and I could see Laura's ears stretching to catch the sounds. I found the volume knob and turned it down, but it was too late. Fresca's message was still audible in the stillness of the Mission. Laura's hand drifted down Mink's neck past her collar.

"And one last thing," Fresca went on. Interminably on, in that sonorous singsong voice, *"Why can lifting belly please me. A rose is a rose is a rose is a rose. Lifting belly can please me because it is an occupation I enjoy."* There was a sound of two lips smacking together, the audio waves of a kiss and a click.

That did it. Laura was laughing out loud now. I could see her lungs filling with air, expanding the fine bleached cotton of her bathrobe, filling her rib cage with chortles which made their way past her lips, a nasty sound, like a car backfiring.

At least Laura had managed to startle the cat. Mink reached out a claw and then it was my turn to smile as she drew a thin line across the fine skin on top of Laura's hand which quickly filled with the sergeant's blood. So much for calling the cops.

CHAPTER THIRTEEN

CLEANING
AND SLEEP

Saturday night and I would be scouring the pages of the *Examiner* for news of Tracy Port's demise and scrubbing my kitchen floor. It was time for the chore of thinking and guessing, which might, just might, be facilitated by cleaning.

I found heavy-duty trash bags, anonymous gray sacks, for everything that was broken and ruined. Rubber gloves and earth-friendly cleaning compounds. A new mop and three bags of auto-mechanic rags. I'd had no time, yet, to look at the negatives. Gurl Jesus, murdered. Tracy, taken out. Laura was right. There was no order, just chaos. No conspiracy, just circumstance. Gurl Jesus was a speed freak and speed freaks get dead often enough. Meth heads, the busiest criminals in the business. They kept the fraud department at SFPD busy all the time. They could stay up later and think faster than any dope-free inspector trying to chase them on the telephone. Speed freaks, zooming along in the middle of the night. Not only did their brains work at remarkable speed, but worse, they always thought their plans would work. Laura was right. There was no conspiracy, no CIA. Just someone who wanted to kill Tracy Port.

I could use a little speed right now, I thought, starting in the bedroom and hanging up all the clothes. My retro, sports and second-hand clothes. The dapper pair of Oxfords with the plaid shoelaces. Sweatpants and sleeveless silk shirt. Cut-off T-shirts and old hand-knit sweaters. Sweaters that Frances had knitted for me. One double-breasted pinstriped suit with matching skirt for the fortunately few times I had to make an appearance in court. Gurl Jesus, I pray I didn't leave any fingerprints in your apartment.

Then there were Frances's dress-for-success clothes, the rows and rows of hangers with the little double clips on each rung, row after row of carefully hung dresses, slacks and skirts. There were the communal ski coats and bathrobes; I slipped hangers inside them all. I worked quickly, not thinking about the fingers that had turned every pocket inside out. There was a lot of change and small wads of paper on the floor. Everything horribly strange and familiar at the same time.

I popped a Deee-lite CD into the player.

"Deee-lite-fully" drowning out the vacuum cleaner, I swept into the kitchen. Some strange collection of sounds competed with my jangling thoughts and won, distracting me from all the things, the many things that I had said good-bye to as they went into bags. I began to feel clearer as I saw the linoleum emerge.

I looked to my watch. Midnight. Everything was clean. But completely different. All of the cracked knick-knacks gone. An empty refrigerator. Not much of our crockery

171

left. I was tired. I was very, very tired. If Frances had thought before that I liked a sparse house, she would be convinced when she came home from Seattle. If, indeed, she was in Seattle.

My feet took me to the front door where I'd left the bag with Gurl Jesus's negatives. I peered inside. The squares of curling film rustled softly as I shook the bag. My feet automatically took me upstairs and into the guest room.

I laid down on the counterpane bedspread and turned the bag upside down. The curling leaves of negatives fell out.

There was a foot and a shot of the mural far behind the cleft of a clean-shaven chin. One group photo showed hundreds of black-faced men with identical white moustaches. Our table shouldn't be too hard to find.

I perused last night's strange events in reverse, my eyelids becoming heavy. Was that Helen talking to some people at a table? The negs had no numbers and no order anymore. But surely *that* was Carla Ribera's long curls falling down the middle of her back. There was shot after shot of unmistakable mojos on the bulbous belly of Renquist Falkenberg, whose face was as white as the driven snow.

How many people were angry with Tracy because she made use of the Archive to further her own career? How many people had ambitions of becoming executive director of the premier research source of lesbian and gay material in the world? How many would want her out of the way? Was Allen really as civic-minded as he seemed? And anybody who knew anything about the les/bi/gay literary scene knew that Helen wore, or purported to wear, a necklace with a poison-filled crystal. Publicity, Rose had snorted, and Rose was, herself, beyond suspicion. Unless she was schizophrenic and had become completely *un-*screwed by Carla Ribera.

Would I become unscrewed, unglued without Frances?

Laura Deleuse was right. There's no order here. Only the carefully orchestrated chaos of my unconscious and the demise of the relationship with Frances. Somehow that was my fault, too. My eyelids were heavy.

I had no home in San Francisco. I floated about the city, through the clouds of pollution and was pulled into a dark cave, Red Dora's Bearded Lady Cafe. I found a beautiful brown lady in the bathroom. She was shooting junk. The bathroom was painted with flowers, its pipes were big arms, strong arms, arms covered with flowers. There were no track marks on those arms. They were the arms of Deborah Dunton.

There was no way out, out of the flashing and spitting of blood that was suddenly coming from Fresca's arm and her mouth. The room was small and getting smaller. Fresca, I realized, wasn't shooting up heroin. I had been mistaken.

Fresca was building a bomb and Deborah Dunton was giving her instructions. Deborah's words were visible and filled up the room with tiny print, diagrams, arrows and words which buzzed around my head. Like gnats. Like insects that would sting and bite. Wasps and yellow jackets that would keep my hand away from the bomb that Fresca was building, the bomb that was being made according to Deborah's instructions.

Time was ticking, throbbing to the rhythm of a Bronski Beat, beating with the rise and fall of the ruby at Fresca's neck and with the extended hand of Renquist Falkenberg who showed up at the last minute to garner votes. Larry Boznian was riding on his massive shoulders, painting scenes of the Last Judgment on the ceiling; he was working from the curled-up negatives of Gurl

Jesus. But he was painting the photographer herself. She dripped red plaster blood out of an exit hole in her brain. It was getting mighty Catholic and mighty crowded in the toilet at Red Dora's. I was almost relieved when the explosion came and ripped me right out of my sleep.

I lay in the Sunday morning gloom on my hard bed. I was still tired. The insides of my eyelids were featuring gray. I felt Mink jump on the bed; I opened my eyes. Mink was gray. The ceiling was gray. The air I was breathing was gray.

The dream, a draught so potent, so real, that when I woke up, I found the world past my eyelids a dull echo where people were merely murdered and framed, an echo that wouldn't yield clues without a fight. I woke up knowing that sometimes the best of marriages can fail, that falling in love can happen any time, anywhere.

I stood up slowly and bent down to explore the bottom of the bed. I found the little .22 pistol. I double-checked the barrel. I wiped it for prints and wrapped a paper towel around it and put it in a plastic bag with a Ziplock closing. I opened the freezer door and put it inside.

I called Rose, gave her a shopping list and set up an appointment. Then I started putting little devices on the outside doorknobs and window sills. Hairs. Hansel and Gretel crumbs which no one could see except myself. It wasn't a security system, but it would do for now.

The phone rang. It was Renquist Falkenberg.

"Emma, we're planning a memorial for Tracy."

That was fast. I heard someone in the background, the sounds of coffee, a late breakfast being made. "That's nice," I lied. It wasn't nice at all. I was tired of funerals. I had not been a friend of Tracy. But I could feel the dark purple mantle of responsibility landing on my shoulders. Renquist Falkenberg was putting it there.

"I'd really like you to be in on the planning." Renquist's voice was cracked and teary. The memorial for Tracy Port would be one big dreadful show of hypocrisy, I thought. "I'm meeting with Deborah at her apartment." Renquist's voice steadied itself. "She has two clients at eleven."

"On a Sunday morning?"

"Mental emergency."

Couples counseling on Sunday, a ninety-minute emergency that might net me a half hour with Deborah alone.

"Let's meet at one-thirty," I said, knowing what would come next.

"One o'clock." Renquist was a busy man.

I answered in the affirmative. Deborah Dunton. It was time I paid her a little visit on my own.

CHAPTER FOURTEEN

I DREAM
OF DEBORAH

Deborah Dunton lived and practiced the art of living out
of her penthouse at the Victorian Mews condo complex. If
the Castro was Gaylandia, then the Victorian Mews was our
Buckingham Palace. An exclusive den of rabbit warrens
decked out to look like a gothic castle on boundary between the Mission and Castro, Victorian Mews was not immune to the local crime wave which swelled and overran
the neighborhood from the public housing project in Red
Dora's backyard.

From a distance, it was a strange, anachronistic sight,
something medieval, with turrets and towers, but decked
out in a Victorian style that, as you came closer and closer,
was more a Disneyland kind of cuteness than a historical
reenactment.

The real nineteenth century wouldn't have had the tennis courts, the underground gym with three squash courts
and weight room, the Jacuzzi and the residence towers
arranged around a large triangular swimming pool. At

least the tiles weren't pink. Not yet. The residents had put in a petition.

This cooperative venture offered a lot to the single, professional, childless lesbians and gays who could afford to buy property in the Bay Area. Supposed security and bay views. They could leave home in peace, their automatic timers set to turn on the lights, to open and close the curtains. Lawyers, doctors, doctors, lawyers, couples and singles, Tracy Port and my former therapist, Deborah Dunton. One pet allowed. A lot of bickering over the color scheme of the garden. And a lot of hassle for Red Dora's Cafe when Mews residents protested their wine and beer license.

It was twelve-twenty. I had agreed to meet Renquist at one. I should just be able to fit in a chat with Deborah between her last appointment and our meeting with Renquist.

I walked up to the main front door. A super-dense vinyl—the stuff they make suitcases out of and molded to look like distressed, antique wood—covered it and sometimes kept the bad people away. A well-heeled young man was just coming out. I smiled at him, as if I'd lived there for years, and slipped smoothly past him.

Although each apartment looked strictly anonymous, regulated by the homeowner's associations—no pictures in the halls, no hanging laundry from the windows—I felt I knew every thread of carpet, every individual nick on the doorway of Deborah Dunton's apartment. I had stared at it hard enough as a client, while waiting with Frances. We'd paid handsomely to have that particular kind of twentieth-century healing, therapy, practiced upon us. Deborah's outer door had a coded entry. You punched in the code and turned the knob. I still remembered the numbers.

One, two, three, four, who does Frances love the more? Five, seven six, nine? Is her heart really mine? Zero. The electric bolt slid open and I entered the tiny hallway as I had done before, as a client. But now it would be my turn to ask the questions. And "How do you feel about that?" wouldn't be one of them.

With the permission of the homeowner's association, Deborah Dunton had converted a quarter of the roof into a penthouse and established her practice there. Deborah's therapy was quiet. There would be no primal screams coming from her apartment. Just gentle sniffles and a few sobs and some countertransference that made you feel really shitty later.

I entered the vestibule which was made over into a waiting room. My eyes adjusting to the dark mauve, I heard the familiar whistling sound which came from a noise-making machine Deborah employed. Therapy Muzak, a melodic, rhythmic whoosh, like the tape of a bad ventilation system. It was designed to cover up any embarrassing sniffles or cries. "Shhh," it said.

There were lots of quiet prints of flowers in brass frames. I sat in one of the two matched chintz chairs and stared at the reassuring pattern of stripes woven into the maroon carpet at my feet. I listened to my nerves jangle. How many times had I sat in that chair, waiting, with Frances, trying to learn to talk about our relationship. *"Shhhh,"* counseled the noise machine.

Why could other people talk so easily about their feelings and not I? How did they do it? When emotions bubbled up inside of me, they never took the form of words. Sometimes feelings took the form of music, of sex. Even food. But they never took the form of words. The best I ever did was pronounce boundary statements. I had a long way to go, but D. Dunton would never get me there.

The door from the inner sanctum opened.

Four white tennis shoes came out onto the carpet. Stiffly bleached white linen shorts with colorful tennis tops and tennis arms coming out of the sleeves. But the expressions on these clients' faces were nothing alike, and if there was anything they were going to do, it wasn't play tennis.

"Shhhh," counseled the noise machine.

"Thank you, Deborah," a blonde said. The brunette didn't say anything. She was holding on tight, her face taut, to avoid melting into tears. She was devastated.

"Are *you* okay, Jane?" came the dulcet Southern tones of Deborah Dunton.

"Of course I'm not okay," Jane shouted. The noise machine didn't have a chance. "My girlfriend just sprung on me that she's in love with someone else! What is it, you're too much of a coward to tell me to my face, one to one, is that it, huh?"

"That's exactly why I had to tell you here, honey," the blonde said, "in therapy, so I can feel safe, with Deborah!"

"Taking sides again, Deborah?" I asked.

"Emma! What are you doing here?" Deborah's face clouded and it took her a full two seconds to put the peaceful therapeutic smile back on. "Jane, Meg, why don't you go home and do some of those honesty exercises—"

"Hey, why didn't she tell me about Sharon during last week's honesty exercise! Huh? You coward, Meg!" Jane cried.

"It would have saved you a hundred bucks," I said from the sidelines.

"Emma, I don't need your wit."

"You never did."

"Shhhh," counseled the noise machine.

"Call me, Meg, Jane, if you need to. I'm always available for another emergency session." Deborah was shoving them out the door.

"Yeah, and don't forget your checkbook," I cracked, but the door had closed with a sad finality. Dunton leaned against it, making me feel terribly trapped in her hallway. She was wearing an olive-green peasant dress of a thick linen which covered her slight frame in heavy folds. Dark red lipstick was slashed across her tiny lips. A little stripe of red raced across one of her front teeth, making her look like a fox that had been at the chickens.

"What's going on, Emma? Is there something I can help you with?"

"I just want to ask you a few questions."

"Well you have a funny way of going about it. Are you trying to ruin my business, or what?"

"Sorry, I regressed."

Deborah looked at me closely. "Okay, let's talk about regression, Emma. And aggression. A suitable topic, don't you think? But you'll have to wait just a moment. I have to write up my notes." Deborah disappeared behind the famous door of her therapy chamber. I watched the carpet for a while and wondered what kind of notes Deborah took. And why. I had ruminated enough for a few novels when Deborah reappeared.

The bloodred color had gone from her teeth and she had on a feverish version of her therapist smile. She wandered over toward me, the folds of her dress moving rhythmically. "Couples' Counseling." She breathed the words into my face, and I realized she had been drinking. I could have lit her breath with a match. "Oh, Emma, sometimes

I think I just function to take the rap for bad relation-ships!"

"Well, at least you're paid for it."

"Too bad I don't have any friends left. Even *you* won't be friends with me after—by the way, how *are* you and Frances?"

"Deborah, I'm here investigating the murder of Tracy Port."

"*Really?* Who's your client, Emma. Helen Thomas? Good luck. She's guilty, Emma. Guilty as *sin.*"

"A surprising judgment call from a therapist, Deborah. Listen, I just need answers to a few simple questions. You don't need to put a noose around Helen's neck or solve the world's problems." Or drink whiskey.

"I'll try and restrain myself." Deborah's mouth con-torted into a very untherapeutic sneer as she showed me into her office. It hadn't changed a bit.

The child within was not only welcome, but forced out in a caesarean section of the mind by Deborah's interior decor. The room was determinedly cheerful, each corner filled with the reminder of sunny thoughts. Wreaths of dried flowers, nosegays of roses and willow twigs hung from the ceiling; framed mottos and paintings of god-desses surrounded Deborah's clients with their good humor. This surfeit of effort felt ultimately depressing even before you saw the toys.

Hundreds of molded plastic figurines were arranged in a bookshelf that stretched from floor to ceiling. *"Shhhh,"* counseled the noise machine. From Batman to Snow White and the Seven Dwarfs, the Hulk to Cinderella, little by little the rubber beings had multiplied on Deborah's bookshelf, an army ready for the role playing, reinforcing,

I imagined, any cultural narratives one might be unconsciously playing out.

But that wasn't Deborah's idea. Her idea was to identify with one of them and do some acting out with the small rubber dolls, rather than with your partner. It was a way to understand and maybe verbalize your feelings. It had just made me feel like an idiot. And my responses were always classified as "denial."

In these moments my attention had always drifted to the titles on the spines of Deborah's library. There were books. Lots and lots of books. Had she read them all, I wondered?

The author of *Lesbians Who Love Too Much* looked at me directly. "So what can I tell you, Emma?" Deborah breathed at me. I winced.

"I was wondering if you could shed a little bit of light on Tracy's last weeks."

"I didn't really see Tracy much, as you know. Not after the cruise."

"Did you notice anything different about her in the last weeks?"

"Why don't you ask Lee Turgo?" she said bitterly.

"What makes you think Lee Turgo was seeing Tracy?"

"It was obvious, Emma. I was there on that cruise when they got together. And Tracy was still in love with Lee, right up to the end."

"How would you know that?"

"I know Tracy when she is in love, Emma. She was in love with me. Once."

"And?"

"And—she whistled."

"She *whistled*?"

"Listen, Emma, Tracy lives—lived—right down the hall

182

from me. It's not like our bathrooms are connected, but I could hear her whistle in the hallway. I know that she was in love. Because she whistled when she was in love with me." Deborah's eyes had that intensity that people get when they're reaching maximum alcohol saturation. But Deborah was a Southerner. Who knew how much liquor she could take? "There's part of me that is attuned to Tracy," she was saying. "No matter how mean, or deferential, or even rude Tracy's been, she was a good person. I'm sure it was Lee Turgo. I watched them flirting together on that cruise. Everybody on the boat knew Helen was on a book tour. And who wouldn't take Tracy if they were given half a chance?" I could think of plenty of people. "Besides," Deborah continued, "if Tracy were in love, it had to be with somebody married. It had to be. It *had* to be Lee."

"I'm not following you, Deborah."

She said, with the kind of confidence only therapists can have, "There is so little justice in the world, Emma. I see that all the time as a therapist. I see adults that are really damaged children. Tracy had a very unhappy upbringing. She had issues. Intimacy issues. Abuse issues. I believe Tracy was severely traumatized as a child."

"Why do you think Tracy had been abused as a child? Did she ever tell you that?"

"She didn't have to. She kept many, many things to herself. But I'm a therapist, Emma. There are things that I know. Tracy could only give of herself—sexually—when her lover was a stranger. The first time was wonderful. Making love with Tracy Port was the most intense experience of my life, Emma. But she wanted to spill all that love and passion on somebody who didn't care. When you start to care, she cooled off." Deborah sniffed and her little

183

foot drew a pattern in the air. "It's a common pattern. Not just for lesbians. For the whole of society."

Deborah turned to her bookshelf and picked up a molded rubber figurine of Sleeping Beauty. "In a way, Tracy was sleeping, and I, in my own egocentric way, thought I would be able to wake her. But she moved on. On to Lee Turgo." Deborah's gaze was directed toward a rubber snake with large fangs. "A woman who was profoundly engaged with someone else, and, therefore, fundamentally unavailable. At some level, Lee would always remain apart from Tracy—a stranger to her."

"You're on the board of the Archive. Was there any love lost between Tracy and any of the staff? Allen Boone? Connie, the volunteer coordinator? Ever heard of anyone named Ginger?"

"I wasn't on Administration and Finance, which handles management issues, Emma. But Tracy got along with everyone who had a sense of mission—"

"Allen?"

"Made for each other. Allen is the ultimate collector, doesn't want anything to do with administration. He would never even want to get in Tracy's way." Deborah's voice took on a protective quality. I remembered the quiet stuffy sanctuary of Allen's office. "Collecting, Emma, is Allen's way of staving off feelings of helplessness. An attempt at comfort and reassurance. Believe me, that wasn't something that Tracy needed. Well matched, Tracy reached deep into donors' pockets and Allen reaches out for what he sees as protective talismans."

"What about Renquist?"

Deborah leaned toward me conspiratorially. "That will be one of the case studies in my next book, *Gay Men Who Love Too Much*. Title doesn't have quite the same ring, does it? Allen could write the book, if he didn't so miserably star in it. Renquist keeps him deep in the background—"

"I noticed they barely acknowledged each other at the gala."

"I guess they've got a cozy domestic life on the weekends." She shrugged.

"Maybe it works best for both of them. Allen doesn't seem like the arm decoration type. He seems pretty happy with his artifacts."

"Allen was my client, Emma. So of course I know. And I can't really say anymore about him." She paused, her lips tightening together to keep something inside. Over the noise machine, a fly was buzzing, trapped in the windowless room. I wondered how much damage one loose-lipped therapist could do in a small community. "Actually, I don't see what anyone sees in Renquist. He's just too, too *friendly*. I don't trust him," she said with finality, uncrossing her legs and putting both feet firmly on the floor.

"He's got that vision thing," I said, wondering how fast a bullet train could travel to Seattle. "And he's delivering. When's the last time you went to the airport?"

"I'm not saying I don't like his politics. I just don't like *him*. I can't really say any more. If you read between the lines in *Gay Men Who Love*—"

"How long did you and Tracy live in the same building, Deborah?"

"*Shhhh,*" counseled the noise machine.

"You'll find out soon enough, Emma, and I don't mind telling you. I made the down payment on Tracy's flat. It was when we were together. I also helped Tracy out with her last year's tuition at the School of Library Science. I don't have any regrets. Tracy was an excellent librarian. I voted for her as Executive Director for the Archive. It was a unanimous vote, by the way. Everyone on the board thought that Tracy was the most qualified candidate. She had her problems with personal relationships, but she was one hell of an executive director."

"About the down payment on Tracy's flat. How much was it?"

"A hundred thousand." She sniffed.

"A hundred thousand dollars?"

"She was paying it back, a thousand a month."

"She could afford it once she was executive director of the Archive."

"That's not why I voted for her, Emma. You have such a suspicious mind."

"It's my job."

"Why don't you blame Helen Thomas? Tracy went around having hyperdramatic sex with unavailable people. It's not exactly a life insurance policy."

"Did Tracy have any?"

"Sex?"

"Life insurance."

"Well, I may as well tell you. You'll find out anyway. Yes, Tracy had taken out life insurance. It was for the outstanding amount of the condo down payment."

"So she paid you back?"

"More than that, Emma, I not only have the down payment returned to me, but I've inherited Tracy's condo as well. That is, if she hasn't changed her will."

"Has she?"

"I don't know. I didn't keep track once we broke up. I received a copy of her life insurance policy as part of our agreement. But I don't know about her will. I imagine we'll find out once her safety deposit box is unsealed. The police were over in her apartment this morning, looking for clues."

"Do you have a key, Deborah?"

"What makes you think I do?"

"It happens. You live in the same building. You were lovers. Aren't you on the board of directors of the home-owner's association?"

"Yes," Deborah said slowly, her tongue licking her little red lips. She needed that whiskey. She needed it bad. She'd needed it for a long time. But that wasn't all. Deborah Dunton needed something she thought of as love. Desperately.

"Well, do you have a pass key?" I asked.

There was a nice positive silence.

"I can find out from your bylaws, you know."

"Ah—ah don't—" There came that Southern accent again, every time Deborah got nervous.

"I just want to take a little look around, Deborah. The police have already been there. Let's see if there's any caution tape, if the door to her apartment is sealed or anything."

Deborah paused long enough to give me the impression that she was thinking about it. Then she started to shake her head. I'd have to try some magic words.

"The relationship is going really shitty with Frances," I confided. It was just the aperitif for Deborah's appetite.

"It isn't!" Then, "I'm so sorry."

"Really. It's just as you said, Deborah. I think Frances is tired of my intimacy issues."

Deborah looked me up and down. She wasn't a stupid woman.

"You know, I just can't seem to talk, I don't have the words for things that other people have." My performance was getting a little real for comfort. But it was working. Deborah switched on her therapist gaze and knitted her eyebrows in a familiar way that had always made me want to shut up. This time it had to do the opposite. "Feelings for me just don't have words, they're like colors. When I start to talk the colors go all muddy—"

"Emma, have you read my book?"

"No." I tried to sound confessional.

"I'll go get a copy." Deborah turned and smiled at me with the tiniest, most terrifying air of delight. "And I'll bring the key to Tracy's apartment." She hauled herself out of her chair with some difficulty. Her weak arms were no match for her drunken brain.

Deborah opened a door I had never seen her open before. It was the door to her personal apartment. The part she lived in. I peered around her back at a lot of pink walls and pastel accents, as she gripped the sides of the door frame. The apartment was full, as I might have expected, of flowers. Deborah swayed slightly, like a small refrigerator with feet, trying to make it through the door.

I took the opportunity to find out just exactly what kind of notes Deborah liked to take on her clients. I went over to her filing cabinet. It was locked, but its key chain swung above it from a bulletin board. I opened that drawer of Deborah Dunton's with her own key. Inside it I found Frances's *Lesbo-Parthenogenesis* notes.

I pushed the drawer closed.

For a moment I sat down on the couch, the very spot where I had sat so many times with Frances. The experience receded, far away from me. There was something inside me that was turning numb. I stood up and followed Deborah Dunton into her private apartment. Inside I stopped short.

Chintz, needlepoint and hand-crocheted lace. And guns.

Deborah Dunton's personal decor featured a Plexiglas wall cabinet full of guns.

CHAPTER FIFTEEN

TRACY'S TERRAIN

Deborah's apartment had a basic twentieth-century open-floor plan. A corner kitchen with white Italian cabinets, built-in appliances in white: a white dishwasher, trash compactor, microwave, wall oven and stove top. Flowered chintz curtains were gathered on either side of a view of Twin Peaks which was already funneling a blanket of fog into the valley.

The counter was a bright egg-yolk yellow, and there was a pass-through to a dining room where a circular table was covered in primrose print with matching upholstered chairs circled around it, the covers held on by big, fluffy pink ribbons.

There was a long living room off to the right, an expanse of white carpet and lots of aqua wicker furniture. A small dark hallway led to what was undoubtedly a bedroom, where Deborah was probably having another pull for the road and searching for her keys.

I stood in the other dark hallway off the kitchen examining Deborah's gun collection. It was quite a little stash. For a therapist. Or a white supremacist.

Single-shot muskets. Antique revolvers that looked beyond use. A shotgun with a carved mahogany handle, all in a Plexiglas case with a wimpy lock that would be alarmingly easy to pick or pull off.

"Mah daddy," Deborah said from behind my back, her Southern heritage revealing itself again. "He left them to me. Quite a collection, wouldn't you say? You know how we Southerners are about our guns. And our whiskey. How 'bout it?" Deborah's breath was a confession that threatened to knock me off my feet.

"A little early in the day, Deborah—"

"Nonsense, come over and sit by me on the couch, Emma—"

Reports of women accosted by their male therapists were no longer surprising, but we lesbians were supposed to be above all that. Dream on. That gutter rolled all kind of balls. Just less frequently. "Let's talk and drink when we get back, okay, Deborah?"

There was a smile deep in Deborah's eyes that rose to the surface a little too quickly for my peace of mind. She turned her back long enough to take an obvious swig from a hip flask that she had in her pocket. When she turned back to me, her eyes were all hard and glittery, just like before. Then she went over and got a hardbound copy of *Lesbians Who Love Too Much.*

"I'll sign it for you later," Deborah promised with a wink.

As we walked out into the hallway, Deborah closed the door behind her, first pulling out a little button on the inside knob so we could get in again without the key. It was a practiced gesture. Something Deborah had done hundreds of times so she could roam the corridors of Victorian Mews. As we walked down the plush carpet, underneath regulation sprinklers and fire extinguishers, Deborah became quieter and quieter.

Eventually, she murmured, "I have my ears tuned to this hallway, as you can imagine. Listening, still listening for Tracy. I'll probably be listening to this hallway for the rest of my life, Emma."

"Twenty-seven steps!" she announced, wobbling slightly at the entrance to another apartment, identical to her own.

"I wasn't counting." But I realized Deborah *had* been. Maybe for years now. Lesbians who loved too much.

"Is there any other way into Tracy's apartment?"

"There's a service stairway."

"Someone could come and go without being seen?"

"I guess so. The service stairwell serves six units."

Deborah paused, her key in the lock. I sucked in a breath. Why did I imagine that there must be something terrible behind that door?

But the door opened on a Tracy Port I never could have imagined. A Tracy Port I might not have minded knowing. Soft light filtered through sea-foam shades. The walls had been papered in a satiny silk grass paper, a silvery green texture that was like a mattress for the eyes. My pupils slowly adjusted to the dim light. So quiet. So peaceful. Had there been another Tracy Port, someone who was much more likable?

There were smoky green carpets underfoot, high-ticket items stretching out on a blond finished floor in a long living room identical to the one that Deborah had, but so much classier. Tracy had chosen olive-green kitchen cabinets, black appliances and a bird's-eye maple counter. It was almost austere.

The long living room was suffused with green, the blond accents continuing in the light gold reflected in built-in bookcases and coffee tables and a cozy spinet piano in the corner. The whole place was as neat and orderly as a bread and butter note.

Deborah was sniffling. I thought about the frilly fuss of her place and how she must have loved this haven of quiet just down the hall. Deborah had the cash, but Tracy had the taste, that much was clear. Part of that down payment must have gone toward silken wallpaper and handwoven silk carpets.

Had Tracy done Deborah for the down payment? And then dumped her?

Deborah was walking around the center of the big living room, slipping slightly on the carpets which shifted under her weight on the slick floor. Waving her spindly arms, Deborah seemed to be embracing the air of Tracy's apartment. And why not? It was hers now.

I looked at the carpets and the tracks across them. The tracks of professionals, the tracks of tears. Deborah had seated herself on the middle of a bamboo settee in the living room. Her fingers were walking through her hair, grabbing at tufts and pulling them. Deborah was getting a little scary.

I would start my search in the kitchen. The rice and the bulgur and the beans might all have been in alphabetical order. Everything in tidy rows, glass jars, lids clamped on. I picked them up methodically and shook each one. Rice, beans and bulgur.

I looked in the refrigerator. Tracy liked food, good food. Eggplants with organic stickers. Pomodoro tomatoes. Some basil in a bag which had turned black and mushy. A protein drink. Had Tracy been worried about being too thin? You could never be too rich or too thin— an upper-class straight woman's motto. I looked in the garbage can. Recently emptied.

Everything indicated strict control. The rigid color scheme. Not a mismatched cup or saucer. Not a chipped memento or an article stuck on the refrigerator. I checked all the cupboards quickly. The freezer was full of ice cream. Gallons of Cherry Garcia competing with Heath Bar Crunch. Dairy.

"Say, Deborah, about Tracy's allergies—" I said, but stopped when I saw the therapist, an elongated shadow hovering over Tracy's little blond spinet piano. She had lifted the cover and was moving her fingers over the keys, staring at her own fingers, as if, for one second, they could have been Tracy's. I walked to the end of the long room and watched Deborah's face with a wicked satisfaction.

Her eyes widened as she lifted the piano seat. Sheet music.

"She loved music," Deborah was saying with her fingers playing over the stapled edges of yellowed piano books. "Selected Czerny studies," she read. I looked into the pile of music. It was a pile of music. "Achievement Series of Piano," Deborah read aloud. "Tracy would play and play, working her fingers over that keyboard like it was her enemy. Ha, ha! Trills, embellishments, grace notes all came under attack! She was brilliant! I'm tellin' you she was ah genius!" Deborah's voice had fallen to a whisper. She wasn't telling me anything I didn't already know. Her hands were running along the ivory keys of the piano again. It was no time to hear about Tracy's musical interludes; it was time to check out the rest of her apartment.

The bedroom. I walked down the little hallway and slipped inside. Tracy had chosen an almost masculine Glen plaid for her coverlets and sheets. A lamp hooded in dark green glass sat next to a bed, a very big, firm bed. Rubenesque females played with gauze in a framed print on the wall. Had Tracy been a chubby-chaser?

An exercise bicycle claimed the most important spot by the window. I checked the program. The bicycle was set at the most challenging level. I looked at the pedals, remembering Tracy's muscular legs.

It was a good thing Deborah was still busy with the piano, I thought. Who knows what she might do in the bedroom. I shuddered, listening to a few tentative notes being played upon the spinet. An occasional pause might have meant that Deborah was dipping into her flask.

I examined the bedside tables. Reading material: *The Care and Preservation of Manuscripts, The Copyright Reform Act*. Very dry, like old leaves of paper. Like the hands of a dead woman.

There was no soft porn. No strap-on under the mattress. No drugs. Not a sleeping pill or even an aspirin. Only many gallons of ice cream in the freezer. I heard a few more sad notes from the spinet in the living room.

Where was Tracy's desk? She must have had an office somewhere. But where? There were no other hallways, no extra bedroom, just a bathroom. Maybe Tracy had been shortchanged on the second bedroom in her floor plan. Maybe she gave it up for grass paper silk wall coverings. Who knows? Who cared? It just meant that there must be a drawer or bureau where Tracy kept all her little house notes and bills, somewhere I hadn't seen.

I peered into the closet. Also a neat freak, Tracy employed the double-clipped hangers for the rows of her

power suits, just like Frances did. I heard a few more tentative sad notes from the spinet in the living room as I ri-
fled the drawers and learned more than I ever wanted to
know about how Tracy rolled her socks and folded her
panties. Where would it be? The clue to Tracy's secret
love. My fingers searched among sweaters and sweat socks.
Tracy played tennis. I started on the second dresser. The
large drawer at the top yielded the fruit I was looking for.
A drawer with a checkbook and a carefully fanned-out row
of bills to be paid; a plaid folder trimmed in leather with
pockets inside for envelopes, stationery, memorabilia;
scraps of papers, the ephemera that every life collected. I
unfolded and read every receipt, program and shopping
list. There were theater tickets of the opening of a play at
the Rhino next week. Benefit tickets stamped, "compli-
mentary." Slipping out of my fingers, the colored papers
fluttered through the air onto the carpet.

Bending over I saw another piece of paper on the floor.
Had it fallen out of the tickets? Or had it been here all
along? A tiny, four-squared piece of paper. I opened it up.
Little letters, vaguely familiar handwriting.

"*I am completely bloodied,*" it began. I shuddered.
Bloodied. My God. Was it something she had never sent,
or maybe a first draft of the final missal that
boomeranged, poisoning the librarian to death. The first
notes of a song came from the spinet in the living room.
Tracy's handwriting? I remembered Deborah's scrawl
from the honesty exercises. This was not it.

"*I will be taking your life with me.*"

And the rest was gone. Torn off. This was serious business. Somebody had gotten to Tracy, had made good his
or her threat. And it wasn't Helen Thomas. I put the let-

ter in my pocket as I heard a few bars on the spinet come to an end.

"Emma?" A worried tone. Deborah had come out of her morning reverie. Maybe the whiskey had worn off.

"Yes? I'm almost done." I tried to sound reassuring, but my fingers ached to continue their search.

"What are you doing?" Suspicious.

Don't get all noble on me now, Deborah. "Just looking in the bathroom." The bedroom, I figured, was not a good word to mention at this point. And I would quickly be onto to the bathroom. A place that sometimes yielded more clues than anyone would expect.

I could hear something in Deborah's voice that made me think she needed a little supervision. I would have to be fast. I started quickly through the medicine cabinet. Nary a pill nor powder. Natural cosmetics and some mud packs. Tracy used menstrual pads, not tampons.

There was the usual standard twentieth-century plumbing. Nothing hidden in the toilet tank. The shower and the sink ran hot and cold, just like Tracy. I took my penknife and poked around the drain. Black curly pubic hair. Could be anybody's. And I didn't have a lab.

Somebody, maybe the police, or maybe the fastidious librarian, had emptied the trash can herself. There was something sticking to the side, one of those long flat pulls from a sanitary napkin. But then I looked more closely. The pull wasn't right for a sanitary napkin. It was something else, made of a soft absorbent material, the end a pastel blue. I remembered what Deborah had said about Tracy.

"Tracy had a very unhappy upbringing. She had issues. Intimacy issues. Abuse issues. I believe Tracy was severely trau-matized as a child . . . Making love with Tracy Port was the most

197

intense experience of my life . . . She wanted to spill all that love and passion on somebody who didn't care. When you start to care, she cools off . . . She moved on . . . someone . . . fundamentally unavailable . . . It's a common pattern. Not just for lesbians. For the whole of society."

"Emma? What are you doing in heah?" It was Deborah. She was taking up most of the doorway. Then she wobbled past me and looked around the bathroom, opening up the medicine chest. "Whad you find in heah, Emma?" Leaving the mirror flapping open, she looked accusingly into my face.

The whiskey *had* worn off. Deborah's eyes didn't hold any more promises. Something shaky and endlessly freaky was going on in there. I would remember that look in her eyes and the one that followed it for the rest of my life.

Deborah looked behind my back where something loomed. Something familiar and terrifying at the same time. But I didn't have time to look around and see what or who was there. There was a huge explosion.

My ears screamed as my mind struggled to believe my eyes. The entire midsection of Deborah Dunton had turned into a red mist as the cartridge from a thirty-gauge shotgun ripped open her heart.

THE KEY TO
RENQUIST FALKENBERG

You live in New York. You wait for the delivery. The men in white coats are coming, carrying the eggs. You are not ready for this. I feel completely bloodied. Condoms kept in wallets develop holes.

The men push harder, the wheels have turned into squares and the streets are made of cobblestones. You are in New York. You have always been in New York.

The eggs begin to undulate, yolks softening the shells. Lumps crawl slowly over the surface, like cats trapped under the bedclothes. You have eaten off the tops of your fingers. It doesn't matter.

You live in New York. There are clocks on the wall. The time that they tell is never the present. But there is something else.

They will be fumigating your apartment. You live in New York. It's a good idea. The apartments have been built by cockroaches. Rats in the wall recording everything you say. Outside the whining of sirens bounces off the towers, the sounds stretch into infinity. There's a noise. It's Deborah Dunton.

The hands of Deborah Dunton are dark. Her white fingernails, covered with blood, are trying to keep her chest together, her heart

Mary Wings

inside. Her ribs are a broken cage. Inside, a small brown bird is singing, "You always hurt the one you love."

Renquist Falkenberg was in front of me. He made little whimpering noises, like a wounded animal. He was bending over something that might have been Deborah Dunton once, but was now a pool of blood in the middle of some arms and legs. Irregular shapes, candy coated in a red slickness congealed around a white grid of bones. Deborah's chest had been split open like a baked potato, and Renquist Falkenberg had his hands all over her, trying to hold what used to be Deborah Dunton together with his hands. The sounds he made were not human; there was a whimpering and strangling in his throat.

I would have got up and helped him. I would have done a lot of things if I hadn't been puking. Puking on a thirty-gauge shotgun. I did the cowardly thing. I spat the puke out of my mouth and laid down on the floor and stared at the ceiling. Tracy's pale, sea foam-green ceiling only had a few drops of blood splattered onto it. I listened to Renquist.

"Hang on, Deborah," he was saying.

"Renquist?"

"Yes?" Just like we'd met in a cafe. But Renquist was hunched over Deborah Dunton, who no longer had a torso. I staggered to my feet. It was too late to save Deborah Dunton, but Renquist Falkenberg could do with some help.

I felt in my pocket. The little square of the note was gone. *I feel completely bloodied.*

"C'mon, there's nothing we can do." I was standing now, somehow, on automatic pilot, not looking at anything except Renquist's face, which had a strange, a very strange

200

expression on it. "C'mon, Renquist." I had a hand under his huge armpit. I was hoisting him to his feet when his throat started to gurgle.

"Renquist," I said sternly. "Just don't look. Don't look. C'mon, we're going to call the cops. Let's go over here. To this corner of the room." The corner with no blood in it.

Renquist stared at me wide-eyed as if he didn't understand English. It didn't matter. I was just making sounds to fill the air while I got us away from the bloody bag that had been Deborah Dunton.

There were numbers to call for the police. Numbers like 911. I was going to call now. That's just what I was going to do. I was going to call the police.

Then a thought struck me.

I ran out into the hallway and past several doors until I came to Deborah's apartment. The door was still open. I remembered Deborah pulling it closed. I remembered the click of the latch.

I walked into the little hallway, through the office of toys and teddy bears into her chintzy living quarters. Someone had trashed Deborah's place. Her stereo was gone. And there were Daddy's big guns hanging on the wall. All except one. Someone had just pried that little padlock off the Plexiglas and helped themselves.

Back in Deborah's office I checked the desk. The key was still hanging above it on the wall.

I opened the drawer. Frances's *Lesbo-Partheogenesis* notebook was still inside. I closed the drawer, locked it, returned the key and walked back down the hallway, all twenty-seven steps, into Tracy Port's condo.

Renquist was in the living room looking at the couch as if it might start an engine and race with him were he to sit on it. The blood on his hands was dry. Deborah Dunton was still in the bathroom. I picked up the receiver and called 911 for the second time that day. "Hello, I would like to report a murder." As I said it, I became aware of a persistent tapping on my shoulder. I put my hand up automatically.

A sticky red hole that used to be my shoulder let me know that this was going to be a fun telephone conversation to get through. I held onto my stomach for the third time and readied my cords for cogent verbal communication.

"Yes, a murder," I was saying. Renquist Falkenberg was crying. I would have cried, too, except that I had a shoulder to try and hold on to and an address to repeat. A long time later, I hung up the phone. Renquist and I would sit on the sofa, I decided.

The cops would be here in a few minutes. I didn't hear the sirens, yet. They would send an ambulance. They always sent an ambulance. *I feel completely bloodied.* What was it about that note? That handwriting?

First, I had to hold on to my shoulder. Second, stop Renquist from crying before the cops came He *was* the city supervisor after all. *Our* city supervisor. I didn't want him to lose it. *I feel completely bloodied.*

I stumbled toward the kitchen. Nope, that's the silverware drawer. Then I found the towels. Glen plaid dish towels, neatly folded into squares. I dampened one, two, three, four towels and took them into the living room. I knelt before Renquist and started to wipe his hands with the towels.

I had to think. I had a client to protect. I wouldn't want to pull anything that wasn't in Helen's interests. But you don't fuck around with the cops and murder. They are in the business of gutting your thoughts, and by the time they get to be homicide inspectors, they can be sort of good at it.

"Emma, what are you doing here?" Renquist Falkenberg was suddenly all business. He spoke as if we'd come across each other in a strange country, shopping for vegetables at the same market. A thick fog was lifting from his brain.

"Condolence call," I muttered. "What were you doing here, Renquist?"

"The memorial meeting, remember?"

"Oh, yeah." Funeral plans I hadn't wanted to be a part of. "Who else knew you were going to be here?"

"Just you. And Deborah."

We sat there in the silence and tried to make sense of it all. Had someone been stalking the supervisor?

I looked into those red-rimmed orbs that were Renquist Falkenberg's eyes. He had the look of blind ambition. Or maybe that was my own prejudice against politicians. After all, who knows what my eyes looked like at that moment? Then the cops made the scene.

They came inside like they always do, guns drawn, blue barrels flashing like the fingers of the devil. Their eyes and their guns looked around for trouble.

"In the hallway," I said, hating to spoil their fun, but wanting to get the show on the road. They would find the weapon, the body. And then they would try and find out what happened.

They found what was passing for Deborah Dunton, and then it was macho time. Another tree-pissing contest began. I could hear them making jokes about ordering pizza, an opportunity to show off their manhood and their iron stomachs.

Next, the chief homicide inspector appeared at the door. I looked him up and down. A gray cashmere suit and the faint smell of cigars. He would be like a thousand other homicide inspectors all across America. With a wife who picked out his clothes for him, a wife who had ambitions to a higher social stratum, a wife he would have to get away from at least fourteen hours a day. They would have sex twice a year, once on Christmas and once on the Fourth of July, if no one was visiting.

And he would stick the knife in so cleanly, I wouldn't know it was there until he twisted it. Oh, I knew this guy. He was like a hundred thousand other homicide inspectors in the United States of violence and cheap weapons.

Just then a cop signaled from the bathroom and the inspector trudged across the floor. He joined the knot of blue uniforms crowding into the hallway, looking at the mess in the bathroom. His mustache twitched like he was smelling a bouquet of roses. From the benignly curious look on his face, he could have been looking at a portrait of his mother.

"Photo detail will be here any minute," he growled. "Just stay back, okay?" He bent over and slid a pencil into the trigger ring of the shotgun and pulled it toward him. Then he pushed it back. "Let's wait," he said.

He turned and came back across the room toward us. I wondered if he would recognize the city supervisor. No problem.

"Supervisor Falkenberg," he said with a practiced political sheen. "Homicide, Inspector Edward C. Korian."

Renquist shook his hand. Renquist, in fact, shook all over. His hands trembled and his eyes looked almost pleading. "Please, sit down, sir," Korian said, comforting the witness, another traumatized victim of crime. Then he looked over at me.

I wasn't going to get the pillow treatment, I could tell.

"So which one of you called?"

"I did."

"Okay. Who are you? Let's start there."

"My name is Emma Victor."

"Emma Victor, oh yes." His blue eyes narrowed. It wasn't a good sign. Name recognition with cops is not what I hoped for. Inspector Korian held his hand out in what might have passed for chivalry and put it under my elbow.

"I won't break, you know." I pulled my arm away.

"Sure, Miss Victor." He waved me over to the breakfast nook with a quick, "Excuse me, Supervisor." But Renquist was on his cellular phone now, talking to Allen Boone.

Korian pulled out a chair for me from the high-gloss Formica table. I sat down carefully and took my hand away from my shoulder. I decided not to look at whatever might have been on my hand. I kept my face still. It was real meditation. I just put that shoulder way into outer space. Inspector Korian's eyes held something that might, just might, have passed for respect.

"Okay, Miss Victor. Now, let's get to the story."

Miss Victor. It bode ill.

"I was in the bathroom and Deborah—"

"That's—?" His head flicked toward the hallway.

"Yes. She called me from the living room. I went out and she came toward me. She moved past me and looked at me from the bathroom. Then I saw her being shot. She was shot from behind me. The next thing I knew, there was a shotgun at my feet and Renquist had appeared."

I was getting a headache from trying to keep my face still. The front of my skin seemed to stiffen and harden.

"And then what happened?"

"I lay down, puked a few times on the gun, stood up again, drew Renquist away from Deborah's body and brought him to the living room. I called nine-one-one and then I wiped off his hands."

"That's all?"

"That's all."

"Hmm!" The inspector seemed amused. He looked around the apartment, at Tracy's neutered interior, the blood spatters on the wall, the wallpaper, the back of some side chairs. His eyes saw everything: the bay view, the books, the blond spinet piano. Then his eyes turned to mine.

"So this Deborah. She lived here?"

"She lived down the hall."

The inspector smiled. "You know whose apartment this is, Miss Victor?"

I nodded.

"I suggest you start from the beginning. And don't leave anything out. I like the details. Details make me happy."

I told him I had been at the Howard Blooming Lesbian and Gay Memorial Archive Gala Dinner—the one where the murder had taken place. Korian didn't twitch a muscle or flick a lash, but I knew being a lesbian wouldn't exactly endear me to him. I told him that I remembered that a photographer by the name of Gurl Jesus had taken photos of our dinner table. I had gone to Gurl Jesus's apartment that morning and found her dead. I called 911 at 10:23 and reported the homicide.

Inspector Korian's face was carefully composed granite now. "This is your second homicide call this weekend, Miss Victor?"

"Yes."

"You've witnessed three murders in a weekend?"

I didn't say anything.

"So, you left this Gurl Jesus's apartment about ten-fifteen. Why did you go there precisely, Miss Victor?"

"I was hoping to find some negatives of the photos taken at the gala."

"And?"

"Gurl Jesus used a Polaroid."

"And then you came here?"

"I went home first. Then Renquist called me to say that there was a meeting at Deborah's to organize a funeral—a public memorial—for Tracy Port. That gave me an idea. I thought I would drift by and ask Deborah a few questions first. I knew that she had had a romantic involvement with Tracy, one that didn't turn out in her favor.

"I thought I would ask Deborah if she remembered anything suspicious. We talked and she agreed to show me Tracy's apartment."

"Just like that." Korian did something with his lips that might have been called a smile. But it wasn't nice.

"I think she wanted to see the place. She was drunk; she had alcohol breath."

"Take me back to Gurl Jesus, Miss Victor. You came across a murder scene, walked around it for a while, and then you were kind enough to let us know about it."

"I wouldn't call it kindness."

"I wouldn't call it smart, Miss Victor."

"I don't have anything to hide. I'm investigating on behalf of a client."

"Oh, a *client!*" Inspector Korian leaned back and nodded his head slowly.

"I work for Willie Rossini—the lawyer? She's defending Helen Thomas against the charge of murdering Tracy Port."

"Really! Isn't that interesting? Tell me more about it."

"I picked up Helen this morning from jail."

Korian sighed, "Listen, Miss Victor, this isn't a detective novel. And you're not Mickey Spillane."

"Did I ever *want* to be Mickey Spillane, Inspector Korian? I don't get your point."

"My point, Miss Victor, is that you are tripping over too many dead bodies to make anybody comfortable with the idea of letting you wander around loose." He jerked his head at someone behind my back. I looked around and saw a paramedic standing behind me. Korian waved his hand and I knew what was going to happen.

A guy from photo detail licked his lips as the paramedic carefully clipped away what was left of my shirtsleeve. There was a long black gouge on one side of my shoulder with burnt threads of white T-shirt sticking out, hard with dried blood.

Men murmured in the background. There were no women at this crime scene. My female arm felt exposed in this world of men and blood.

Snip, snip, snip. I could almost see inside now. Something had been burnt. It reminded me very strongly of hot dogs on a grill and I realized it was my upper arm.

When the wound was fully revealed, I felt the flash of a camera bulb as someone took a mug shot of my shoulder.

"Let me tell you something, Miss Victor. You keep your smart-ass out of this case. You hear me? I don't want to hear about you at any crime scenes or asking questions of anyone involved in this case, you understand me? Or I will get a court order to cool your heels in jail with the kind of company that would just love to burst that lovely poker face of yours."

"Now, Supervisor Renquist." The inspector turned away from me as easily as a knife through warm butter. "I think we need to talk about diplomatic protection." Korian was already over with Falkenberg, a fraternal arm around the huge city supervisor. Then a cop emerged from the bathroom with a slick triangle of paper, dripping red off the edge of his tweezers. A little cellophane bag, ready to receive the piece of evidence, hung loosely beneath it. A little blood had dripped into the bag and was making a red line at the bottom of the plastic.

"Look what I found!" the cop muttered, happy as a kid with his first trout.

He turned his head at an impossible angle and read words that were apparently inscribed there. *"I feel—"*

"I would like to put you in touch with Dignitary Duty, Supervisor, if only for the next few days," Korian was telling Renquist. "We think you need some extra protection."

Inspector Korian walked Renquist away, and I felt the paramedic slapping a bandage on my wound. My naked shoulder, my beautiful naked shoulder had a bite out of it, and Frances, the woman I loved, was nowhere within reach.

From the bathroom, the cops were cracking jokes.

"You know what they call a gay cemetery? Har, har, har."

"No."

"Out and *over.*"

Ha! Ha! Ha!

Detective Korian looked over at me. "I guess I'll be seeing you later," he said. I managed to look totally blank.

I continued to hold my face rigid and keep myself moving until I got out of the building.

I sat down on the curb and tried to let my face relax. When I finally succeeded, my face felt like it was breaking up like concrete floes and crashing onto the asphalt and my view of the Bay Bridge was awash with tears.

CHAPTER
SEVENTEEN

BLIND
DATE

Someone followed me to the Castro, someone with squeal-ing brakes. I took a circuitous route. The individual fol-lowed.

The likelihood of the same car taking the same route from the Mission to the Castro was too small to make this coincidence. Or to make him that careless. This was not exactly a tail. This was someone who wanted to make con-tact. Someone with a mustache and a late-model Ford.

I plunged into the intersection of Eighteenth and Castro Street, the busy valley full of buses, cars and pedes-trians. I pulled into a truck-loading zone in front of the twenty-four-hour Walgreens. My newfound friend got a space in the parking lot just beyond.

Walgreens was busy. I went to the back and picked up some packages of sterile gauze and first-aid tape that sup-posedly *breathed*. Then I checked out the section with con-doms, gels and spermacides and made my choice, leaving the drugstore with the goods in a small plastic bag.

I drove down Market, my friend a cool stoplight behind

me. Pulling into a red zone just outside Cafe Flore, I put an old parking ticket under my windshield. Let the mustache man find a legal parking space. If he had to. I would take my chances on a red square. Three-fifteen. I hoped it would give me time, time to make a few phone calls.

I ducked behind the wood dividers that fenced the patio section of the cafe from the street. The outdoor phone booth was free. I dialed my own number and scanned the patio crowd. The patio crowd, some of them, scanned me. I punched in my answering machine code and heard the rewinding voice of Rose Baynetta.

"Emma, for your information, Eleanor DeWade, the name on Fresca's license, was a 'DB.' "

"DB." A dead baby.

"Born 1968, died 1970," Rose continued. *"Youngstown, Ohio."*

So, Fresca Alcazon had constructed an identity for herself out of the death of an infant twenty-five years ago. *"See you later, Emma. Let's try for a quiet evening."*

But it wasn't likely. I thought I saw mustache ducking behind a corner at the front of the patio, where small one-person tables were shielded from my view. Popping in the back door, I found the restroom free. The rest was easy.

I opened the Walgreens bag, found the box inside and read the instructions carefully. I tore the box open. Sliding the silk boxers off my waist and letting them drift to my knees, I completed the task. The result was as expected. The color pink.

Returning to the bar, I stood in line for a double cappuccino. I hadn't had a meal for sixteen hours. But I was far too wired to think about food. Eyeing the backs of heads outside the front window, I watched a line of people hunched over tables, staring into their coffees. I would stay inside, I thought, picking up my drink and warming my hands as I walked over to a tiled table.

An offering of old and new magazines lay in the corner. I picked up an old *Out* magazine, one with k.d. lang on the cover. I held her up in front of me, like some kind of talisman, some kind of protection. I waited. I waited. I looked at the pictures. I saw nothing. Time passed reluctantly.

Out of the smoke and conversation someone emerged and sat down next to me. *He* carried a *New York Times* and wore a blue work shirt and khaki pants. When I felt comfortable enough to lower my magazine, I found a wary-looking person who needed a shave. He didn't like me, either.

"Nine-four-one, thirteen-forty-seven." He barely moved his lips.

It took a moment to sink in. 941-1347.

I nodded.

"In ten minutes. Now point outside at that window."

I pointed outside, across Market Street to the Baghdad Cafe. Mustache thanked me, finished off his espresso in a gulp and was gone.

I stared at some glossy fashion pages. Time passed even more reluctantly. Ten minutes later, I returned to the phone booth and called the number.

"Hello?"

"Hi. This is Emma Victor."

"Emma, old gal, hey, what's doin' man? Georgette told me ah should look you up when I pass into town."

"Georgette, yeah? How's she doing?"

"Fine. You going to be home about five o'clock? I want to stop by, say hello."

"Sure. It will be nice to see you."

I called Rose again and left her a message. "I've got a date. Five o'clock. Hope you can make it."

First, I wanted to see Carla Ribera. It was the kind of thing that would get me in trouble with Inspector Ed Korian, but what the hell.

The fog had engulfed Glen Park, where Carla had turned a storefront into a photography studio. I hadn't called earlier. I wanted to be a surprise. I wasn't.

Carla's dress had been recently pressed and her lipstick was fresh. She licked her lips when she saw me at the door.

"Emma! Come in!"

"I've always wanted to see your place, Carla," I went inside to the tune of Carla's phone ringing.

"Oh, excuse me." Carla's charm bracelet jangled as she threw a few jet black curls over her shoulder, turned and raced down a hallway. "Have a seat. I'll be right back."

Carla's huge sofa, shaped like two big red lips in the middle of her showroom, was the only available seating. I settled myself into it. It was like a kiss, a kiss that would eat me. I stared at the walls that featured Carla's work.

Photographs, mounted on boards, were suspended along a curving wall. The figures of women printed on metallic paper seemed to float in the middle of the room.

Runway models, anyone? Carla had had them all in front of her lens. Seductive waifs. Voluptuous sluts. Fashion skeletons with barbed hips. Rounded young girls fresh from the shower.

"Can I offer you something, Emma?" Carla was striding back into the room. She looked at me, her arms folded. "Beer, wine cooler?"

"Soda pop. Any kind."

Carla turned her attention to a section of the wall. As

she tapped on an almost hidden seam, a door slid noise-lessly open, revealing rows of liquor bottles. A small re-frigerator, lined with glasses, was held in place by rounded brass rails.

Carla didn't stand, she planted herself, like a two-hundred-year-old tree, feet spread wide apart as she poured herself a Scotch. I remembered how much Rose had been in love with Carla. There was a way the woman pulled the tab off my soda with a casual flick of the wrist and a certain tenderness as she listened to the bubbles flow over the ice. Tenderness or calculation. Carla had chosen a cutthroat business.

Carla brought me the soda with a twist of lemon. She juggled the glass for a moment before she turned around.

"How's Frances?" Carla asked.

"Fine. Carla, can I ask you a question?"

"Sure."

"I want to ask you about the baptism at the Universal Community Church."

The room was suddenly so silent, the bubbles in my drink sounded like a geyser.

"I don't know what you're talking about."

"The scrapbook that Berniece said you stole."

"Berniece is getting Alzheimer's," Carla said.

"Deborah Dunton was murdered today."

I watched Carla's face. It moved and twisted. Nervous fingers stretched and plucked the last Gauloises out of a cellophane packet. She curled the outer cellophane wrap-per into a ball in her fist and tossed it into the garbage can. She turned around toward me, balanced one leg over another, twitched her foot a few times impatiently, lit her cigarette, shook the match out and asked me what my business was.

"Rose told me that you took the photographs at the Universal Community Church baptism."

"Rose talks a lot."

"Yeah. Sort of endearing, really."

"Endearing?" Carla snorted. "My God, that woman is her own worst enemy."

"The scrapbook, Carla, do you have it?"

"Nope." Carla leaned against a marble table and crossed her feet. She regarded me thoughtfully.

"I'd like to look at it."

"I said I don't have it, Victor." Carla squinted. "With a little lighting, Emma, I could make you every dyke's dream."

"Without any lighting, I've been a few dykes' nightmare. Listen, Carla, are you going to show me the scrapbook?"

"I really don't have it, Emma. Jesus!"

"Okay. How long have you known Larry Boznian?"

"What is this, the Inquisition?"

"You have a problem with answering questions?"

"Larry?" Pause, sucking on her Gauloises. One, two quick drags. "Eight, maybe ten years." She looked down, tamping her cigarette in the ashtray. "I met him at a furniture exhibit in Barcelona. He was showing chairs that year."

"Do you know anything about where he's from? Originally?"

"Manchester, Leeds, one of those places."

"Bully for you, chilly for me?" I imitated the painter.

"I've known Fresca since she was a baby, she needed—a mother. Stop looking at me like that."

"Like what?"

"I know what you think about the business I'm in."

"What do I think?"

"That I'm making out like a bandit in the world that grinds young girls up."

"Ah, the brief and commercialized blooming of their youth, just another global marketing ploy."

"I'll tell you, Emma, they're still better off with me as a photographer than they are with a lot of horny lens jockeys that couldn't care less what happens to them next. And I'm a happy, successful size sixteen. And forty. Actually, I wouldn't mind having my own agency someday. To help the girls make that transition. Get the right education. Think about their future. Manage their money."

"And Fresca?"

"Be careful, Emma—"

"*Of* her, or *with* her?"

"Both. She's still like a daughter to me, even though it feels like she's a million years old sometimes, doesn't it?" Carla showed me to her stainless steel door. "Goodbye, Emma." Carla gave me a brief peck on the cheek that left me smelling of cocoa butter.

I walked to my car, started it and drove around the block. Garbage night in Glen Park. The bottle collectors would be coming as soon as it was dark. Charles Dickens's California.

I opened the car door quietly, slipped outside and crouched behind a skirt of eucalyptuses across the street from Carla's studio. From between the fringe of curling leaves, I saw lights going on in her room. *Snap! Snap!* Then Carla came out of the back door and deposited a big bag of garbage. I could see her silhouette as she raised the lid of the can. Then there was a heavy bang and the rattle of the lid being shut.

Carla paused for a moment, peering out through the fog. She locked her door, got into her white Maserati and drove away. I watched the car purr off into the distance before I came closer.

Carla's garbage can was a gift indeed. Inside a big black opaque bag was a nice collection of Newcastle Bitter bottles. And underneath those, and some long ribbons of exposed negatives, was Berniece Able's scrapbook.

I couldn't make it back to the car quickly enough. I drove down the block until I found a deserted spot. Hands shaking, I leafed quickly through the scrapbook. There it was. The Universal Community Church baptism. The event which had sent Jeb Flynne over the edge.

I remembered that day. It had been warm and sunny, a Sunday morning with a gospel chorus. Renquist Falkenberg had been glad-handing the crowd while Howard stood, almost shyly. And Allen was there, too. The first hate notes had arrived that very morning.

I peered closer at the photo. At the people stepping up to have their infants baptized. There was one white woman with a baby. She looked familiar. One of the first lesbian mothers, perhaps? And then I looked closer at her child. The infant was beautiful. A brown baby girl with a small gale force of squall coming out of her mouth. People were actually clapping their hands on their ears! The baby's mouth became wider and wider as I moved in closer. And then I saw it. There was no mistaking the birthmark on that tiny neck, a deep, rich, ruby-red stain.

Then I remembered the handwriting on the note and why it was so familiar.

And now I knew why Carla had stolen Berniece Able's scrapbook. And I knew why I wasn't going to give it back. I put a finger underneath the photograph of the baptism and tugged at it. The gummed cellophane, which Allen found so objectionable, loosened and the scrapbook gave up one of its memories. I folded the photo into a piece of index paper, tucked it inside my jacket and headed home. After all, I had a date.

He showed up at a decent seven minutes past five. Seven minutes for me to sweat through my deodorant and wonder if I could take up smoking and still live in California. I opened the door. The individual who stood there was around five foot eleven, a middleweight. He would be strong. "Ralph Chesterton," this charmer said formally, and held out his hand.

I grabbed his forearm and pulled as hard as I could. Rose wheeled up right behind him and had Fresca's little .22 somewhere below his neck, still slightly cold from the freezer. She backed slowly away. It wasn't easy in a wheelchair. But Rose did just fine.

"Don't move," I barked. "The woman behind you is familiar with firearms. The revolver is cocked and there is a shell in the chamber. It's a .22. Doesn't do a lot of damage, but she wouldn't mind putting you in a wheelchair. I believe she's aiming for your spine."

"Okay, okay, but—"

"Shut up." There is nothing in the world like having a gun trained on someone. Every little move could be a checkmate that gets somebody killed.

I patted the man down, emptying his pockets. It wasn't fun. I turned up an ankle holster with a Smith and Wesson in it on the first round. After I'd relieved him of that, I found his money clip, a thousand dollars in notes and some change.

"Hey, look—" he started again.

"Shut *up*," I yelled and jerked my head for Rose to wheel closer. "Listen, buddy." I pushed him into a chair. "I'm really angry with you, you understand?" I had his hair in my hand. It felt terrible, but there was a hate inside of me that made me not want to let go. This was the character that had trashed my house. I was sure of it.

I reached behind me for the duct tape and secured his hands behind the chair. I worked quickly, trying to keep an eye on this joker, on his feet, head, and on Rose, on the windows and door. Only when I had his hands taped behind his back, his chest and feet firmly bound, could I take a breath. Looking him over, a big beefy character I could have never taken, I felt myself getting angrier.

"Emma," Rose cautioned.

"What's your story, dickhead?"

"Listen—" His face was red.

"Why should I listen to you, creep? Why shouldn't I just let Rose give it to you. An intruder against a woman in a wheelchair."

"I'll tell you why you'll listen, Victor. There are a lot of reasons. And some of them have to do with why you made the date with me in the first place. I'm interested in someone you've just gotten to know. And if you can give me a lead on the person, I've got a thousand dollars, right here. For you."

"Why shouldn't I just take it?"

"Because, Miss Victor, you want to know who I am. Don't you?"

"Yeah, shithead, I really want to know. Who the fuck are you?"

"I'll give you a number and you dial it," he said coolly. "If you hold the phone by my head I'll say something into it, okay? They'll get a voiceprint identification. They'll clear me, okay?"

"Shall I give him the phone, Rose?"

"Sure. Why not? Give him the phone." Rose's voice was a monotone. The man recited some numbers. I dialed the unfamiliar area code and the following seven digits according to his instructions. I held the phone to his craggy face, wary little eyes looking far down the phone line to home.

"Okay, Chesterton for clearance," he said clearly into the receiver. "Give them a description."

"Hold." I took the receiver back. It was an automatic voice. A few seconds later, it parroted a description of the man sitting in front of me. *"Twenty-nine, five foot ten, one hundred and seventy-five pounds, blue eyes, pale complexion, large mole under right armpit, scar on both large toes at base of nails. Chesterton is on duty with the Treasury Department."*

"Let's *not* take off his shoes," Rose said.

"Treasury Department." I looked the guy up and down. It was really going to be hard to *un*tape him. "Really?" I tried to look impressed.

"Yep," he said confidently.

"You know, it's really not polite to go calling on ladies with guns."

"You're no lady."

"Careful, Emma," Rose cautioned quietly from her chair.

"You two intend to untie me now?"

"Sure."

I cut the tape and started to tear it off of his clothes. When enough of it was loose, he stood up and pulled off the rest with a pinched expression. I invited him to sit down on the couch. I offered him a Scotch. I even gave him back his gun.

"Okay." He took the gun first, then the drink. "Miss Victor, we believe that you know someone who is involved

221

in a sophisticated money laundering operation. We have reason to believe that you know this person." He showed me a xeroxed photo. It was Fresca Alcazon.

"Ramona Hurst," he said. "Sound familiar?"

Footsteps on the roof. The house professionally tossed. Christ, he had even taken the wall sockets off. What the hell had he expected to find in there? I shrugged my shoulders.

"Come on, Miss Victor. We saw you with the suspect. We followed you both here to your residence. Where you kept her busy for a number of hours."

"She looks like someone I met the other night," I admitted grudgingly.

"What was her name?"

They could find out her name anyway. She'd been introduced all around the table. Although she had handily avoided giving her name to David Sing.

"Fresca."

"That's it?"

"Yeah."

"Well, she was driving a BMW motorcycle which was bought with cash in Switzerland, from a less-than-reputable dealer. The cash she used came from a bank robbery twenty years ago. A bank robbery where four people were killed. A thousand dollars for a pointer, Miss Victor. Just tell us if you have another date with this individual. A phone number, perhaps?"

"Hell would freeze over before I gave you any number, bub. Get a subpoena. Get a warrant. But most of all, get the fuck out of my house." I pushed him into the doorway.

"Miss Victor, these people are armed and dangerous. That's why there's been careful surveillance. We don't want them to know we're onto them. And we don't want to endanger you. We have to stop them, Miss Victor."

"*You're* armed and dangerous. Who's stopping you, the enemy of democracy?"

I slammed the door, missing his fingertips by a nanosecond. Rose and I sat there in the silence, listening to Chesterton thunder down the stairs.

"I hope your tax returns are in order, Miss Victor!" he shouted.

"Congress just isn't doing its job, Emma," Rose said, shaking her head sadly. The phone rang.

It was Fresca Alcazon. Or Ramona Hurst. Or Eleanor DeWade. It was of the greatest urgency that she meet me at the Archive. And that I take public transportation to get there.

VAULTING
FRESCA

I wore a big raincoat, big pockets to hold small tools, a tiny transistor radio, a few of Gurl Jesus's negatives and the baptism positive. I took the Mission Street bus. It started and stopped. People got off and on. And some people got on when I did and stayed.

He was a bit overweight, but I wouldn't let his stocky build fool me. He would be fit, strong. And possibly armed.

I got off the Mission Street bus at 18th. I was in luck. The 18th Street bus was waiting for me. It set off right away, but it was a slow bus route. I sat in the back and watched my tail catch up with us at every stop.

He was six feet tall, with a buzz cut, a baggy gray hooded sweatshirt and a backpack making a hump in the middle of his back. His baseball hat was screwed on backwards. He had Converse sneakers and the loping walk of a teenager. He was the image of thousands of other teenagers. But this one was meant for me.

He faded from view around Dolores Park. The bus continued through the Castro and went up the steep hill on the other side of Market. When it reached the top, it stopped. I got off and looked around me. I started down the lane that would lead me to the Archive. It loomed large and gray and evil, like a Transylvanian castle. I stepped into the shrubbery.

Then I heard him. The snapping of a twig. Someone rustling through the pine-needle carpet. I moved toward him, the branches scratching my cheeks. I didn't care. When the baseball cap fell off, I felt no sadness. When she held me in her arms, tightly, expectantly, I didn't feel the fog or any impending sense of doom. My hands ran over the corded muscles that rode along the top of her leg. I looked into the caraway seed eyes, at the expectant smile that was stretching large across her face. Her face seemed as big and bare as the moon, now that she had no hair.

Fresca Alcazon had shaved her head. Had transformed herself into a boy. Her hug revealed extra padding in her shirt, hiding her breasts, but her breasts were there. We did a slow dance, feverish with reunion, the moon and the danger. She pulled me down onto the pine-needle carpet, spreading her sweatshirt upon the ground.

"Emma. God, I'm so glad to see you. I brought you something."

"Fresca. I brought you something, too." There was no way to hide the warning note in my voice. No way to break it gently.

"What?"

"A photograph." I watched her face take care of itself. "A photograph of your baptism." The lips pressed together, the eyes fled behind a thousand doors. She turned around and I heard her fill her lungs with fog. Then, slowly, she let the long breath out into the night. When she turned around, she was someone new. Someone who wasn't quite Fresca Alcazon anymore.

"Fresca." I unfolded the piece of index paper. It was white and clean, the precious image nestling inside. I handled it carefully. I wanted to show respect for the image of a moment in history which could ruin lives.

There she was in the photos, with that ruby-red birthmark on her neck. Very recognizable. Less instantly recognizable, but obvious enough when you looked at the photo closely, was the identity of the woman holding Fresca in her arms. Fresca's mother was Laurie Leiss. And Laurie Leiss looked familiar in more ways than one. She was the woman I had seen in the parking lot years ago. She was also Larry Boznian. Fresca's mother.

I pressed her to me and felt what I thought was fear underneath twenty years of name changes, passports and packing up in the middle of the night. "What's it been like, babe?"

"Life on the lam? I wake up in the morning and I like to drink coffee from freshly ground beans. I go shopping for organic vegetables and I make a mean quiche. We celebrate birthdays. My life on the run. Just like anybody else's. Except that I never know when I have to pick up and move."

Fresca reached out for the photo.

"Uh-uh, not so fast." I pulled the photo out of her reach. "I want some answers. Let's go back. Back to when I gave Laurie the twenty thousand bucks in the parking lot in El Cerrito."

"Yes, that was the final step," Fresca said. "I was a baby, but I remember a blur of old farmhouses, hideouts. Mom wanted out of the country; she wanted to take the final step. She wanted to go to Sweden and have the operation.

She wanted to live and be an artist in Europe. She knew it would be easier as a man. She enjoys being a *man*."

"Why did Howard give Laurie the twenty thousand dollars? It wasn't family loyalty, was it?"

Fresca snorted.

"Your mother took the explosives for her group's revolutionary agenda from Howard's labs, didn't she, Fresca? During the visit when you were baptized. And Laurie had some proof of this, didn't she? Proof that she used to blackmail Howard."

Fresca nodded. "She saved receipts with his name on them."

"And all to blow up that brownstone in New York. But it's dangerous living in a bomb factory, isn't it, Fresca? Bombs can go off during nap time. And that's how you got your quilted leg."

Pause. "That's right. I've seen a lot of pretty strange doctors in my day, Emma."

"I'll bet." I imagined Fresca as a baby, being taken to medical men who'd mend wounds without questions, guys who'd lost their licenses, a botch job. Looking at her leg again, a patchwork of pain. "How," I asked, imagining the barrels of fuel, the timing devices, the tricky plastic explosives that would tear innocent bodies to shreds, my fingers grazing the strange flesh on her leg. A pattern, an abstract painting. Something like a camel's head. "How can someone make a bomb? Set it off? I don't understand."

She pulled my hand away from her leg. "What makes you think I know? Because Larry is my mother? She made bombs and blew people up a long, long time ago. He sees my leg every day and within my burnt repaired flesh, he sees the families of the people who worked in the bank and there's not a day that he doesn't try to drink it away."

My heart wasn't exactly breaking.

"Why doesn't Larry just turn himself in? Is it really worth the running? Giving up your life for—"

"Larry? A transsexual prisoner in a federal penitentiary? He'd never last a week."

"The way he's drinking, he won't last long either."

"He'll dry up. I know some places. Dusty and hot and windy. We can live in tents and he'll dry out all right. We'll listen to the Koran at night in a language we will never understand. There will be people with Kalashnikovs and I will never look them in the eye and they will never know I am a woman. A winter in the Sudan. Eventually, who we are, Larry and Laurie and Fresca and Eleanor and all the people that we are, will blow away in the desert air."

"Fresca, soon I'll have the other key to Howard Blooming's safety deposit box in the Archive. I'll give you thirty seconds to look inside to see if there's anything you want. Then you give me back the key. That's what I'm doing and that's all I'm doing."

"Why would you do that for me, Emma?"

But we both knew the answer to that. "What do you think you're going to find in that box? What was worth you and Larry mugging me for?"

"We were afraid," she began slowly. "We were terrified that Howard had gotten hold of the documents of the sex change operation that Mom had had in Sweden. I don't know how he got them. Or if he really ever had them. But once, when Mom called him, he said he knew what her real identity was. And if she didn't keep away from him he would blow her cover wide open. And we knew David was back from Paris. We've been waiting for years, and there you were with that hatbox. I felt the wound that night, I kissed it, I swear, like I have never kissed flesh before.

Emma, I wounded you. I don't ever want to do anything like that again. I've watched Larry. It's not my kind of revolution. And it's not his, either. You've got to believe me."

I let the historical facts jiggle around in my head. Events assumed new places, people new identities. The past was a different place than I'd thought I'd inhabited.

"Okay, Fresca, I'll meet you here day after tomorrow. The library opens at nine. The Archive at eight A.M. I'll manage to get us in."

"Honey, you are *hot*," Fresca said appreciatively.

"No kidding. We're both hot."

"What do you mean?"

"I've got a homicide inspector on my ass. Somebody blew away Deborah Dunton today with a shotgun. Got any ideas?"

Fresca knew just what I meant. "Larry is—was—a revolutionary. He didn't just *kill* people—"

"No, he killed them for a cause." I almost smiled, almost, but not quite. But I didn't think Larry Boznian was Deborah Dunton's killer. I just wanted to check the facts on Fresca's face. Larry Boznian was a drunk on several lams.

"And you've got the Treasury Department on your ass, Fresca."

"What?"

I nodded slowly. "Someone came over to my house to offer me a thousand dollars for your phone number."

"Fuck!" Fresca stamped her foot on the ground, hard.

We both stood there and let the implications sink in. Fresca wouldn't be sticking around for long. No wonder she needed to see me so fast. She had to have Howard's box and she didn't have time to waste.

Fresca gave me a sudden hug. "Hey, Emma, it's really

fun to tail you, you know that?" She was nuzzling my neck, her hands reaching inside my raincoat. "I have a present for you." She reached for her backpack. Inside, carefully wrapped in a white linen tea towel, was a book, a brown book with bright gold lettering.

"*The Making of Americans,*" I read. "It's lovely, Fresca."

"Open it up, Emma." Fresca put the parchment like vellum against my cheek. "It's cool, almost soft, isn't it?" She opened the book and displayed the signature: "Gertrude Stein" in a bold stroke across the inner board. "One of five," I read. "It's beautiful." I turned it over in my hands. "It must be very valuable," I mused. "How can you part with it?"

"Darling," Fresca said softly, "for every*thing* that is yours there's a second price." Pulling my raincoat off my shoulders, she slipped her hand inside my shirt, found my breast and rubbed her fingers against my tightening nipple. "Ownership."

Our shirts both came off, and there was no fog at all. Fresca peeled my jeans, kneeling in front of me. Her breasts were silken and they hung, loose, gifts of soft fruit, charcoal nipples in the moonlight. As she worked her way down my body, fingertips and lips in precious counterpoint, I could feel the volume of Stein next to me, the deckled edges of the pages tickling my legs.

> *Lifting belly with me*
> *You inquire.*
> *What you do then.*
> *Pushing.*
> *Thank you so much.*
> *And lend a hand.*

What is lifting belly now.
    My baby.
Always sincerely.
    Lifting belly says it there.
Thank you for the cream.
    Lifting belly tenderly.
A remarkable piece of intuition.

And so I came.

RIOT!

Sirens interrupted a final embrace. Fresca pulled away from me. I saw lights flashing on her face. Red, black, red, black. A cherry light whizzed down the street alongside of us, toward the Civic Center.

That's when I heard the familiar sounds. Distant chanting. Loud and fierce. An ocean of rage. People were running down the street. Glass was breaking. A police car zoomed by, summoned to a barrier position perhaps. A central command had already been set up. "God, Emma, I want you to have me." She nibbled my lip, but was throwing on her clothes. The leaves rustled as she promised. "You will fuck me later, baby, I promise."

"Promise?" I would never be able to find her. To look for her.

"To live outside the law you must be honest." The sirens picked up behind her.

And then Fresca was gone, leaving me with a Gertrude Stein first edition swaddled in a plain brown wrapper.

*   *   *

There were voices all around me now. Clots of people, planning, laughing, angry. Within seconds my treadless tennies hit the pavement.

I remembered this part. You saw the flames. You ran *toward* them. Toward, of course, the temples of government, those pompous sugar tart castles in the center of town. The dome of City Hall—taller even than the Capitol dome, as the tourist guides proudly pointed out—came into view. From the Civic Center, a flame gushed forth into the night. People were yelling, a flat backdrop of chants. What were they saying? *"Sheebbeeen! Sheebbeeen!"* A rhythm against the running feet. I moved, hypnotized, toward the conflagration, holding the book to my chest.

All around me police cars exploded, their gas tanks popping; shattered shells formed vicious shrapnel which rained all around us. Gallons of gas added to the fountain of flame which threatened to engulf the entire Civic Center.

It was nearly seven o'clock. I looked behind me. A new generation of twenty-nothing dykes and an army of young men who had nothing to lose in this economy were running around in groups that looked almost happy. *"We're here, we're queer. Get used to it!"*

The crowd seemed to thin out as I got closer to the center. The heat from the flames made the small street an oven. And then I saw the front line. Four separated groups of people, in perfect concert, had picked up a large construction railing. They had stripped the legs from the thirty-foot metal barricade. They held their communal spear, gripping tightly, listening to the chants.

The crowd was split now. Some cried, "No violence! No violence!" and someone else yelled, "Fuck you!" A cheer went up as the spear bearers aimed the jousting lance at the very door of the federal building.

The door was covered with a grill featuring the golden goddess of justice and a bald eagle above her head. The goddess was blindfolded, and the bald eagle seemed to look down slyly at her breasts.

As the spear was aimed at the door, the crowds roared in approval. Even the "No violence" faction was silenced by the sight of this mighty beam aimed at the mockery they thought justice to be in America.

More people took hold of the beam. Men and women, black, brown and white, old and young, a self-selected rainbow group, hugged their lance and started to march forward.

They picked up steam as they ran toward the door and with a deafening roar of metal, "Justice" was punctured through the stomach. The crowds cheered. More battering rams were hoisted and more than thirty-foot spears were aimed at the windows. One by one the heavy glass sheets shattered.

"*Shebbeee! Sheeebeee! Shebfee!*"

Other groups marched toward the federal building, climbed up on the embankment and crawled inside. Chairs, paper, computers and keyboards flew out of the windows and crashed onto the pavement. Inside my raincoat, the Stein volume was warm against my breast.

I turned on my transistor radio and tuned in to the twenty-four-hour news channel. I listened to the din around me echo inside the little plastic box, and then I heard the voice of a journalist frantically describing the scene before us.

"*In front of me tonight, one of the worst civil riots in the history of San Francisco, the result of an attempt being made on the life*

234

of City Supervisor Renquist Falkenberg. Official sources, who decline to be identified, have confirmed that a threatening note at the scene of a recent murder was written by assassin Jeb Flynne. Although Flynne was believed to have committed suicide, several murders recently in San Francisco have been linked to the assassin."

"I feel completely bloodied." The handwriting had been familiar. But it had not been Tracy's handwriting. It had been Jeb Flynne's.

That's when I realized that the two-word chant had been Jeb Flynne. Jeb Flynne.

The original battering group was still going at justice. The "no violence" chants were weaker. Photographers were arriving at the scene. The popping of breaking windows was counterpointed with flashbulbs, white blasts against the inferno of bursting gas tanks and the black, acrid smoke of cop-car tires.

A fax machine landed at my feet with a crash—cracked plastic, glimmering circuit boards and a lot of little screws. I pulled back behind the corner of a building, out of the line of fire and, just like everyone else, watched the battering group break into the temple of justice.

A flurry of burning papers flew out of the building. I picked up one of the papers as it drifted by on the wind. Through the smoke I could read, "Workmen's compensation," and an address in Modesto.

There was a bright pink glare and someone screamed. The tactical squad had arrived. I watched them moving forward as one, a slow, relentless march of faceless creatures, with helmets. Gas masks covered their features, triads of eyes and mouth making them look more like insects from a B-movie than human beings.

The street stilled; the crowd looked at the squad for one

long second. The battering ram was hoisted up higher under the rebels' arms. Sweating brown, white, tan, purple faces reflected anger and utter determination.

"Sources close to the police force have leaked the news that the handwriting on notes received both by the city supervisor, Renquist Falkenberg, and by the police has been positively identified as that of assassin Jeb Flynne. Flynne, who allegedly committed suicide while in a jail in Los Angeles five years ago—Here! Wait a second. Here is Supervisor Renquist Falkenberg now! The supervisor has been busy with aides preparing a statement since the rioting broke out which nearly destroyed the Federal Building."

I was standing at the Civic Center. The tactical squad had done its work. The riot was over, the demonstrators gone.

And then the unmistakable tone of Renquist floated over the airwaves: the deep reasonable, velvet voice, speaking from the Howard Blooming Lesbian and Gay Memorial Archive. *"I would like to ask the lesbian and gay communities, all of the communities of San Francisco, to try to come together in this difficult, difficult time. There are those who say that Jeb Flynne is alive. If that is true, then he will be brought to justice. In the meantime, we must continue to live our lives with the kind of integrity that will help our community achieve its aims and receive its own justice. This community has lost some of its best and finest leaders in their finest hour. Let the violence stop now."*

A new voice came over the airwaves. It was Berniece Able, her strong seventy-year-old voice ringing out with words which stopped me in my tracks.

"History there = is no disaster = Those who make history = Cannot be overtaken = As they will make = History which they do = because it is necessary = That every one will = Begin to know

that = They must know that = History is what it is = Which it is as they do =."

I knew who the murderer was now. The cloud of suspicion which had engulfed Helen Thomas and Lee Turgo and Berniece Able would be lifted. They could continue their lives of happy productivity.

I didn't think that Renquist was in any danger. In fact, I thought that the whole series of murders, of Tracy, of Gurl Jesus, of Deborah, were to protect Renquist and further his career. Renquist. The protégé of Howard Blooming. The mantle of gay politics had fallen too early upon his shoulders. Renquist had never lost any weight on his public jogs with Tracy Port. And now I knew why. My conclusion was not a happy one.

I waded through jagged floes of glass that were once department store windows, climbed blackened whales of beached cars. The wave of white-hot anger had broken upon the shore, leaving a sea of civic debris. There would be a fury and fallout, retribution and rebellion in the days to come. Many would always want to believe that the assassin, Jeb Flynne, was alive, protected by the federal government. But I knew who the real killer was. The person I had least expected, and had least wanted, to be the murderer. I readied myself for a hike up to the Castro and the Archive. The Stein volume felt much heavier than it should have.

HISTORY,
PART II

The gray metal door marked STAFF ONLY was guarded now.
Outside, David Lamble, a local radio commentator, was
pulling his equipment out of the doorway. A clenched mi-
crophone was still screwed into its stand. The guard was
being polite, holding the door open.

"Hi, David," I said and walked right past the security
guard into the linoleum hallway. At the end of the hall was
that anonymous back door of Allen Boone's office. I
knocked and waited. The door opened and Allen Boone
stood there, face white, hands shaking when he saw me.
Behind him, Renquist Falkenberg was rising to his feet
like a bad sunrise. In front of them was a copy of *The Yale
Gertrude Stein*, and the assorted clutter of Allen's desk had
been swept to one side for the radio interview.

"Hi, Emma," Renquist said, slowly, quietly.

"Hi, Renquist. Hi, Allen," I said and sat down, putting
the Stein volume on the desk in its brown wrapper.

Allen was sitting now, too, squeezing Renquist's palm
between both his hands. Allen was wearing black slippers,

238

black sweatpants as if he'd been hauled out of bed. He was wearing a T-shirt that said, "The Sixteen Pleasures." The gold chain on his right wrist twinkled.

"What's up, Emma? What's that?" He indicated the package, a trembling smile.

I looked slowly from Allen to Renquist. "I know who the murderer is," I said.

"You do?" Renquist whispered.

"Yes. I have a negative right here—well, actually it isn't a negative. Polaroid film doesn't make a negative. But it records the ghost image of the original picture. You can't make any more prints off of it—"

"Stop rambling, Emma." Renquist swallowed hard.

"The negative clearly shows the chain of the amulet around Helen Thomas's neck, the chain that held the so-called poisoned necklace in place—the chain that was broken by Allen Boone."

"Allen—you—" Renquist's mouth fell open to his chest. "*You* murdered Tracy?" Renquist's face collapsed into the big palms of his hands. His shoulders shuddered and a terrible strangled noise came out of his throat. "Of course," he said.

But Allen was almost laughing. "Ghost images, Emma? Renquist, don't listen to her!"

"You've left more evidence, Allen."

"Evidence?"

"Yes, you know, trace evidence. Haven't you been watching the O.J. trial?"

"The O.J. trial?"

"Had your tuxedo from the dinner dry-cleaned, yet?"

"No, I—"

"Get ready to donate that Quill Collection to the

239

Archive. You are going to jail, Allen, for the murder of Tracy Port, Gurl Jesus and Deborah Dunton."

Renquist's face, gray and waxy, emerged from his hands. Acceptance of denial. His own denial. Allen's denial. A web of secrets that became untangled.

"You were too clever, Allen," I continued, as much to hear my own voice fill the room, full of carefully kept secrets and love crushed beyond repair.

"The necklace of Helen's was too easy, too romantic, Allen," I said. "You set me up to hear the argument between Tracy and Helen before the dinner."

"You'll never be able to prove—a negative—a Polaroid —a *ghost* image—" Allen stuttered.

"No? Let me suggest your weapon of choice, Allen. Let me see." I walked over to the case of pens. Walt Whitman and Lizzie Borden. There. The fountain pen of Daphne du Maurier, who wrote in sepia ink.

I slid my hand under the glass and pulled du Maurier's pen out, silver clip glowing, I pulled off the softly rounded cap and looked over at Allen. His face gave me the answer I was looking for. Holding the pen aloft, I pulled the tiny metal lever which depressed the bladder inside. Liquid squeezed out onto the ribbed feed tube and through the little air hole onto the nib where an amber tear formed and hung, glimmering. I could smell it from a foot away. Almond-scented ink.

"Daphne du Maurier." Allen's eyes seemed dilated. Far away. Perhaps the past would be even more real to him now that he had no future. "I had to use her pen. She was the only one who used sepia ink."

"Why didn't you throw the pen away?" I asked him, but I knew the answer, as I gazed around his office, at the beloved Queer Quill Collection, the napkin collection, the portraits, the books, the letters, the ephemera of history. Allen could never throw anything away. History. The history of assassins is the history of madness. "Allen, let me bring you into the Hall of Justice. I can help make sure there's as little fuss as possible."

"You killed Tracy." Renquist's eyes were tearing and I wondered if he knew. "You killed my baby." Tracy had told him.

"What?" Allen's eyes filled with a sense of reality. His eyes were bulging out of his head and his hand combed his beard over and over again. "No—" he breathed.

"Tracy was pregnant."

"Tracy was . . . " Allen whispered and his hands curled together, tight fists, ascending to his face, uncurling, his fingernails digging deeply into his skin. I stepped forward and pulled his hands away from his face. It wasn't a pretty picture.

Renquist had walked over to one of Allen's portrait-filled walls. He had his back turned to us. "Call." Renquist's hand reached up to touch the portrait of John Maynard Keynes. "Call my car." Scratchy words I would never forget. And then gushing sobs took over, the unstrangled cries of a man who had lost two lovers and one child. They were the only sounds in the room until we heard the honking of Renquist's car.

STRETCH

CHAPTER
TWENTY-ONE

Stretch limos. I was watching the dawn through smoked glass, sitting in the back with Allen. The driver was invisible beyond a curtained window.

Allen was curled up into a fetal position on one side of the car. I didn't look at him. There were some tight little sobbing sounds that never quite made it out of his mouth. The car took a turn.

They used to make stretch limousine Cadillacs, but the extra weight burned engines up. I remembered riding in a few limos during the apex of Howard's career. The leather seats, the big sofas, but, most of all, I remembered the eerie feeling of not moving at all. The smoked windows, the length of the vehicle, a shock absorber system designed by God, all made me feel that we were perfectly still as we were rolling down Market Street to the Hall of Justice. We stopped at a red light outside the Norwegian Hall. Through the smoked glass, it reached out with a sign. "Bingo Tonight."

"Berniece got us a good deal on rings," Allen was saying,

words making it past the sobs. Strange words. His voice a disconnected thread in the interior of the car. "Her uncle . . . a jeweler . . . in Philadelphia. The Philadelphia Fish Market." Allen's voice was absorbed by deep leather. I didn't look at him. "The march on Washington," he continued. "We went to it—the march. We pooh-poohed the mass wedding, of course. But then we were in a sea of thousands of happy couples. The vows. Somehow it all made sense. It was very emotional. And then we came home. And it was all over."

We'd stopped by a light at the Orbit Cafe. Dark inside, out of orbit. Up the hill, I could see the UC San Francisco extension. The parking lot was empty.

"What's that bridge called?" Allen was saying. "In Florence? The *Ponte Vecchio*," Allen was saying to himself. "That's where we got the Henry James pen. Very touristic, of course . . ."

Nowadays, stretch limos are party cars. Roses and a free gift. Champagne bars, televisions and VCR's built into the solid walnut dashboard. Renquist, I saw, had only a clock. Market Street was still sliding by my window.

"I thought Deborah suspected," Allen was saying. "After all, she'd been my therapist—she was the therapist to all of us. But I never felt really comfortable with her . . ."

The car was gliding down Bryant Street now, past SOMA cafes where early workers managed to drink cappuccinos in the wind that came up with the dawn. Projection, projection, projection. It got Deborah Dunton dead. To my right was a panel with remote controls for the sun roof, the car door locks. I had locked them when we'd gotten in. I kept my nose pressed hard to the window, my eyes reflected in the bullet-proof glass.

"You know, the funny thing is, Emma—" For the first

time Allen was talking directly to me. We were pulling up to the Hall of Justice now. I would take Allen inside the building. He would be booked. Photographed, finger-printed, searched. Housed in a special security cell. Sprayed with insecticide. He would polish the handles of his own cage. "The funny thing *is*—" Allen's voice picked up, he sounded almost cheery. He could have been talk-ing about pasting photos into an album with little black corner mounts. "I almost enjoyed killing Tracy."

I didn't turn my head. Tracy probably would have dumped Renquist just like she dumped every other lover she had ever had. A wisdom that would make no differ-ence now. The driver opened the door. Someone from the sheriff's department was waiting for us. Renquist had called ahead. Renquist, a bisexual body trapped in a ho-mosexual movement. "But Deborah, no, that wasn't easy, and I—" I looked at Allen for the first time since we'd stepped into the limo. The San Francisco fog infused with the salmon light of dawn made Allen Boone look for all the world like he was covered in blood.

Two deputies jerked his arms violently. His T-shirt, the Sixteen Pleasures, rode up, and I noticed that Allen had an aqua-green bullet-nosed fountain pen clipped to the elastic band of his pants.

CHAPTER TWENTY-TWO

TWIN
PEAKS

Seven A.M. I was sitting in Rose's van on top of Twin Peaks, where the limo had dropped me off. I needed the view, the bracing fog and my friend. I needed to tell her about Allen Boone. She passed me a steaming latté which she'd picked up at Cafe Flore on the way up.

We looked down upon the city. A big smudge smoldered in the middle of it. Through Rose's windshield, we stretched our eyes across the aqua bay. Mount Diablo was a black dinosaur on the red horizon.

"I can't believe it—Allen Boone—Emma—are you—"

"I was only really sure when I heard that notes of Jeb Flynne were popping up with regularity. I didn't believe that Flynne could be alive, but the FBI had been pretty clear about the authentic handwriting. I began to wonder if someone had saved the notes, sent so very long ago. Of course Allen came to mind."

"Allen?" Rose whispered, her hands finding their way around her waist. I pulled one of her hands toward me and held it.

"Allen had found out that—Renquist Falkenberg and Tracy were having an affair. He's bisexual. I always thought Howard—"

"Renquist, bisexual. *Okay.*" Rose took a deep breath. "But Allen a murderer—"

"Tracy was pregnant. I found the fragment of leftover pregnancy test in her bathroom wastebasket. It was positive."

"And he never lost any weight on those jogging expeditions—"

"I remember finding condoms in his wallet. And everybody knows you can't keep condoms in your wallet. They develop holes."

"But, Allen, please, don't tell me my little buddy—"

"Accept it, Rose. You can imagine what he felt. Allen, the man who liked to be so close to history. Renquist, never quite acknowledging Allen as a public partner. Meanwhile, Allen was collecting napkins, memorabilia from every gala, brunch and reception. He was always there, not wanting to be in the limelight himself, but needing to be in the thick of things.

"If he lost Renquist Falkenberg, he'd be just another librarian. And it looked like he might be losing him. To Tracy Port. His boss. His overly officious boss. His *bisexual* boss. And then he saw his opportunity. Helen Thomas's amulet, Helen Thomas's manuscripts.

"He encouraged Helen to donate them, to bring all of them to the gala that evening. He arranged for Tracy to meet Helen at the loading dock. My appointment was timed to coincide with theirs. Allen paged himself from his own office and then left me there alone to witness their conversation."

"Allen was always so good with details."

"It was a marvelously staged argument. Poor Helen and her cyanide amulet. I suppose it is possible that Helen's necklace had poison in it. I'm not sure that a poison would remain viable for ninety years. Still, it looked good in the planning. Amidst the hugs and congratulations and bad food, Allen must have snipped the chain of Helen's necklace. She was so overwrought about her fight with Tracy and the speech, she didn't even notice that the amulet was missing. Allen was carrying the cyanide in a fountain pen. A few drops of poison in Tracy's potatoes and a drop on Helen's necklace. *Voilà*. Instant cozy murder scene. Much too cozy and perfect. It had been too *literary* a plan. And Helen the perfect suspect. I never believed it for a second, but it looked like a good case to the D.A.

"What Allen hadn't counted on was the photographer, Gurl Jesus, who had captured one of the moments on film. I don't know what she had, but I may have a negative somewhere. A moment where Allen pulled at something on Helen's neck? Gurl called him. Her big card, of course, was that she would tell Renquist unless Allen paid her off. But Allen needed to keep Renquist—that was what it had all been about. He would have been absolutely desperate. What he didn't know was that the negative of the print—that chemical transfer paper—accompanies every photograph. I'd fished a bunch of them out of Gurl's wastebasket. I never did find the incriminating one, but it was easy enough to bluff Allen into believing I had it."

"Allen, Allen." Rose stared at the city.

"He shot Gurl Jesus in the back for a Polaroid print, Rose."

"And Deborah Dunton? How'd she get in the way?" Rose's voice was dull.

"Renquist had called a meeting to discuss Tracy's memorial at Deborah's house. I don't think Deborah liked Allen.

"Allen was starting to freak. He was convinced that Deborah knew; he'd been a client of hers. All the guilt was making him see pointing fingers everywhere. Remember, Allen read every newspaper in the city, the two dailies and the four weeklies. And he knew there had been a well-publicized shotgun murder in the Mews complex. He decided he had to get to Deborah before Renquist did."

"And he almost got you in the process."

"But Deborah was close to the truth. I don't think she would have fooled herself that much longer about Lee Turgo. In fact, I think Deborah had pretty strong suspicions about Tracy's pregnancy."

"What makes you think so?"

"She'd stolen Frances's *Lesbo-Parthenogenesis* notes. She must have taken them at the Archive dinner—I admit I was pretty careless with them. I suppose she thought they might contain some sort of insemination records including Tracy Port—but, of course, they didn't.

"In any case, Allen came calling, not thinking I would be there so early. Perhaps he overheard Deborah talking about Tracy in the hallway. He went into the gun case, pried off the lock and took one of the guns. He followed our voices down the hallway.

"My suspicion is that he knew all along that the guns were there. Deborah was always holding those dreadful benefit brunches in her apartment.

"After killing Gurl Jesus, Allen must have been thinking double-time. That's where he tripped up. He veered away from the Helen Thomas motive. He was afraid someone would make the connection with Gurl Jesus and the gala.

He had the notes of Jeb Flynne, the original threatening notes written in the name of the Family Values Society. Murder. Blood. Shame. Guilt. It was all in Jeb Flynne's notes.

"Jeb Flynne was an extreme right-wing fundamentalist, remember? The whole concept of baptizing the children of homosexuals attacked his religion. His way of life found its way into vicious prose and vicious acts. He felt "blood-ied" by the whole experience. I got to thinking that David Stimpson was right. Maybe we should have paid more attention to those notes. To Jeb Flynne. So this time around, I made sure I did."

"Oh, Allen—" Rose's hand left mine and gripped the steering wheel.

"Allen slipped into Tracy's room and simply threw a fragment of one of Flynne's notes on the floor, where someone was sure to find it. He watched as I picked it up. Allen started up a real campaign to convince everyone that Flynne was alive. He sent notes. Too many notes. Flynne's notes were sent sporadically, in response to a per-ceived ideological threat. He just wasn't a murder and mayhem kind of guy."

"And Allen was in the apartment while you were there? With shotgun in hand?"

"Waiting for Deborah. Who surprised me in the bath-room. The gunshot came from the bedroom. Allen hit my shoulder. Single shot. He didn't have time to pump the barrel and I was probably on the floor anyway. So he ran."

"What about your friend Eleanor-Fresca-DeWade?"

"A little tax evasion. She declared too many depen-dents." At least that part was true, I thought; a very de-pendent Larry Boznian had bought the ticket and taken her along on the trip.

"The modeling business? She looks a little fleshy—"

"Money in buckets. I told her to get a good tax lawyer. Just a red herring."

Rose's eyes reflected the sun which had finally risen over the crest of Mount Diablo. "How does Carla Ribera fit into all this?"

I wasn't going to tell Rose how red the herring had been. Carla Ribera's politics were more radical than any of us could ever have imagined. That Carla may be involved in an international underground to protect political prisoners. That maybe the fashion photography and the long-legged models *were* just a pose. That Carla still loved Rose.

Fashion, turn to the left, turn to the right. I wouldn't stick my finger into that mess.

"Oh, Emma." Rose's hand left the wheel for my shoulder. "Thank God you're sitting here beside me in the van, not spread all over Tracy Port's floor." An airplane roared through the sky overhead. "We may never get to the airport on public transportation." Rose twisted the key, starting the engine.

Once I arrived home, I turned off the phone ringer and slept for twenty hours.

CHAPTER TWENTY-THREE

WHAT ELEANOR ROOSEVELT SAID

I had been standing in front of the Archive since seven forty-five, holding onto a safety deposit key which had come in the mail yesterday morning. Standing wasn't accurate. I'd been walking, sitting, chewing on my fingernails. Waiting for her. Taking note of all the cars, pedestrians, loiterers like myself. Holding that key. Looking for her. Everything looked copacetic. Safe. So where was she?

I lurked behind the windows of Laundromats. Doing everything that might make me inconspicuous enough to be approachable. At nine A.M., I gave up. At ten, I felt foolish. The sea gulls were laughing at me now. It was time to go home. San Francisco was too hot a town for Laurie Leiss and her daughter, Fresca Alcazon. Dysfunction on the run. I didn't really need it in my life. But I wondered what Larry Boznian would be painting next. Would I see Fresca's face, framed in some museum, made up in macaroni?

When I got back to my apartment, I found Frances's

Mary Wings

Miata parked in front of the apartment. The hood was up, the engine was warm. And the back seat was full of luggage. Somehow I had known.

I slipped quietly into the apartment. A lot of Frances's back was showing through a deep V-cut in a beige cotton dress. There was an empty vermouth bottle by her elbow and she was stirring a drink with an anxious percussion. I watched the swing of her hips, the tapping of her foot. When the blender stopped, I watched her pour the mixed martini into the glass and lift it to her lips as she stared out the kitchen window. She would need that drink when she realized I was standing right behind her. Finally, I said something. She jumped and dropped the glass.

"Emma!"

"Little early, isn't it?"

"Emma, my God, I didn't know you were—don't ever—" And then Frances stopped and looked at me, and if I had any doubts left, they were gone.

"Don't ever what?"

"Sneak up on me!" She looked angry, but only for a second. "What happened here anyway? The dishes are gone—have you been defrosting the refrigerator? Are you flea bombing? What's been going on?"

"A lot. A lot has been going on."

"And you—you got your nose pierced." Frances looked at my face in what seemed like a very different way than during our entire marriage.

"You like it?"

"Yeah!" She cocked her head and laughed in a strangled way. "I do like it." She sounded like her heart was breaking. "Emma, oh Emma, oh, Emma, I—I don't know how to tell you this."

"You're leaving me, aren't you?"

252

We stared at the broken glass on the floor. Somewhere a car honked and in the distance schoolchildren were screaming.

"Yes. I'm leaving you."

How to hold on to tears, face, lips. I looked out into the garden. I buried my feelings there in the warm, black, fetid soil.

"I don't really want any answers," I managed to say. I'd forgotten that I hadn't asked any questions.

"Yes. Let's not—"

"But, Frances, on the other hand, I don't want to make it *too* easy."

"Please?" Frances asked quietly. "Don't."

"Well, who is she?"

"Let's not do that, either."

"You're leaving me after five years?"

"We haven't been close for a long time."

"Hey, *you* kept *me* on ice, remember?"

"Emma, let's not."

"I knew you'd say that."

"Yeah, I knew I would say it, too." She smiled. It made me angry.

"I suppose you're trading me in for an upscale model, something in government, perhaps?"

"Emma, sarcasm isn't going to help."

"Well, it's helping me right now."

"I want to leave now, Emma. This serves no purpose. We—we'll have to deal with the house; I'll pay the mortgage—"

Guilt money. There was a violent moment in my brain, but it was better to look out the window. I'd grow dinner-plate dahlias this time. Big, fluffy white ones. Better camouflage.

"Emma?"

"What?"

"Do you want me to apologize?"

"Huh?"

"Do you want me to apologize?" She repeated more quietly.

"Will it make you feel better?" There were sticky weeds crawling from under the neighbor's fence. The kind of weeds that get caught in cats' tails. Were we going to split up the cats?

"I'm sorry, Emma. I really am."

There was a long pause, and then Frances asked, "Didn't make *you* feel better, did it?" She was crying now. I could hear it in her voice.

"Nope." I shook my head. A swallowtail butterfly floated along the marguerites.

"Good-bye, Emma." And then I listened to Frances's footsteps going across the newly cleaned floor, down the stairs, avoiding the squeaky tread like she had done so many times. Always so considerate about that stair.

I went back into my apartment, my very own apartment, and searched under the guest room bed. I found the bud of the plant that Fresca had failed to drown and located some cigarette papers.

Twenty minutes later, I was sitting in the garden, feeling that glorious California sunlight with all its UV rays shining on my skin. I took a long toke and surveyed the garden. Something that Eleanor Roosevelt had said came to me. What was it?

"After forty, everything bad has already happened once."

Certain truths were self-evident.

I was sitting in the sun planning next year's flora.

I'd had a weekend of heartbreak, murder and mayhem.

I had turned in a killer of three. I had let loose a killer of four.

I was the proud owner of a Stein first edition. My nose was pierced.

I would see Fresca Alcazon again. And she would have the other key.

Frances was, in some way, leaving me.

I would get beyond it.

And I truly believed that every woman in this dyke life must have a garden.